"Jodi draws the reader into her stories from the first page...She's one of my favorites."
—Debbie Macomber

The novels of Jodi Thomas are:

"Exceptional." —*Booklist*

"Exciting." —*Midwest Book Review*

"Entertaining." —*Publishers Weekly*

"Thrilling." —*Rendezvous*

"Your heart will be moved."
—*The Oklahoman*

continued . . .

TO TAME A TEXAN'S HEART

Winner of the Romance Writers of America
Best Historical Series Romance Award

"Earthy, vibrant, funny, and poignant . . . a wonderful, colorful love story." —*Romantic Times*

THE TEXAN AND THE LADY

"Jodi Thomas shows us hard-living men with grit and guts, and the determined young women who soften their hearts." —Pamela Morsi, bestselling author of *Something Shady* and *Wild Oats*

PRAIRIE SONG

"Thoroughly entertaining romance." —*Gothic Journal*

THE TENDER TEXAN

Winner of the Romance Writers of America
Best Historical Series Romance Award

"[A] marvelous, sensitive, emotional romance . . . spellbinding." —*Romantic Times*

Titles by Jodi Thomas

THE TEXAN'S WAGER
TO WED IN TEXAS
TO KISS A TEXAN
THE TENDER TEXAN
PRAIRIE SONG
THE TEXAN AND THE LADY
TO TAME A TEXAN'S HEART
FOREVER IN TEXAS
TEXAS LOVE SONG
TWO TEXAS HEARTS
THE TEXAN'S TOUCH
TWILIGHT IN TEXAS
THE TEXAN'S DREAM

THE
TEXAN'S
WAGER

JODI THOMAS

JOVE BOOKS, NEW YORK

THE TEXAN'S WAGER

A Jove Book / published by arrangement with
the author

PRINTING HISTORY
Jove edition / November 2002

Copyright © 2002 by Jodi Koumalats
Excerpt copyright © 2002 by Jodi Koumalats
Cover design by George Long
Cover photograph by Wendi Schneider

Visit our website at
www.penguinputnam.com

ISBN: 0-515-13400-7

A JOVE BOOK®
Jove Books are published by The Berkley Publishing Group,
a division of Penguin Putnam Inc.,
375 Hudson Street, New York, New York 10014.
JOVE and the "J" design
are trademarks belonging to Penguin Putnam Inc.

PRINTED IN THE UNITED STATES OF AMERICA

10 9 8 7 6 5 4 3 2 1

PROLOGUE

August 8, 1883
Halfway between Fort Dodge and Santa Fe

BAILEE GRACE MOORE WATCHED AS THE LAST FEW stragglers of the Roland wagon train disappeared into the fiery sunset. The dust from fifty teams of oxen pulling huge Conestogas settled around her along with the shattered remains of her final dream.

She thought she heard the wagon master, Broken-Hand Harrison, yelling, "Catch up! Hold tight!" But the call she'd listened to every day since they had left Independence, Missouri, was no longer meant for her or the two women standing beside her. Their one wagon and four oxen now had no place in the long line heading west. The three of them had been cut from the group and abandoned as easily as a drover cuts the weak from a healthy herd.

"They'll be sorry," Lacy Dillavou whispered behind Bailee. "They'll all wish they hadn't kicked us off. Someone will turn around and come back for us, you'll see. And then they'll apologize." Her voice trembled.

"No." Bailee fought back her own tears as she faced the girl ten years younger than she. Bailee's father had always insisted she be practical even when the truth hurt.

Lacy, though in a woman's body, was little more than a child clinging to hope when none existed.

Bailee tried to soften her words. "No one will turn back, Lacy. No one will come for us."

"Then we'll follow from far enough behind that they won't know." Lacy gulped back a cry and tried to act older than her fifteen years as she glanced at her two companions. "We can't just stay out here in the middle of nowhere without anyone to help us."

"We can't follow." Sarah Andrews's calm voice cut across Lacy's sobs. "Even if the three of us could manage the team, there is no one to hunt for food. In a week we'll be out of supplies. In two weeks we'll be starving."

Bailee looked into Sarah's sad eyes. Though only twenty, Sarah's pale blue depths lacked any spark of vitality. She believed herself dying, and despite Bailee's efforts, Sarah grew weaker every day. Her face was as pale as her white-blond hair, and her eyes were almost void of color. She reminded Bailee of a faded painting of an angel she'd once seen. It almost seemed cruel, forcing her to live and remain on an Earth far too harsh for her nature.

In the weeks since the wagons rolled through Fort Dodge, Sarah had lost first her baby, then her husband, to fever. When she became ill, the wagon master ordered her wagon burned, along with everything she owned. A few days later Bailee insisted on giving her a ride and was ordered to the back of the train. Lacy joined them to help nurse Sarah back to health. A week later all wagons stopped and a council was called. A council bent on ridding itself of all undesirables.

"I wish I were a witch like they say I am!" Lacy shouted at the thin line of dust in the distance. "I'd turn them all into crows. They should've shot us outright. What chance do we have?" She leaned against the wagon wheel and gave way to sobbing.

Bailee couldn't stand to watch Lacy cry or Sarah draw into herself. Yet, Lacy's question echoed in her mind as she began making camp just as she had done every night for weeks. It would be dark in an hour, and a fire had to be built. Without weapons or protection the light from the fire would be their only defense.

As she gathered wood, Bailee forced down her fears and tried to think. Be logical. Be practical. Be sensible. She could almost hear her accountant father lecturing her with his glasses low on his nose. But logic made her hesitate when Francis Tarleton asked her to marry him. She'd told herself she was being practical when she insisted he go on without her. He'd make his way, build a home, and send for her.

Bailee dropped a load of wood on the ground a few feet from the wagon and headed for the stream to find more. She made several trips before finally stopping to wash. In the stillness of twilight she pulled Francis's tintype from her pocket and faced the truth. It had been three years. He wasn't going to send for her. He hadn't written for months, and, even before that, his letters gradually stopped mentioning her joining him in Santa Fe. He hadn't gone on ahead of her, he'd gone on without her.

Even if he were somehow waiting in Santa Fe, he'd never accept her as a bride when he learned of the trouble she'd caused the night she left Independence. She hadn't left with her father's blessing, but with his curse. Francis wasn't the kind of man to overlook a mistake.

In a gust of wind the thin image on tin flicked from her fingers and splashed into the water. Bailee didn't even try to grab at the treasure she'd held dear for so long. She let it float away, along with her dream of marriage and family.

She stared down at the outline of herself in the dark water. She would be twenty-six her next birthday. Her father always said she was lucky: being sensible was far more important than being pretty. It was time to face the truth and stop running toward a man who wasn't waiting for her. The one dream she'd ever let herself believe in was that she'd marry, and now that would always be a dream, nothing more.

Slowly Bailee stood and walked back to the others. Lacy had stopped crying and was building a fire. Sarah already curled into her blankets, so thin beneath them her body appeared more a twisting of sheets than a person.

"We have beans and cornbread," Lacy said as the fire sparked. "If we're careful and eat only once a day, the supplies will last a few weeks. By then another train is bound to come along." Hard times were nothing new for Lacy; she'd told of being on her own since her mother died five years ago. She'd had her cry, now it was time to get on with surviving.

Bailee shook her head. The Roland train left late in the year. Some said if they didn't reach the Rockies by August first, they'd never make it across before snow buried them. The chances of another wagon train following so late in the year were slight and cattle drives that crossed this trail heading north mostly traveled in the spring.

Lacy worked around the campfire, building her hopes as she built a meal. "I know they feared Sarah has the fever, but she won't give us nothing. I can feel it in my bones."

Bailee managed a smile. "Your feeling it in your bones is one of the reasons you got left behind with Sarah and me. They feared Sarah might give them the fever, but they knew you gave them the shakes with your talk."

Lacy made a face. "Hush your teasing or I'll cast my evil eye on you."

"And what?" Bailee laughed out loud. "Make me an old maid, lost out here in the middle of nowhere with a sick woman and a girl?"

"I'm fully grown," Lacy corrected. Huge brown eyes turned up to Bailee. "Do you really think we're going to die out here?"

"No." Bailee made up her mind about an idea that had been rolling around in her thoughts all afternoon. "And we're not staying here hoping someone will save us."

Catching Bailee's determination, Lacy nodded.

"Come morning, we're loading up with wood and water and heading back the half day to where we saw the red barrel for mail at that crossroads. From there, we'll turn our wagon south."

Lacy's smile faded into panic. "South?"

Bailee tried to sound determined. "That's right. Come morning, the three of us are heading straight for Texas. We've got two weeks to get there before we starve."

Lacy's mouth opened, but no sound came out.

She didn't need to say a word; Bailee read her thoughts in her stare. She'd just named the one place lower than hell in Lacy's mind. The one fate that might be worse than starvation.

Texas.

ONE

THE WINDS HOWLED ACROSS THE OPEN COUNTRY. Bailee slept little, feeling she had to keep watch over the others. She was the oldest, therefore somehow silently appointed the leader. Sarah and Lacy were her family now. Her father had turned his back, and she knew, no matter what, she could never return home.

Just before dark Bailee had found a board down by the stream. It had probably been left from some other abandoned wagon that camped as they did, beside a stream too small to be worthy of an entire train stopping. Or maybe the piece of wood fell from one of the supply buckboards that followed cattle drives through this area. It was weathered and rotted in a few spots, but her grip molded around one end perfectly, and it stretched the length of a cane at her side. She'd found her weapon. She could stand guard.

Sarah Andrews, despite her weak condition, insisted on sleeping by the fire with the others. Bailee couldn't help but wonder if Sarah felt the loneliness from the missing wagons as dearly as she did.

They'd traveled in a village for weeks now, always hearing the sounds of people and animals moving about them. Now the air was no longer thick with smells, and the invisible safety blanket that came with the crowd had disappeared.

The three women formed a triangle around the small campfire. Three souls holding to one another when no one else wanted them.

The board lay beside Bailee's bedroll as she watched the stars arrive and listened to the haunting sounds just beyond the campfire's light. During the day the vast plains seemed empty, but at night Bailee heard movement in the tall grasses and splashing at the water's edge. A lone wolf cried somewhere in the blackness. His howl carried on the wind a homeless echo. An owl circled back and forth across the moon, then plummeted to earth. Bailee covered her ears, not wanting to hear the scream of its tiny prey.

"Tomorrow," she whispered, "tomorrow, we'll go to Texas." Her one hope was no more than a flicker, but it was all she had.

"To Texas?" Lacy asked from a few feet away. She didn't sound like she had been asleep, either. "I hear there are Indians in Texas and men so mean they'll shoot you for talking too much. I heard the only people who live in Texas are folks nobody else would put up with. The cast-offs of all other places."

Bailee laughed. "That's us. We should fit right in."

Lacy didn't see the humor. "We ain't bad. You know I ain't got no witchin' in me, and Sarah's just heartsick, that's all. She doesn't have the fever, she just lost her fighting spirit since her baby died and she ain't got no man to hold her while she grieves."

Lacy stared at Bailee through the dying fire. "I don't

know what you done to get left behind with us two, but I'm sure it's not any more true than our crimes." Lacy hesitated in her attempt to cheer herself up, then asked, "What did a right proper lady like you do, Bailee, to make them so mad at you?"

"Does it matter?" How could Bailee ever tell them, or anyone, her crime? Even Broken-Hand Harrison, when he was ranting to the council, only said that she was undesirable, no more. Maybe he figured if he told the truth about being paid off to take Bailee along before the sheriff arrested her, the council might have voted to hang her and not simply dump her at the watering hole. Harrison had known the truth when he took the money from her father that night before the wagons pulled out. "I'll see she gets to California," he'd promised. "And never returns," her father had added.

"No," Lacy answered with the honesty of a true friend. "It doesn't matter what they think you done, Miss Bailee. I saw what you did for Sarah, trying to help her, even letting her ride in your wagon after they burned hers to get rid of the fever. That alone is enough to let you tiptoe right into heaven, no matter what anyone accused you of doing."

"Thanks." Bailee took a deep breath and relaxed for the first time since all the trouble started. Maybe this time she could leave her past behind. Surely, no one in Texas would know or care that she was a criminal on the run. Harrison was the last person to know she might have been charged with a murder if she'd stayed home, and he was already miles away into the sunset.

He'd be the last person who would ever know, she swore. Let people guess, if they must, but she'd never tell anyone.

"Bailee?" Lacy whispered. "Do you think they want us to die out here? I heard one of the women say the council wasn't doing nothing but throwing out the trash when they dropped us off. 'Let them rot in the sun,' she said without looking me in the face."

"They probably do," Sarah answered from across the fire. Her voice grew softer with each day of her illness. "But you're going to fool them, both of you." Sarah sounded determined to believe. "You'll go to Texas and catch you a wild man, and make a husband out of him, and have a herd of kids."

Bailee agreed, knowing Lacy loved children dearly. "You'll have so many kids, Lacy, you'll run out of names and start numbering them."

Lacy giggled. "I heard someone say you have to bite the ear of a wild mustang to tame him. You think the same thing might be true of Texans?"

Suddenly adventure danced into Bailee's soul. The flicker of her dream sparked amid the ashes. "I'll do what I have to do," she swore, enjoying the game. "Even if they start calling my husband 'Nibbled Ears.' "

Lacy giggled again, forgetting her troubles as only the very young can do. "There's bound to be three men in a state so big who need wives."

"Two men," Sarah whispered. "I've had my chance at love. I'll not marry again."

"I'm almost past the age of marrying also." Bailee forced herself to be practical. She might be able to wipe the slate clean of the crime she committed, but she couldn't change her age or make herself pretty. Once she'd asked her father if she was beautiful, and he'd said her black hair was prettier than most.

"Since I'm having lots of kids, then you'll both come

live with me," Lacy answered. "I'll need help with all those babies. I swear, as long as I live, my house will be yours."

"And mine will be yours," Sarah answered. "If I ever have one."

"You'll both be welcome in mine." Bailee said the promise as though she believed she might someday have a place to call hers.

"Go to sleep." Sarah's low voice sounded deadly tired. "We've got a long day ahead of us tomorrow."

"I agree. Before we find Lacy her wild man, we've got to get to Texas." Bailee closed her eyes and let the spark of hope die within her as she echoed Sarah's words. "Tomorrow will be a long day."

Neither woman knew how hard the next day would be. By nightfall they were all too exhausted to undress before crawling into their bedrolls.

Hitching the team had taken half the morning. A job that looked easy when watching the Roland wranglers do it now proved near impossible. If Sarah hadn't climbed from her bed to help, they might have never pulled away from the stream.

Once moving, Bailee followed the tracks back to the red barrel at the crossroads where people often left mail. Cattlemen would pick up letters from folks heading west and drop them off in Dodge. Folks on the wagon trains would leave papers they'd left with for others to read.

From the barrel the three women turned south. Bailee guessed they were a hundred miles from Texas and should make it easy in a week. If it didn't rain.

She stared up at the endless blue sky. It never rained here, she decided. Never. Late summer had been so dry she could sometimes hear the wind snapping the tall grass.

The land had turned from green to brown. Drying in the sun. Dying in the sun.

The days passed without any sign of civilization. First they rationed food, then water. Lacy and Bailee agreed Sarah should have a double portion, for her body had thinned to bone.

By the end of the second week they were out of food and following a trail so faint Bailee couldn't be sure if it had been made by men or animals. They saw antelope and buffalo, but without a gun, had no way of killing them. The rabbits were long eared and thin, never drawing close enough to catch.

They crossed shallow streams that allowed them to re-fill their water supply, but no one had the energy to stop and do laundry. The few clothes they owned faded into the same red-brown color of the sandy earth.

Bailee tried to keep up everyone's spirits, but even the joke about biting a Texan no longer made Lacy smile. Bailee didn't bother carrying the board she'd found by the stream. After the first few days, the fear of starvation be-came far greater than anything that might attack in the night. She knew there were ways to survive in open coun-try, but she was the daughter of a bank accountant, not a mountain man. She'd grown up keeping house for her father and knew nothing of building a fire in open country or living off the land.

Sarah, though only twenty, knew more than the others, but she was so weak she made little effort to talk. She wanted to help them survive, but had no desire to live herself.

One morning Bailee sat alone by a cold fire and watched the dawn. She'd lost track of how many days they'd been on their own. Was it twenty, or twenty-one?

Sarah and Lacy were still asleep. It seemed cruel to wake them from dreams. At least for a few hours they weren't tired or hungry or frightened.

For the first morning in two months the sky didn't lighten bright and warm. Clouds hung along the horizon like a white mountain range in the distance, and the breeze smelled of rain.

As the air slowly thickened with moisture, Bailee watched a lone figure moving toward them from the south. At first she didn't respond, unsure if it were man or beast. But the creature ventured closer, growing bigger as it neared.

"Lacy," Bailee whispered. "Lacy, look. Someone or something is coming."

The young girl rolled from her blankets and squinted in the direction Bailee pointed. "A man!" she shouted. "We've reached civilization."

But as he drew closer, neither woman felt so sure. A light drizzle distorted him, making it seem as if he weaved back and forth as he walked. Covered in animal hides, they smelled him long before they could make out the features of his face. He looked hairy enough to keep warm without clothes and so dirty it would take more than a drizzle to clean him. A beard the color of mud covered half his broad chest.

Sarah climbed in the wagon to keep dry while she watched, but Lacy and Bailee stood in the rain waiting to greet him. Lacy tied back her hair, trying to be more presentable, but Bailee knew she could do nothing that would matter to change the way she looked. In Sunday best she was plain. She'd be the same in rags and dirt.

"Howdy!" the stranger shouted, raising his hat high. "Name's Big Zeb Whitaker. Howdy to the wagon!"

Lacy waved, but Bailee waited. Though his voice was friendly enough, she didn't miss the fact that he kept his gun at ready. In his furs he looked more predator than friend.

The stranger drew closer. "Where's your menfolks?" he asked as he lifted a huge rifle a few inches.

Cumbersome saddlebags hung from both shoulders, making him seem wider than his already considerable girth. The gun he carried was long-barreled and old.

"We ain't got any!" Lacy shouted before Bailee could stop her.

He didn't lower his weapon as he drew closer.

"Why are you afoot?" Bailee changed the subject as he reached the oxen. "Are you lost?"

"Never." Zeb Whitaker's laughter chilled the air between them. "We're not more than a good day's walk from Cedar Point." He glanced in the direction he'd come and nodded once. "I had to put my horse down about a half mile back."

"I didn't hear a shot," Bailee said more to Lacy than the man, but she guessed he heard her. Something about Big Zeb didn't make sense. If he'd had to shoot his horse, wouldn't he head back to town? No sane man would walk into this open country without horse, or bedroll, or any supply of food or water that she could see.

He ignored her stare. The oxen interested him more. "You wouldn't want to sell me this wagon and team, would you, ladies?"

"No," Bailee answered without taking her eyes off him.

He ignored her answer and continued appraising the merchandise. "You ladies must be headed toward Cedar Point. It's the only place for a hundred miles. You won't be needing this wagon once you reach town, I figure.

Might as well take it off your hands." He helped himself to the water barrel as he passed, not bothering to use the dipper, but dropping a dirty hand into the supply.

"The wagon's not for sale," Bailee said firmly. "But we will offer you a ride back to town." It was the right thing to do, she told herself, even though the idea of riding beside him didn't appeal to her.

The man's black gaze shot her direction. The hardness in his stare startled her.

"I'm heading in the opposite direction, ma'am." His words were polite enough, but his stare made her shiver.

Without asking, he swung up on the running board of the wagon and checked the storage box below the bench. From the way his shoulders relaxed, Bailee guessed he searched for weapons.

"What's wrong with that one?" He pointed toward Sarah who was wrapped in several blankets.

"She's sick," Lacy volunteered. "But she ain't got the fever."

"She looks more dead than alive." The stranger didn't seem to care if he offended Sarah. "Get out here with the others where I can have a look at you."

When Sarah didn't move fast enough, he grabbed her by the arm and pulled her onto the wagon's bench seat. She glared at him with fever-ringed eyes, and he moved away, wiping his filthy hand on equally filthy clothes.

He jumped to the ground and rested his rifle across his arm. "Look, I need your wagon. You can walk to town in a day or so. I'll even unload it and leave all your belongings right here so you can come back for them." His effort to be nice never changed the cruelty in his eyes.

"No." Bailee was starting to believe the man might be hard of hearing. "The wagon's not for sale."

Zeb Whitaker swore under his breath, as if he were talking to a child who couldn't understand logic. "I'll pay you a hundred dollars."

"No," Bailee answered. What good would a hundred dollars do Sarah? Even if she and Lacy could make it to Cedar Point, Sarah couldn't walk that far, and they wouldn't leave her.

"A hundred and twenty!" The man puffed out his chest trying to intimidate them.

"The wagon is not for sale."

Zeb Whitaker slowly turned his rifle toward Bailee's middle. "I didn't want to do this, but you leave me no choice. I have to have your wagon, and the matter of your surviving is of no importance to me. So step back out of the way so I can be gone. If you three are no more trouble than gnats, I won't have to waste a bullet on you."

Bailee didn't make a sound, but Lacy let out a little cry. "You can't take our wagon, mister! You can't!"

"I'm not taking. I said I'm willing to pay. I never stole from no woman. Or shot one. Leastwise, not when I was sober and can remember doing such a thing. I just need to be traveling, so don't bother me, girl."

She grabbed his arm trying to stop him.

He raised his hand suddenly as if to strike her, then looked Lacy up and down carefully like she were also something he considered buying. When he turned back to Bailee, she caught a glimmer of lust in his black eyes. She had no doubt in her mind that he'd kill her if he had to, but what he had planned for Lacy was far more evil.

A smile slowly wrinkled across his dirty face. "Ladies, there's probably a rope waiting to stretch my neck, so I'll have to cut this bargaining session short." He stared at Bailee. "You can sell me the wagon and stand aside, or

I'll leave your bodies rotting in this rain. One way or the other, don't matter much to me."

Bailee's mind raced as fast as it once had when her father badgered her at the dinner table over some small fact in her lessons. *Think!* he'd shout, as if his demand would help reason.

"Two hundred," she said as her hands balled into fists. They'd all be dead in a few minutes if she didn't think of something. "We want two hundred for the wagon."

The man blinked, seemingly surprised she had the nerve to speak. "What?"

"You said you'd pay." Bailee stood solid, knowing that if she took her eyes from him, she'd fall apart.

"What?" Lacy echoed. "Bailee, you can't be serious."

"It's my wagon." Bailee forced her words to be cold. There was no time to explain to Lacy, and she didn't want the girl getting in the way. "Two hundred is as low as I go."

The man raised an eyebrow, debating whether to spend money. "All right," he finally said. "I don't like the idea of killing women, even ones as poorly looking as the three of you. There's not enough meat on all of your bones to feed a crow."

He lowered one of his saddlebags and began unstrapping the laces. "Besides, I just come into a considerable amount of cash, and I can afford to pay. For that kind of money, though, I'm taking the girl with me." He winked at Lacy as though he considered her the lucky winner. "She's young, but I don't mind training her. Already a full handful of breast busting out of that dress. That'll make her worth the trouble of feeding."

Before Lacy could react, he grabbed the front of her blouse, tearing the material almost to her waist.

As she backed away in horror, trying to hold the scraps of her clothes together, he laughed. "You'll do, girl."

Lacy's mouth opened in shock. For a moment only little sounds of panic came out, then she screamed, "I'm not going anywhere with you!" She snatched her shawl hanging on the wagon and tied it around her. But he'd touched her. Panic washed across her face.

Zeb laughed. "You'll get used to me, girl. Might even start liking my handling you after a while. If you don't, it won't matter none because where we're going, no one will hear your screams but the buffalo."

Lacy's gaze darted to Bailee. "He can't take me! He can't!"

"No," Bailee answered with her teeth clenched tightly together. "He can't."

Zeb wasn't listening to their chatter. He smiled, proud of his own plan. "I'll work you so hard during the day, you won't even fight what happens to you at night. Two hundred for the wagon and the woman is high, but I'll pay. When I reach the Comonchero camps, I might be able to make some of my money back." He smiled at Lacy. "You'll know how to lie real still for a man by then, girl."

He knelt on one knee and began digging in his bag. Bailee reached her hand behind her and felt the board leaning against the water barrel.

Lacy backed away a step. The man grabbed her wrist with his free hand and pulled her to her knees paying no attention to her sobs. His beefy hand forced her head down, then patted her face in more of a slap than a touch.

"Yes, sir, you'll go with me, girl." He bragged to himself as he slapped her once more as though daring her to try and move. "You'll go with me and we'll get along just fine once we understand one another."

Lacy gulped for air, too afraid to even look up.

He knotted a handful of her hair into his fist and jerked her head up. "There ain't nobody here to stop me from taking you, girl, so don't get any ideas. These two friends of yours are half dead anyway. And you will be if you don't make up your mind to be real good from now on. I ain't long on patience."

He grinned as he let go of her hair and hit her again to prove his point. When Lacy tumbled backward, Whitaker reached for her as if angry that she'd moved when he'd told her to be still.

Bailee saw her chance. Her fingers closed around the smooth wood of the wet board. It was her only weapon. Her only choice. Lacy's only chance. With one swift movement Bailee swung the board with all her strength.

Wood met his skull with a mighty crack. Lightning popped far above them, echoing the sound.

Screaming, Lacy jerked her arm free of his grip.

The stranger glanced up in shock, then melted to the ground as though made of butter and it was an August noon. Gold coins spilled from his bag across the dirt as he tumbled.

Lacy kept screaming as she jumped to her feet. She ran about as though the earth had grown suddenly hot and she was testing for a place to stand. Her words came out in broken fragments. "You, you! Oh, Bailee . . . You killed . . . He . . . He was going to . . . He hit me . . ."

Bailee didn't move. She stared down at the man with the board still in her hand. "I've killed again," she whispered, making no effort to stop her tears from tumbling down her face with the rain. "Again."

Sarah, looking more ghost than human, slowly moved through the rain to Bailee's side.

Lacy ran to her. "Sarah! Did you see? Oh, Sarah, Bailee killed . . ."

On bare feet Sarah crossed between Bailee and Zeb Whitaker's body. Red mud clung to the hem of her nightgown, forever staining the lace. Her thin hand covered Bailee's and pulled the board from Bailee's white-knuckled fingers. Without a word Sarah lifted the weapon in the air and let it fall across the back of the stranger's head. Like an echo once more the thunder rattled the sound skyward.

Lacy screamed again as if all had suddenly gone mad, but Sarah only raised her pale eyes to Bailee and said, "We killed him, Bailee. My blow may have been the deadly one, not yours. It wasn't just you doing what had to be done. I killed him, too."

"But he . . . he was already . . ." Lacy froze, letting understanding filter into her panic.

She moved forward and took her turn with the weapon. Her blow hit his shoulder, but she stood back and lifted her head. "*We* killed him. All of us. He said no one would stop him, but we did."

TWO

"Get in the wagon!" Bailee shouted over the thunder. "Hurry."

Sarah climbed into the back of the Conastoga, taking the bedrolls from Lacy as Bailee pulled the oxen in line. The dawn air grew silent and still around them, almost as though morning held its breath until they could get away from the body crumpled in the mud. Then, when the harnesses jingled, the thunder resumed and lightning brightened their path.

The three women followed nearly washed-out tracks Big Zeb Whitaker had made when he'd stomped into their camp. The sun hid behind a wall of clouds, but they knew they were heading south. South, to the only town within a hundred miles.

"We won't stop for anything but to water the oxen," Bailee reasoned aloud. "If Zeb Whitaker said it was a good day's walk to town, we should be able to make it by nightfall with the wagon."

Sarah and Lacy nodded their agreement.

"But we can't waste a minute. Each time we stop,

everything has to be done fast." Bailee didn't have to add that since there was nó food, they didn't have to bother with a noon fire.

"What'll we do when we get to town?" Lacy held the board they'd used for a weapon as if she expected trouble to come toward them at any moment.

"We confess," Bailee answered. "It's the only thing we can do."

Lacy climbed onto the bench beside Bailee. "To a priest? I never done that before. I don't know if I can talk to one."

"No, to the sheriff." Bailee tried her best to sound determined. "It's only proper. We killed a man. If this Cedar Point is big enough to have a lawman, we go there first."

"They hang murderers," Lacy whispered. "Don't they?"

"Not us." Bailee tried to sound sure of herself. "I'll explain that my killing him was self-defense. After all, I have you two as witnesses."

"And I have the two of you as witnesses when I killed him again," Lacy added.

"I'm not sure you can be a witness to the same murder you're pleading guilty to," Sarah mentioned from the back of the wagon. She was given out. The thought of being tried and hanged didn't seem to worry her at all. She'd used all her energy carefully building her nest in the tiny space between Bailee's crates so she could sleep. For her, she'd only done what had to be done, and there was no point wasting time thinking about it.

Twelve hours later the sheriff of Cedar Point, Harman Riley, asked the same question Sarah had. "Now, let me get this straight." He paced in front of the women like a lawyer. "You three ragamuffins claim to have killed Big

Zeb Whitaker, a man who told you he was due for a hanging?"

The three suspects nodded.

Harman Riley considered himself a hard man, but he'd been gentle with these three women because they reminded him a little of his daughters back in Tennessee. They'd pulled into town well after dark and looked near drowned when he'd opened his office door to them. It had taken him ten minutes just to get them all three to stop talking at once and almost a half hour to get the office warm enough for them to stop shivering.

"That's right." Bailee spoke slowly, as if beginning to believe the sheriff might have permanently fogged up his mind with the stink of his own pipe tobacco. "We murdered him a day's ride from here. He was a big man and he said his name was Zeb Whitaker." She pulled the blanket the sheriff had given her around her thin shoulders.

"And are you sorry?" Harman scratched his bald head and tried not to swear in front of the women. He hadn't had a good night's sleep in a week, and tonight had lost all promise. "Are you truly sorry?"

The three looked at one another. "No," they answered in unison.

"Does that mean we hang?" added Lacy, the youngest one. " 'Cause if we do, I'm thinking I'm beginning to feel *real* sorry."

The sheriff leaned back in his chair. "Zebadiah was one of the worst, lowdown, no-good drifters in these parts. He did everything short of murder, and, if the truth were known, he probably did that in the dead of night, leaving no witnesses to his crime. But still, it ain't right to kill a man, ladies. Surely you know that."

"We know," Lacy said. "If we promise not to do it again, can we go?"

The sheriff gave her his meanest look. "You're startin' to bother me, girl."

"I have that effect on most folks," Lacy answered honestly. "My momma used to say I was a curse waiting to happen. It must be true, 'cause she up and died on my tenth birthday, and my pa left the day I was born, and ever' cat I ever had died for no reason. . . ."

Harman Riley raised one eyebrow and glared at her, stopping her as suddenly as if he'd tapped her on the head with his pipe. She reminded him of one of those toy tops you twist and wind up, then when you let go you think it'll never stop.

Lacy made the sign of the cross awkwardly over her chest, obviously just learning the habit. "But I swear, Sheriff, I didn't put a curse or the evil eye or nothing on that man. I just hit him as hard as I could with a board Bailee calls 'the weapon.' I guess it's 'the murder weapon' now. Anyway, I killed him flat out. There he lay, them gold coins spread around him in the dirt. I thought about burying him, but I figured we should leave him alone. We'd done enough to him."

Sheriff Riley rubbed his forehead. He hadn't heard so much confessing since he found out MayBell Howard over at the saloon was pregnant. There was such a shortage of wives out here, every man in the county wanted to make an honest woman out of her.

"Gold coins?" The sheriff looked at Bailee as though he suddenly realized the story was pure fiction. All three women struck him as squirrely, but Bailee seemed closest to the ground. "Did you take his money?"

Bailee looked surprised he'd even asked. "We're not thieves . . . only murderers."

Riley needed a drink. He'd spent enough time with the women to make him remember why he'd left Tennessee. One female in the house is heaven, two tolerable, but three will drive a man to drink every time. "No robbery. That's a blessing," he mumbled. "We kill a man, or woman, twice around here for stealing."

None of the women seemed to understand his attempt at humor.

"Look, ladies, I'm going to have to lock you up until we get this straightened out. I don't believe for one second that you three killed Big Zeb Whitaker, but until I find out the truth, I have to hold you for questioning."

He stood and motioned them toward the only cell, a large one, built to divide the office almost in half. Usually, when it was empty, like tonight, Harman would sleep there. The bed in the jail was better than the one over at the boardinghouse. But tonight he hadn't had time to think of sleeping. As soon as he got them settled in behind bars, he had to find someone dumb enough to ride out and look for a body.

The youngest, Lacy Dillavou, began to cry, making the sheriff put down his pipe and rub his whole face as he opened the cell. "It's not so bad," he said. "I'll have Mrs. Abernathy bring a meal over for you and water so you can wash up."

Lacy cried louder as she walked into the cell.

"Lots of water," Sarah added as she looked around the cell as though she thought she was renting it and not being arrested. "Enough so we all can have a bath."

He frowned, remembering that bathing was one of the pestering habits his wife tried to spread.

"And I could probably round up a few blankets to put up around the bars to offer some privacy." Riley smiled, proud of himself for being so thoughtful.

But Lacy continued to cry.

The older one, Bailee, comforted her friend as they sat on Harman's cot. "It might help, Sheriff, if you could send over a pie. That would probably cheer her up. We haven't had anything but beans for weeks."

"And milk," Lacy gulped between sobs. "Milk always makes me feel better."

Sheriff Riley grabbed his hat. "I'll be right back. Mrs. Abernathy will have to make do for tonight, but she'll have biscuits and gravy ready for you all at dawn." He waited, hoping he'd cheered the young one up a little.

She did stop yelling, which was an improvement.

He took two steps toward the door and stopped. "Anything else?"

Bailee stood and faced him. "Yes, leave the cell unlocked so we can get our things out of the wagon. And we'll need soap and towels if you can manage them."

Harman nodded. Even if they thought of escaping, where would the three of them go with oxen? "All right. Anything else?" He took another step toward the door.

"Can someone take care of our animals?" asked Sarah, the usually silent one.

She was as close to an angel as Harman figured he'd ever see, so he nodded. "Anything else?"

All three women looked at him. He was through the door before they could ask for more. As it was, he wasn't sure he could remember everything. If he hadn't already let his no-good deputy go off to his nightly drinking, Harman would have asked Wheeler to run the errands.

An hour later Riley was ready to saddle up and head

into Indian Country for some peace. The women unloaded half their wagon into his jail. In fact, they'd made it look downright homey.

Mrs. Abernathy had brought a tray of bread and butter, complaining loudly that it was far too late to ask her to deliver food so they would just have to take what she had. She did, however, take her six bits in payment.

To make matters worse, half the men in town had been by to offer their support as either witnesses to how Zeb deserved to die, or as jurors should there be a trial. They all stood at the door hoping to get a look, as if the women were freaks at a tent show. Riley finally had to answer the door with his Colt in one hand to discourage visitors.

Adding to Riley's misery was the problem that all three women cleaned up to be fine-looking ladies. Bailee with her black hair, green eyes, and matter-of-fact ways. Lacy, young, impulsive, with warm brown hair and a body that promised heaven. And Sarah. Shy, frail Sarah. If she ever turned those light blue eyes on a man, she'd melt even a stone heart.

There wasn't a man in the state who'd find them guilty. The jury would be more likely to fine Zeb a death fee for dying in front of them.

Riley had his hands full, for above all, he couldn't let them go without at least a fine. After all, killing was illegal, even in Texas. They'd already told him they didn't have more than a few coins between them. He couldn't keep them in jail. Judging from the way they ate tonight, he wouldn't be able to feed them for more than a week.

He had to think of something, and he had to think fast.

THREE

Long after Lacy and Sarah fell asleep, Bailee stood at the jail's barred window and watched shadows move across the muddy rut this town called Main Street.

To say she'd hit bottom would be an understatement. She'd sunk to what must be the lowest level of hell . . . a town called Cedar Point. She could almost smile and remember the morning she left home, without a single person to bid her farewell, as being the bright point during the past few months. Even being kicked off the wagon train didn't seem so bad compared to her present predicament.

Overlooking the fact this town hadn't discovered soap or paint, the dust seemed never to settle. Not even on rainy days. Bailee guessed the few respectable citizens she'd seen, the ones not staggering, had never been inside a barbershop. Zeb Whitaker, whom she thought part animal, must have felt among his own kind here.

Her grandmother always used to say, "Look at the bright side." Bailee thought hard. When they found Big Zeb's body tomorrow, at least she'd be hanged in clean clothes. The sheriff, true to his word, offered plenty of water to his prisoners. Bailee saw no need in rationing the small amount of soap she carried in the wagon. It would only go to waste if left among these folks. So, she'd used all her soap and half of what the sheriff brought her before she'd felt clean.

A year ago she'd been organizing small dinner parties for her father, waiting for Francis Tarleton to send for her, and learning to quilt. Tonight, she was in the ugliest town in existence, and she had committed more murders than she'd completed quilts.

Bailee saw the North Star between the dark outline of two shacks. She couldn't help wondering how her life had lost all direction. At some point she'd opened the wrong door and fallen into the root cellar. She felt she could write a dime novel, *One Year's Journey of Destruction*.

She watched as a drunk wandered across the pale light between the buildings. He staggered a few steps and tumbled into the mud, as if it were his feather bed.

"Good night," she whispered, thinking he'd probably sleep better than she would.

"Did you say something, miss?" the sheriff asked from half a room away.

"No," Bailee whispered as she moved to the bars separating their cell from his office. She glanced at Sarah and Lacy, but knew they were so tired, shouting wouldn't wake them tonight. Sarah had tried to be strong, had stayed awake longer than she had since her husband died. The day drained her so completely, Bailee swore she'd seen the woman asleep on her feet more than once before they got the beds made.

Lacy cried herself to sleep like a child, sobbing until

exhaustion took over. But the nightmare of the day only kept Bailee awake.

"I can't sleep," she admitted to the sheriff. "I keep wondering what will happen to us."

Harman scratched his short beard. "Hanging, I suppose. But don't you worry, miss. I can tell you're a proper lady. I'll tie a rope around your knees so your skirt doesn't go up when you drop."

Bailee looked up at the old man. He was as strange as the town. Did he really think he was making her feel better with the comment?

"Hanging's better than going to prison," he added. "Texas ain't got much of a place for women. I hear the only way out of the women's wing is in a box or to be transferred to the state asylum. And that state asylum is worse than any prison North or South."

That's it, she thought. The sheriff was starting early on his mission to drive her insane, just in case a jury decided not to hang her for the murder. Maybe, in some strange way, he thought she'd go quieter if she were driven mad first.

The old man stood and walked slowly over to the cell. He chewed on the tip of his pipe while he sucked air through his teeth. Varying ages of tobacco stains spotted his shirt, but his leather vest appeared fairly clean. The star pinned to it looked worn thin from being polished. He was a man who wore his position proudly.

"I've heard said," he began, "that if the screaming and crying don't get to you at the state prison, the feeling of bugs crawling across you in the blackness of night will." Harman Riley leaned closer. "You ain't afraid of bugs, are you, miss?"

Bailee almost wished she had her board. Then, a moment after the thought of clubbing Harman registered, she decided she must be some kind of mass murderer. She was no better than a female Jack the Ripper. Killing someone was crossing her mind far too often of late.

"You know." The sheriff pointed the gnawed end of his pipe toward her. "I've been thinking there might be a way out for you three girls, but it would take guts, and you'd all three have to agree to it."

"It's not something illegal, is it?" Bailee decided she shouldn't care. Even if it was, they could only hang her once.

"No. It's legal. All on the up and up, or I wouldn't even suggest it."

"I'm listening." Whatever he had in mind couldn't be as bad as hearing her neck snap or lying awake in some prison waiting for the bugs to parade across her flesh.

"Since you three confessed and all, I might could get the judge to see it as more self-defense, like you three claim. But of course, since it was three against one, he would have to at least fine all of you a large sum."

Bailee frowned. "Even if I sold my wagon and team, I couldn't raise much money. A hundred at best. And even if we had enough to pay the fine, we'd have no money to live on and no wagon to travel." The thought of staying in this town seemed another level of hell she hadn't thought of yet.

"But someone, say a father, a brother or . . . a husband could pay your fine for you." The old man smiled. His teeth reminded her of piano keys, almost every other one black.

Bailee didn't see his logic. "Sarah is the only one who had a husband and he died. Lacy's all alone and so am I. No fathers. No brothers. No husbands."

"But there could be." He moved closer. "If the three of you are willing to marry, I know a hundred men in these parts who'd step up and pay the fine."

Bailee listened in disbelief. "You'd sell us?"

"Never." Harman acted insulted. "If we had more than three show up with the money in hand, we'd do it fair and square. I'd have the men put their names in a hat and each of you ladies could draw for your man. You'd do the picking, not me."

"But we wouldn't even know them."

"A man never knows a woman until he lives with her. I grew up with my wife living not a mile down the road from me, and I can tell you there were a great many things I didn't know about her until after we'd tied the knot. After a few years, reasons why we never should have married seemed to pop up daily." He scratched his way across his thin hair. "Time came when I couldn't even remember one reason we got together, and, from the way she complained, she couldn't, either.

"I figure if you marry a stranger you got a fifty-fifty shot at liking him." Harman nodded as if he thought his plan grand. "There'd be no time for courting or even meeting, for that matter. I won't have a good night's sleep until I get my jail cleared out."

"We're to be raffled off?"

"Not raffled. More like a lottery. Each man only gets one chance, an equal chance for a wife. So long as he has the money in hand to pay your fine. Any man who has the money to pay probably can support a wife, so you've got the main reason couples argue out of the way."

"But we could get anyone! Someone terrible! Someone dishonest." The drunk in the street ran through her mind. "Or maybe Zeb had a brother."

"I'll talk to the winners. Make sure you both agree on a few rules. So be thinking about what's important to you in the bargain. I'd check up on each couple, too. I figure I'd come by once a week and ask you and the other two if you want to return to jail. If you say 'no' three times, you're the husband's problem from then on and no longer mine. I'd mail the marriage papers to Austin, and you'd be married all legal like."

"But he could be a criminal. A liar. A drunk. If I agreed to this, I'd have no idea what kind of man I'd be getting for a husband."

"Well, one thing's for sure." Harman headed back to his chair. "He'd know what he was getting. A confessed killer."

Bailee rattled the bars in anger. The old man was right. Why was she worried about such a stupid plan? No man in his right mind would step forward and be willing not only to pay the fine for her, but to marry her. She might as well practice choking. It was only a matter of days before she'd be wearing a rope around her neck.

No man had stepped up to ask for her hand when it was free. No one would step forward now. The only man who'd ever been interested in her put thousands of miles between them. He'd promised her a life of marriage and family, a love that would stand forever, but he'd left without her. Francis had known all her strengths. The way she was organized. The way she liked to cook and take care of little details. If he hadn't come back for her when she was free, how could the sheriff believe some man would be willing to pay to marry her?

One week later Bailee watched in shock as fifty men, obviously not in their right minds, stood in line outside the jail and registered for the sheriff's "Wife Lottery."

FOUR

CARTER MCKOY STOOD OUTSIDE THE SHERIFF'S OFFICE in line with four dozen other fools. Rain didn't have the energy to pour, but slowly dripped on him, soaking him to the bone. He had money in one pocket to pay the woman's fine, and a note written on brown sack paper in the other. He was as ready as he figured he'd ever be to apply for a wife.

No one spoke to him. No one would admit to knowing him in daylight, much less after dark. Except the general store owner, who always spoke to Carter, even though his frown told Carter he'd just as soon not. But money had a way of friendlying some folks up.

"Something is wrong with that Carter McKoy," people whispered when they thought he couldn't hear. Only they never said what it was, and he never asked.

The line in front of the sheriff's office moved slowly toward the porch, with each man showing his money and putting his name in Sheriff Riley's hat. Only a few handed over letters or notes they wanted presented to the future wife, should their name be drawn.

When Carter finally reached the front, the sheriff looked at him and shook his head. But he took the letter and put Carter's name in the hat.

"Sure you want a wife, Carter McKoy?" Sheriff Riley laughed quietly. "You might have to talk to the woman if you took her home."

Wheeler, the sheriff's deputy, giggled and repeated Riley's question.

Carter didn't answer. He never answered. He'd learned a long time ago most people only talked to themselves anyway. He moved to the side, to wait with the other idiots who thought finding a wife would be as easy as paying a fine.

The sheriff mumbled something about being glad he didn't have to choose from this sorry bunch. "Let luck do the picking." His voice rose above the crowd. "And pray whoever wins doesn't frighten the woman to death at first glance." The sheriff's gaze met Carter's stare. There was no doubt to whom the old man referred.

Carter fought down a growl. He wasn't some animal to be talked about as though he couldn't hear, couldn't understand. Though he'd never been told, he assumed it wasn't polite to growl in public, so he continued to stare until the sheriff looked away.

A few hours ago the idea of getting married never crossed his mind. Maybe once in a while when a man dreams, but never in the light of day. Never in the real world where Carter forced himself to stay most of the time.

Once in a while some man would go back East and return with a wife. But Carter didn't know anyone, anywhere, but here, and these folks wouldn't introduce him to a single woman even if they knew one. He'd also heard of ordering a bride by mail, but he could never do that to a woman. At least this way, if his name were picked, she'd have a look at him before she said "I do." She'd have a chance to run, even if it was to jail, rather than marrying him.

He'd brought a wagon full of fruit into town this afternoon and unloaded it at Willard's store like he always did. Willard would weigh it light, as he had for ten years, and price it low like always. Then he'd add that amount to Carter's credit.

Willard usually stood on the loading dock and talked while Carter worked. The old storekeeper liked to run through the happenings of the town, adding his own comments along the way. In truth, Carter had only been half listening when Willard told him about the three women who wandered into town claiming to be murderers.

"Virgins." Willard chuckled when he said the word. "We got three real virgins in this town. Imagine that." Being a murderer was no label of distinction in a place where half the population had done their share of killing on one side of the law or the other.

Carter glanced up from the unloading, which was all the encouragement Willard needed.

"One's barely grown, but full woman from what I've heard. One's frail, won't last the winter, but looks like an angel. The third is old, maybe twenty-five." Willard grinned. "If I was under fifty, I'd try for any one of them. There ain't nothing like the feel of a good woman laying next to you in bed on a cold night."

Carter raised one dark eyebrow, and Willard hastily added, "Oh, not that the saloon girls ain't nice and all, but a good woman does something to a man. She makes him want to be better than he knows he is by nature."

Carter hoped his thick beard hid his grin. He doubted Willard ever got near a "good woman" in his life, and women in these parts were generally considered virgins till they ran out of fingers on which to count their lovers.

"You should go over and take a look, Carter," Willard encouraged. "You're of marrying age. A woman would spend some of that credit you keep building in my store."

Willard didn't look like he expected an answer. He was one of the few people in town who had ever heard Carter talk, but it had been so long ago Willard wasn't sure if it had been words, or just a mumble. Whenever Carter came to town, he always had his order written down.

"All you have to do is pay her fine and one of them might be yours." Willard galvanized the possibility. "Sheriff said you can write her a letter. Tell her anything you like. Tell her what you expect. What you want. She'll pick a name from a hat tonight, but if she doesn't like you, or what your letter says, the sheriff said he'd let her pick again."

Willard laughed. "That ornery old Riley's got daughters back East. He believes a woman's got rights, even one confessing to murder."

Four hours later Willard's words still rolled around in Carter's thoughts. He'd written what he wanted out of a woman on the sack and given it to Riley, but all Carter could think about now was getting the letter back and going home before this crazy dream turned into a nightmare. He could imagine all three women pulling his name from the hat and putting it back at the first sight of him.

Sheriff Riley appeared in his office doorway. He carefully sat two lanterns on barrels on his porch, straightened to official statue, and called a name out through the night. The lottery had begun.

A tall man dressed in black materialized from the steady downpour. He wore a long greatcoat and a hat pulled low against the weather. Without a word he walked into the office.

The crowd was silent. Carter moved a few feet closer to the porch, telling himself he'd catch Sheriff Riley when he stepped outside again and withdraw his name before another paper could be pulled from the hat. He'd been missed once in the lottery. He might not be so lucky a second time.

But Carter hesitated. To withdraw, he'd have to talk, not to the sheriff alone, but in front of half the town. Carter's fingers moved at his side.

The stranger in black stepped out of the office. His greatcoat was now wrapped around the thin frame of a woman whose hair looked almost white in the shadowy light. As they reached the edge of the porch and the curtain of rain, the tall man swept her into his arms and carried her to a waiting buggy.

A moment before she disappeared into the folds of the two-seater, the young woman glanced back at the sheriff. Her pale eyes were wide with fright, but she didn't call back. She'd agreed to her fate.

Everyone watched, ready to help her if she only asked. But she didn't. Someone behind Carter whispered, "The angel's been picked."

Carter shoved his way toward the porch. This had been a mistake. He didn't want to take some frightened creature away in the night. He'd have no idea how to comfort her. And if the women were frail and died on him, folks in this town would only talk more.

But before he could reach the sheriff, Riley called another name.

Carter hung back. He'd never be able to withdraw his name in time, but two men had been called. One more and Carter could go home without having to say a word. His chances of not being chosen were good. There had to be at least forty names still in the hat.

An old man, with a bowed back, limped through the crowd toward the porch. Even in the rain, Carter could see that his hands were knotted and twisted. When several of the waiting commented, the man turned around to face the gathering. "I put my son's name in the hat!" he shouted. "If the lady agrees, she'll marry him by proxy tonight. He's fighting with McKinsey in the Indian Wars, but when the trouble is over he'll have a wife to come home to."

If the men in the crowd thought the old man's statement strange, none commented. A few had fought in the War Between the States, others as Rangers along the border, and someone to come home to, even a wife a man had never met, might be a reason for staying alive.

The old man followed Riley into the office. Again the crowd waited in silence, as though on church pews at a wedding. They might not be able to see or hear anything, but they all knew what went on inside. A woman was agreeing to marry.

A young girl finally appeared in the doorway. She didn't look frightened as the angel had. She smiled and nodded at the men as she lifted her left hand. The gold band might forever be the only part of a real marriage she'd have.

Her new father-in-law joined her. He offered her his

arm as he tried his best to straighten slightly. With a trembling hand, he held a lantern before him.

The girl placed her hand on his arm, then turned back to the doorway. "I'll be living in my own apartment over the print shop until my husband comes home. Promise you'll come see me, Bailee."

A tall woman appeared in the doorway. "I promise." She waved until they disappeared into the crowd.

Carter didn't watch the girl and the old man. He couldn't take his eyes off the woman at the door. She was tall, very tall for a woman. But then he'd only seen a few dozen of the creatures in his entire life. Her black hair was tied behind her head in a knot, and her eyes were the green of full summer.

While the other men waved good luck to the girl, the woman in the doorway stared directly at Carter. He saw no fear in her eyes, and wondered if she saw none in his. If the angel and the girl worried him, this one sent panic dancing along his spine.

He should have pulled his name. He wouldn't have known how to treat the angel, or what to do with the girl, but this one . . . this one was no child or mouse. This one was old enough and smart enough to know what she wanted in a man. And judging from the strength he saw in her eyes, she'd settle for nothing less.

"Miss Bailee?" The sheriff pulled her back to her duty. "Will you draw?".

Without hesitation, Bailee reached into the hat and pulled out a paper. Without opening it, she handed her choice to the Riley.

Carter noticed the sheriff glance his direction a fraction of a second before he unfolded the slip of paper. Riley didn't turn toward the light to read the name, which surprised Carter, but no one else seemed to notice.

Riley thumbed through the letters and handed Bailee a brown paper sack.

Carter knew. His fingers moved silently, nervously at his side.

As everyone waited, Bailee turned toward the light and read his note.

The men were silent. Waiting. Fearing. Reconsidering.

Bailee nodded once at the sheriff.

"Carter McKoy!" Riley shouted loud enough to be heard over the rain.

Carter didn't move. He didn't even breathe while every other man standing around him went wild. Some shouted, a few swore. Most let out a long-held sigh as if they'd dodged a bullet after they'd been dumb enough to stand in front of the gun. Like one living body they all shifted and migrated away from the sheriff's office, as though the air had suddenly chilled and it was time for the herd to move. Most headed toward the saloons. For them the evening's excitement had ended.

The woman the sheriff called Miss Bailee searched the crowd for a moment, her eyes full of question. Her gaze rested on Carter almost as casually as it had before she'd pulled a name from the hat. She knew he was the one, he had to be. He was the only man standing in the rain, not leaving.

To her credit, she didn't flinch. She just stared at him with those deep green eyes.

He stepped onto the porch, all muddy, hairy, six feet of him, almost expecting her to scream and run inside.

But she didn't. She just squared her shoulders and said, "I'm the last one." Her voice shook slightly. She bit her bottom lip before continuing. "I was kicked off a wagon train last month for being unfit to travel with good folks. I think I killed a man, but they are having trouble finding his body."

Her fingers trembled as she pressed them against her lips and forced herself to finish her list of shortcomings. "I'm twenty-five, so I guess that makes me an old maid. I've no money and only a few things in my wagon to bring to a marriage. But if you're willing, I'm willing to do what you wrote."

She lifted the paper sack where Carter had scribbled simply, "Be my wife, all my life."

He hadn't been able to think of anything else to write. Looking at her now, he decided she should have had a poem or something grand like Keats or Shelley would have written, not one line scratched on a paper sack.

"I've nowhere else to go," she stated more than begged.

She'd told him how little others valued her, and with her last words she'd made it plain that he was her last choice, her bottom of the barrel.

"Time's a-wasting." Riley hurried them into his office. "If you're both agreeable, I'll marry you and take the fine money. I'd like to get some sleep while this rain keeps trouble away."

Carter opened his hand, palm up to the woman. Her long slender fingers brushed across the calluses. He had the hands of a hardworking rancher. Hers were those of a lady.

Thunder shook the building suddenly, as though a stampede were just beyond the door. But all he would have felt if a hundred buffalo flattened the building was her fingers resting in his hand. She was a lady, the finest he'd probably ever see, yet she planned to give herself to him forever.

He closed his fingers in a gentle grip as Riley quickly read the necessary words. The sheriff looked as if he hadn't slept in a week. He didn't bother with anything except the pronouncing. The time for questions or proclamations had ended.

Carter didn't turn loose of Bailee's hand when he paid the fine.

The rain pounded on the roof so hard the sheriff had to shout, ordering them where to sign. "I'll check on you two in a week. If you're not treating her right, Carter, I'll see there's hell to pay. I'll come ever' week thereafter with the same question in mind. Has she changed her mind? The third time, if she elects to stay, I'm sending in the paperwork to Austin, and there'll be no turning back. So you better be good to her."

Carter raised an eyebrow. He'd known the sheriff for most of his life, and the old man had never accused him of a crime. The woman was a confessed murderer. Yet the sheriff warned *him*.

"You will be good to her?" The sheriff put his hand on Carter's shoulder.

Carter nodded, unsure what that would be.

The old lawman turned to complete the paperwork as he ordered Wheeler to carry the lady's two bags to Carter's wagon.

The lazy deputy groaned, but lifted the two small bags. He didn't seem at all surprised when Miss Bailee told him to carry them carefully.

When Deputy Wheeler was gone, she turned back to face Carter. "May I have my hand back?" Bailee asked without tugging to free her fingers.

Carter released her hand, feeling foolish for keeping it so long. He watched the sheriff, checked the rain at the window, glanced at his feet. Anything to avoid her watchful eyes.

When he did look at her, his fears were grounded. She stared right at him again.

"I think we're supposed to kiss." She said the words with no emotion.

He knew without question that his new wife was a woman of order. Everything in it's place. Everything right and proper. Before he could think of what to do, the woman stood on her tiptoes and touched her lips to his. He didn't lean down, or embrace her. In fact, she probably thought he turned to stone.

In a moment the kiss was over, and she stepped away to collect her few belongings and tell the sheriff she'd be back soon for the few boxes in her wagon.

Carter just stood in the center of the tiny office and watched her. She seemed to have no hint of how she affected him with her slight touch. He wouldn't be surprised if gravity suddenly gave way and he fell off the Earth. After all, stranger things had happened—a woman had just kissed him.

FIVE

"ARE YOU SURE HE'S ALL RIGHT?" BAILEE WHISPERED to Sheriff Riley as they stood on the porch and watched Carter drive the wagon through the river of mud that once was Main Street.

"He's fine." The sheriff added his spit to the wet street. "Strong as an ox, and smarter than most around these parts. Old Willard, over at the general store, says sometimes he gets in two or three books a month that Carter orders. Imagine that. Wonder what a man would do with so many books in such a short time?"

She stared at the lawman for any sign he might be joking.

None.

Bailee tried again. "But he hasn't said a word. He can talk?" She was starting to wonder if she'd married the village idiot, but she was relatively sure, after a week's stay in jail, the sheriff had the title sewn up.

"Carter can talk. He just doesn't have much to say." Riley scratched his head as if trying to decide how much to tell her. "He hasn't said more than a few words since the day I found him out on his parents' ranch twenty years ago. He couldn't have been more than four or five that winter."

Riley sucked on his cold pipe and mumbled as though the words bubbled unsummoned from his lips. "They were both dead, his folks. Had been for days. The cabin was freezing inside and without food or supplies of any kind. Whoever killed the couple must have taken all they could haul off, 'cause it weren't like the McKoys not to be prepared for winter coming on."

Bailee watched the man who was now her husband as the sheriff continued. "Somehow Carter got both his folks laid out in bed." Riley lowered his voice as Carter pulled the wagon closer. "We found him asleep between them. He was half dead himself from cold and lack of food."

Bailee felt a chill crawl all the way to her spine. There was no time to ask questions. Carter McKoy waited for her in the rain, and he was taking her to the very ranch where his parents were killed.

Without a word she stepped into the downpour and took his hand. He helped her onto the bare-board seat of his work wagon. The rain washed the town to muddy brown, and the few lights were blurred into hazy dullness. Bailee huddled into her coat, feeling as if this place had somehow swallowed her, and she would be forever trapped in monotones, without color, without true form, without life.

They rode past the few businesses. Two saloons, a questionable hotel, and several little stores with fronts that looked as if they might tumble in a good wind. The tinny sound of piano music clanged in the air like a cheap wind chime. Laughter, hollow and forced, crackled through the night sharp as dry lightning. Glad she was leaving this town, Bailee tried not to think about where she was going.

This had been her only choice; she'd not waste time regretting it.

Without turning her head, she glanced at the man beside her. He was tall, but his coat concealed his width. His hair could have been brown, or black, but for certain it was long and wet. He held the reins in big solid hands that wore no gloves. To his credit, he drove better than most.

"How far?" she asked as a sudden wind fought to take her coat.

Carter showed no sign of hearing her above the storm.

Bailee settled back, trying not to touch him as the wagon rocked. Did her destination matter? She was already soaked, and she had nowhere else to go. This was her fate. She told herself she wouldn't cry, but a few of the rain drops streaking down her face felt warm. She wasn't in prison, or hanging by her neck from some tree.

She was married, and for the past year married was all she'd prayed to be. She thought of adding a few amendments to the request, but knew it was too late.

In her mind she composed a letter to her father, knowing there was no need to ever write the words, for he would refuse to open any mail from her. But in her thoughts, she wrote: I'm doing fine, Father. Killed another man, this one not so much by accident. I didn't run this time, I confessed. My sentence was for life, not in prison, but in marriage.

Bailee closed her eyes and pushed thoughts of her father aside. He was her only relative, yet his last words to her were that she was dead to him. There was no looking back, she told herself. It was time to look forward. She glanced once more at the man who had just become her next of kin.

Carter stared straight ahead. Not because he needed to,

but more from fear that if he glanced the woman's direction, she'd talk to him.

He must have gone mad for a day, like someone given opium. Or like a man he heard about once who was kicked in the head by a mule he'd tried to shoe. The poor fellow didn't know where he was for days and thought his mother-in-law was his wife. Luckily, he suffered another blow during an argument with his not-so-willing bride, and recovered.

The idea of marriage had sounded good to Carter this afternoon, and the fine he paid seemed a fair price. He hadn't thought about what would happen after the lottery. He couldn't just take her home, bed her, and wait for children to pop out. Somewhere in between, he'd have to talk to her.

He ventured a quick glance.

To his surprise, she looked as frightened as he felt. When his leg brushed against hers, he could feel her shivering even through the wool of his trousers. Carter wondered if it was from the cold, or from the thought of going home with a man she didn't know.

He tried to tell himself that no one forced her to marry him. She'd done so of her own free will. But he wasn't sure that was true. If marrying him was her best choice, what had been the alternative?

Carter could never remember having to consider another person's feelings. He liked his aloneness. Among the few men in town he dealt with, he knew where he stood. And, except for an occasional saloon girl greeting him on the street, Carter didn't remember ever having said anything to a woman, much less worrying about how one felt.

Fighting down a growl of frustration, Carter reached

behind the bench and pulled out a tarpaulin he had used to cover the peaches that morning. He draped the stiff material over them both, cocooning them together.

"Thank you," his new wife whispered as she leaned against his side and folded into the tarp.

He had opened his arm to cover them, and now he left it resting hesitantly across her shoulders. She shivered for a few minutes more, then stopped as the space they shared grew warmer.

Carter wanted to pull away, telling himself he needed both hands to drive, but in truth the horses knew the way as well as he did. With the storm clamoring and the horses splashing through the mud, he could hear little. The night was so black they might have been moving through a river of ink, but he could feel her breathe. And the feel of her against his side made all else minuscule.

At the sheriff's office she'd looked tall, but, with his arm around her, she was hardly enough to hold. He felt as if he gripped a sparrow, all feathers and hollow bones.

She didn't say a word when they finally pulled up to the house. He wasn't surprised. In truth, all they could see of the place came in flashes of light muted by the rain. She couldn't tell that the barn was solid, or that a tack room stood next to it. She probably wouldn't even notice the small bunkhouse he and old Samuel built one year, more for Sam to stay in than anything else. She couldn't see that he kept up his mother's flower garden as well as a vegetable garden out back.

The three yard dogs poked their heads out from under the porch, but they didn't bother with a greeting.

He offered to help her down, but she seemed determined to manage on her own. Her skirts were so wet he didn't know how she walked in them. He grabbed both her bags with one hand and hurried to open the door for her.

Except for a few thin rays of watery light drifting through the windows by the kitchen, the house was dark. To its solid credit, the large room held warmth from a long dead fire and a silence from the storm that Carter always found comforting. His father had built the house, and Carter had been grown before he realized the fine workmanship that had gone into its design and building.

He set her bags down just inside the door to the bedroom, the only other room in the house. Crossing through the blackness of the large living area to the fireplace, he kindled a blaze to life.

When he finally turned around to face her, his new wife had disappeared. For a moment he almost believed she'd been a dream and nothing more. But then he saw the closed door leading to the bedroom and knew she was very much a reality. A reality he'd have to deal with. If she ever came out.

He didn't have time to stand around guessing, or waiting. There was work that had to be done. Carter crossed the room in long strides and opened the front door. The cold wind was almost a relief. He'd deal with his new wife after he brought in a few boxes of supplies and took care of the horses.

Carter stepped into the rain.

From the shadows of the darkened bedroom, Bailee watched Carter step off the porch and head toward the wagon. The man didn't seem to notice the pounding rain.

She felt her way to a table and found a candle and matches.

The light formed a tight circle around her, allowing little view of the room, but lending enough comfort to steady her hand. She moved slowly, trying to see through the darkness to what would be her new home.

The bed was made in best company fashion with a hand-crocheted coverlet. She crossed the room in baby steps. Everything seemed in order. An ivory-colored washbasin and pitcher. An embroidered lace cover over the nightstand. Music boxes carefully positioned along a ladder of tiny shelves climbing either side of the mirror. Every item in its place. The order and care surprised her.

Too much in order, Bailee thought as she tested the pitcher. Empty. She opened the nearest music box. It was unwound. When she ran her hand across the bedcover, a thin layer of dust clung to her damp fingers. Not a man's room. Not anyone's room.

No one lived here. No one had in years, she'd guess. Maybe not since the murders happened.

Bailee could almost see a small boy curled between the bodies of his parents in the shadowy room. He must have been so frightened, so alone.

She set the candle down and tugged off her wet clothes one layer at a time. For a moment she hesitated, thinking she should redress, but her other good dress was damp. Only her gown and robe, tucked away in the bottom of her bag, were dry. This was her home now and a woman could walk around her own house in a robe if no company were present. Carter wasn't company, she reminded herself. He was her husband.

By the time Carter returned, she'd made coffee and found a loaf of bread among the supplies he'd brought in. He opened the door and stood watching her for a minute before he thought to close the door and step inside. He lifted the bolt and twisted a lock.

Bailee watched him, also. He pulled off his coat and

hung it on a peg by the door. His shoulders were broad, his arms thick beneath the thin layer of his shirt. Nervously he toyed with an apple on the table before setting it aside on a small shelf by the door. There seemed nothing soft about him. Nothing of the little boy remained.

Except, she thought, the silence.

He walked to one of the two chairs she'd pulled up to the table and waited. When she sat down he did the same, and she couldn't hide a smile. His simple politeness gave her great comfort. A man who waited for a woman to be seated was probably not the type to beat his wife. Or at least she hoped not.

"I haven't had time to look for everything, but your kitchen seems in order and well stocked." She sliced the bread to keep her hands from shaking. Talk to him, she thought as she placed one slice on a plate and passed it to him. Just talk to him. There had been no jams or preserves, so she guessed he must like his bread plain.

He looked at the bread as if he'd never seen anything like it before, then stared back at her.

"I hung my things up in the bare wardrobe in the bedroom. I hope you don't mind?" When he didn't answer, she continued. "I know we are married, but I thought it would be best if we give ourselves time to get to know each other before we ... before we ..." How could she say "share a bed" to a man she didn't even know?

She opted for skipping that part and hoped he was smart enough to fill in the blanks. "I was thinking I could live alone in that bedroom for three months, maybe six before we ..." She had no idea where he would sleep, but apparently he slept somewhere else anyway. He must have expected her to take the room, for he'd placed her bags inside the door.

She finished pouring his coffee and looked up at him, proud of herself for setting the rules.

The bluest eyes she'd ever seen stared back at her. Winter blue. The color of a cold night sky. They caught the firelight in their depths, but didn't warm.

"So after three or six months or so when we . . ."

He raised one finger.

"One?" she questioned, then glanced down at her coffee when his meaning registered. "One month."

That wasn't enough, she thought. Not when they hadn't even started talking to each other. But at least he was willing to allow her *some* time. She'd feared that he might attack her as soon as they were out of the sheriff's sight. On the wagon train she'd heard tales of mail-order brides wedded and bedded before they'd had time to say a word. The first sound the husband heard from his wife was a scream of terror.

One month, she thought. One month to learn not to scream.

Bailee laughed to herself. No man had ever attacked her, and she doubted one would start now. She wasn't the type, she guessed. She was more the type men asked to accompany their mothers to the church socials than the woman they tried to lure into the shadows for a stolen kiss.

She glanced up at Carter. He stared at her with one eyebrow lifted, as if he'd never seen the likes of her before in his life.

"Oh, I was thinking of something else." Her cheeks warmed. He must think her a complete fool for laughing. "One month would be acceptable, Mr. McKoy. And if you've any rules, please feel free to express them."

They drank coffee in silence for a while, listening to

the fireplace crackle and the wind tap on the shutters.

"I'm a good cook," she finally said. "And I ran my father's house since I was twelve. I'm almost twenty-six, which I know is quite an old maid, but I'm not set in my ways. I'll try to adjust."

The thought that he might turn her out suddenly occurred to her. After all, he'd drawn the last woman. The one left. "I know I'm not as pretty as Sarah and Lacy are, but I can—"

His hand covered hers. When she tried to pull it away, he held tight until she met his gaze.

Slowly she lifted her chin and squared her shoulders. Without breaking his stare, she whispered, "You want me to stay?"

He nodded slightly.

Bailee closed her eyes and took a deep breath. Finally, maybe for a while she could stop running. By marrying him, she had taken a first step toward something rather than away. Even when she'd told people she would someday be going to see Francis Tarleton in Santa Fe, she'd been running from the truth about him. He hadn't come back for her. He probably hadn't waited for her a month, and had already married another.

At least this Carter McKoy would wait a month for her.

Bailee opened her eyes and looked at the stranger before her. Her husband.

"Then I'll stay." She smiled when he squeezed her fingers in his warm grip.

SIX

CARTER WAITED UNTIL HE HEARD NO MORE STIRRING from the bedroom where Bailee disappeared. He finished his coffee before banking the fire, then walked the perimeter of the large room, as he did every night, checking locks and bolts. He stopped at her door. Logic told him her windows were bolted, but before walking away, he fought a habit of almost twenty years to check.

The windows were locked, he reminded himself. He had no idea how she'd react if he opened the door to look, but the odds were not with him. The windows were locked, he almost said aloud, and with the rain she wasn't likely to open them. He forced himself to step away.

She made a good cup of coffee, he decided, better than any he'd ever boiled. He put his cup in the washtub. He wasn't sure what he'd been supposed to do with the one slice of bread she'd passed him. The action reminded him of a little girl playing with a tea set. He thought of telling her not to waste the bread. He only bought a few days' supply every month when he went to town. She seemed on such a mission as she cut and served it to him. For all he knew, she might be performing some kind of wifely ritual. She was the first woman to cross the threshold since the doctor and Sheriff Riley carried his mother out years ago.

Carter would have to talk to the woman sometime, but "Don't slice the bread" didn't seem like it should be the first thing a husband said to a wife. Before he could think of something appropriate, she started setting rules down as to where they should sleep.

A month, he thought. That wouldn't be so long. He could hardly expect her to join him in his room the first night. The poor woman didn't even know where it was.

Carter walked to a corner where the flooring changed slightly in color. He slid a rug aside and lifted a trapdoor that had been invisible a moment before. "What would I have done with her if she had come to my bed?" he mumbled as he stepped down wide stairs.

"My duty?" He reached the basement that looked little more than a tiny root cellar for storage. Extra supplies lined the rough shelves. Potatoes, squash, and other vegetables were stored in bins cushioned with sand. With a touch, he shifted a few planks on the cellar wall and turned into a narrow hallway, tapping the overhead door frame as he passed. The planks rocked back in place erasing all light as he moved farther into the passage, tapping his way along well-known beams.

For once he didn't close the trapdoor to the main room upstairs, just in case she needed him during the night. The bolted doors and windows and the storm would keep him safe from intruders tonight.

The passage widened into the first of his private rooms. His footsteps silenced as he stepped onto a rug.

Once the month was over, Carter decided, he'd bring

her downstairs and breed with her. That's what married people did, he supposed. Otherwise, where would all the children come from? He'd read about love and passion, but it didn't seem like something that would ever stir a simple man like himself.

Once the breeding was over, she could go back to the upstairs room if she liked. He had no idea how long bedding a woman would take. Not more than a few minutes, he'd guess. He figured he had the basics of the act down, but there were probably things he should say or do before he started.

When he touched her hand tonight, that was the first time he'd felt a woman's skin since a year ago when he'd wandered into one of the saloons in town just to look around. A girl with painted lips, and breasts pushing out of her dress, grabbed his hand and tried to pull him upstairs.

"Wanta go upstairs?" the painted woman kept saying, but her expression seemed to say more, almost like the words were some kind of code.

He'd just stood there like a statue being bombarded with the feel of her touching his hand and arm and the way she smelled of near-dead roses. He watched as she pressed herself against his arm and smiled like she'd given him a gift. Her breath fouled the rose smell. Rubbing against his coat caused part of her dress to slip off her shoulder, and he saw the brown sweat-stained cotton of her undergarment.

"Come on, mister. Fanny will take you for a little ride," she'd whispered with a whiskey slur. "You wanta go upstairs, don't you?"

When he didn't answer, one of the men at the long bar yelled for the woman to back away. "He don't like none of us living," the man said as he drew most of the saloon's attention. "Lived out on the farm with his dead parents until the sheriff buried them and made him come to town. Ran away from the only family in town who offered him a good home. He don't want nothing to do with a living soul."

Another man joined in. "I remember him. My dad said the sheriff should've sent him away and not let a boy live out there alone. But Riley's got a soft spot for dumb animals, even the ones who walk on two legs."

The crowd closed in around Carter, mumbling about how he never went to school, or came to church . . . or even stopped in for a drink.

"What you doing here?" someone shouted as the mob migrated closer, stealing the air from around Carter.

"He's here for a woman!" Fanny yelled, then leaned nearer and whispered, "It's a slow day, mister. Half price to the dim-witted." She tugged at his coat as if she thought she had the strength to budge him.

The smells of too many unwashed bodies and cheap whiskey closed in around him. Carter thought he could feel the warmth of everyone's breath reach him even before their shouted words registered.

Suddenly he moved. With all the force of a wounded bear, he plowed a wide row through the saloon and out the door, not stopping until he reached his wagon.

That was the last time he'd gone near anything in town except the loading dock of the general store and the livery. At least, it had been until tonight.

Carter crossed the blackness of his study. He didn't need the light. He loved the silence of his underground rooms. The faint odor of earth enriched the air and the smell of books welcomed him. He discovered reading the year he'd been hauled, fighting and screaming, to town and dumped on the preacher's doorstep. The old preacher's wife used him as a servant. She'd insisted he do the wash and all hauling and chopping. No room was ever clean enough to pass her inspection, so most nights he was pulled from bed to redo chores. On weekends they rented him out to the blacksmith to work from dawn to dusk for money he never saw. On school days Carter was allowed to sit in the back of the classroom and watch and learn and read.

By spring he'd read all the books the old preacher allowed his students to touch. There was no reason to stay. Carter walked all night to get back to his parents' ranch. On the way he devised a plan to make his home forever safe.

The preacher came by the next day, yelling for him to show himself. Carter hid. A week later the sheriff left a box of food on the porch. By then Carter had dug a hiding place no one could find. He knew his parents had a balance at the general store, so he began leaving notes for supplies at the crossroads. Other ranchers would pick up the note nailed to a fence post and marked General Store. Whenever Willard got around to it, he'd send the supplies. Sometimes the old man would bring them out himself, adding extra items to increase the order. Books were a slow mover at the store. They were often packed in with the food.

Sheriff Riley would ride out now and then, but Carter was never around. Once in a while the sheriff would sit on the porch and talk about how Carter should come back.

After a few years no one bothered with Carter. He'd harvest his fruit crop every spring for enough money for supplies and more books. An old handyman named Samuel came by the place when work was slow in town. For meals and a bed, he'd work around the ranch showing Carter more about carpentry than actually doing any. He never stayed long, or invaded Carter's privacy with questions. He slept in the barn until he helped Carter build a small bunkhouse. Over the years Samuel came less and less. Slowly the bunkhouse became more and more of a workshop, but Carter left the bunk, just in case the old fellow dropped by.

Carter ran his hand along the volumes as he walked through his study. For years he'd ordered books on how to do or grow everything. But not one told him how to be a husband.

He tapped the archway overhead as he crossed into his bedroom. Over the years he'd learned to move around below without lights by tapping the same places each time, reassuring himself that he was exactly where he thought.

Carter tugged at his shirt. Three steps to the left was a huge chair he often sat in while reading all night. Two steps to the right was his bed. As with everything in his life, all was in order. Blindfolded, he could have picked any of a hundred items in the room. His clothes were always in the same place. A lantern hung from the ceiling so that it offered the best light for reading. The matches were in a box directly underneath.

Only tonight all was not in exact order. A faint light shown from above his bed. When he'd built the rooms, Carter had added two vents. One in the hallway beneath the upstairs fireplace, for warmth, and a larger one in his underground bedchamber in case he ever needed a narrow escape route. The tunnel opening traveled the few feet from the ceiling of his room, to the floor of the only bedroom upstairs. The shaft had been disguised by thin slats of wood matching the floor above. To ensure he never accidentally stepped on the wood and caved the tunnel in, Carter placed the opening directly beneath the huge four-poster bed.

Until tonight he never knew that if a light were left on upstairs, it would filter down. He'd checked to make sure light didn't travel up when he was underground. No one would ever notice his light shinning from below into the shadowy bedroom. But in the blackened underground, he noticed.

Carter stripped off his clothes, stretched out on his bed, and stared at the light above him. The glow was pale, no more than a sliver of moonlight would make through gingham curtains, but it was there. For a man who'd spent years sleeping in total blackness, it was bright indeed.

She was there. She was in the room he'd carefully decorated to look like a picture he'd seen in a catalog. He'd even put the music boxes on the shelves as if his mother had left them there. Only his mother would have had no use for music boxes, and he'd never wound them to see if they worked.

Carter rolled to his side and closed his eyes. With the vent at least he'd know she was safe. He could hear her moving about her room, and from the sounds, he knew what she was doing. Pouring water in the bowl, pulling back the bedcovers.

Carter rolled to his stomach and placed a pillow over his head. He didn't want to think about what the woman was doing. There were enough times she'd be with him, she shouldn't invade his thoughts when he was alone. He'd figured she'd alter his pattern of life slightly, not turn it upside down.

He forced himself to think of how he'd scrubbed the walls of the bedroom for days, trying to get all his parents' blood off and how he'd burned the furniture and bedding. Then slowly he'd begun to rebuild the room as if somehow by making it normal his life would return to normal also. Samuel had helped him build the huge bed on the spot so large it couldn't be moved by one man. He'd also brought Carter flyers from Fort Worth showing all the items he'd bought to place inside the room.

Now the woman claimed it as hers. A woman who was also settling into his thoughts.

Maybe tomorrow he'd tell her how she filtered into every thought. But that probably shouldn't be the first thing they talked about. Besides, telling a woman you think about her when she's not there seemed a rather foolish thing to admit.

Even with the pillow buffering, he heard the latch being released from the shutters in the bedroom above.

Carter sat up in bed. The woman had opened a window. On this cold rainy night she opened the window. The thought crossed his mind that she might be escaping, running away from him, but why wouldn't she use the door four feet away? He'd done nothing to make her believe he'd hold her against her will.

Rolling to his back, he gave up trying not to listen. He heard the bedropes creak slightly as she crawled into bed. The light disappeared above him. She'd blown out the candle.

Carter lay perfectly still trying to hear her breathing. The ropes creaked again. She was settling in, he thought, and she hadn't relatched the window and she wasn't running away.

He'd never been more wide awake.

After several minutes he thought he heard her crying softly, then only silence.

Carter waited half an hour. There was no question of sleep when he knew a window upstairs was open. Finally he gave up and stood, pulling on his trousers with a sudden jerk. The only sound he made was a light tap at the top of first his bedchamber doorway and then a second later at the entrance to the hallway. He stepped between the sliding panels and into the cellar, then climbed the stairs two at a time.

Moving as silently as he could, Carter crossed the main room and stood at her door. He hesitated with his fingers already on the knob. What if she wasn't asleep? The sight of him entering her room might frighten her. Though he'd given her no reason to fear him. The memory of the woman the sheriff had called Sarah flashed in his mind. She'd looked so frightened, and all she'd done was marry, just as Bailee had.

But he had to be safe. Since the night he'd returned home all those years ago, he double-checked every lock every night.

The need to secure his fortress won out. He opened her door and crossed to the windows. Carefully he closed the shutter and lifted the latch into place. Glanced at her, curled up in the middle of the bed, he couldn't help but stare for a long moment. Her hair, unbound and spreading across the pillow, shone even in the faint light.

He left her room as silently as he'd come and returned to his bed. Now he could sleep; all was in order.

Bailee awoke late, thinking it was before dawn. When she sat up, she saw tiny slivers of light through the shutters and knew it was full sunrise. Somehow, the shutter she'd thought she'd opened must have drifted back into place.

She dressed as quickly as she could and hurried into the kitchen. There was no sign of Carter, but a half pot of coffee warmed on a corner of the stove. She went about making breakfast, finding the basics of stores, but nothing for baking, or canning, or even churning butter.

By the time Carter entered with a load of wood for the stove, she had a simple meal on the table. He looked surprised, but took his chair when she pointed to one. They ate in silence on mismatched china and a tablecloth worn thin from washing.

Bright sunlight shown through long thin windows over the kitchen area, and for the first time Bailee saw the room clearly. It was really far more livable than she'd thought last night. The furnishings were finely carved, not rough homemade. A spinning wheel stood in one corner, a rocker by the fire. A few pieces of china were faced out in a hutch, and an empty pie safe stood on the other side of the wood bin. Polished bookshelves framed the rock of the fireplace with copies of Emerson, Hawthorne, Dickens, Tennyson sliced in between catalogs for farming and gardening.

The books looked old, well cared for, and many times read.

A few things in the room seemed odd at second glance. A rifle stood in one corner, almost unseen in the shadows, with a box of bullets next to it. A thin bookshelf almost as tall as Carter stood near the door, but was empty except for an apple sitting on one shelf as though it were some prized heirloom.

"I have a few boxes in my wagon in town. Dishes and things I've made." She didn't add that they were things she had to pack in an hour's time while her father bought her a wagon and team. "Maybe the next time you're there, you could pick them up for me. I'd like to have them."

She raised her gaze and wasn't surprised to find him staring at her. The blue of his eyes hadn't changed. She thought she saw an intelligence in their depths and wondered if he loved these books or if they were just decorations in his house like the music boxes no one wound and the china washstand that looked as if it had never been used.

Suddenly nervous, she stood and took her plate to the wash pan. "I made a list of a few things I could use from the store." As she set a scrap of paper on the corner of the table, it suddenly occurred to her that she had no idea if this man she married had a dime to his name. What if he used all his money to pay her fine?

Bailee tried to be practical. "Since we're married, I guess the oxen, if they're still alive, belong to you, and the wagon as well. You can sell them if you wish, but I'd really like to keep my boxes."

She fought back tears. They were stupid oxen, she'd swore at them many times on the trail, but they were hers. If he sold them he'd whittle her belongings down to a few crates. And if he refused to bring the boxes, she'd be left with broken mismatched dishes. Her father had only let her pack a few things that she'd made or had belonged to her mother. She'd stuffed them into crates so fast she doubted much of the china was still whole, but he'd wanted her out of his house before dawn.

Carter stood and collected his plate and cup. He brushed her arm slightly as he sat them in the sink. Without a word he downed his hat and rain slicker.

Bailee wasn't sure what she was supposed to do. The married couple who lived across the street from her father always seemed to be laughing. There was nothing funny about the silent man she followed out the door.

As he stepped off the porch, Bailee caught his arm. "I'll have lunch ready at noon."

He nodded without raising his eyes from where her fingers rested on his sleeve.

Bailee did what she'd seen the young wife across the street do a hundred times. "Have a good day, husband." She leaned close and kissed him on the cheek.

Carter stepped away suddenly and almost ran for the barn. The three mangy dogs she'd caught a glimpse of the night before hurried after him.

Bailee smiled at her own boldness, feeling suddenly better than she had in weeks. If he didn't like her actions, he was going to have to tell her. They might never have long talks by the fire, but somehow they'd settle in together. He might just offer the very thing she needed most in this world. A quiet place to rest for a while and heal.

She walked back into the house and laughed aloud as she noticed that the slip of paper she'd scribbled a grocery list on was now missing.

A few minutes later she heard the wagon pass the house and head up the road toward town.

SEVEN

THE SUN MANAGED TO DRY A THIN LAYER OF HARD dirt over the muddy street by the time Carter pulled into town. He gave Bailee's list to one of the girls at Willard's general store and walked over to the livery. He felt people watching him, staring even more intensely than usual. A few smiled at him, and to his surprise, a saloon girl passed him glaring as though looking right through him. It appeared that by marrying he'd become acceptable to some and off-limits to others.

"Morning!" Angus Mosely, the livery owner, shouted to Carter as though he spoke to him every day. "How's the little wife?" he asked in a voice people could hear all the way to the saloon.

Carter nodded once and stopped while still several feet upwind of Mosely. He had no idea how he should answer such a greeting, or why the man suddenly seemed concerned about his wife. He'd had to deal with the livery owner a few times over the years, but Mosely was usually too drunk to say much.

Though only a few years older than Carter, Mosely

moved like a man twice his age. Old age had settled into his bones early. He had a lazy eye, or more accurately he had one good eye in a body otherwise consumed with little or no activity. The one alert eye took in everything around him while it dragged the rest of his dirty face and smelly body along behind.

Mosely's only friend in town seemed to be Wheeler, Sheriff Riley's deputy, who could match both Mosely's work habits most days and his drinking habits most nights. Willard had often told Carter stories of finding the pair passed out in front of his store at dawn.

"She must be fine and dandy." Mosely tried again to make conversation, interrupting Carter's thoughts. "I'll bet she sent you into town after her things or you wouldn't be here pestering me." He laughed in short little sounds that lifted one side of his mouth only briefly. "Better face it, mister, from now on you can stop thinking and just wait for orders. Your carefree days are over."

Carter didn't answer as he followed Mosely into the barn. Willard told Carter once that the whole town couldn't decide if Mosely smelled like the barn, or if the barn smelled of Mosely. Either way most men breathed shallow once they stepped inside the livery.

Mosely's rambling about carefree days made no sense. Carter hadn't had a day free of worry in his life. Why should having a wife make it any different?

Mosely talked on, greeting the horses in the same tone he greeted most people. He needed no return fire of conversation from Carter or the animals.

He finally led Carter to Bailee's wagon behind the stables. If the schooner were in any worse shape, Carter would have suggested using it as firewood. The hand brake had fallen completely off and lay in the mud. There were holes in even the patches of the canvas, and one of the corral horses had gnawed a crescent shape into the wood of the bench seat.

Carter looked inside. Several boxes, layered in mud and dirt, were lodged against one end. A small bed was wedged into the other. Empty boxes and barrels that must have once held supplies cluttered the middle of the wagon. Everything was soaked from days of rain.

"You owe me three dollars for storage and feed for the animals." Mosely scratched his beard. "I'd take a pair of the oxen in trade, but I've no use for the wagon."

Carter shook his head and handed the man a gold coin.

Mosely shadowed him as Carter walked around the wagon. "For another four bits I'd drive it out to your place."

Carter agreed without bartering and walked away. He went back to the general store and was relieved to see his supplies being loaded. Even minutes in town made him feel closed in.

"I got everything," Willard boasted when he noticed Carter checking to see that the boxes were tied. "Mighty glad to see you married. It'll be more business for me. She ordered a few things you never put on your list."

Carter tilted his hat an inch in thanks and climbed onto the bench. Before he could release the brake and urge the horses into action, a woman came running from across the street. She jumped the ruts like a child told to keep clean.

Even though he'd only seen her once, and it had been raining, Carter recognized her. The sheriff called her Lacy last night when he'd married her off by proxy to a soldier. She was so short, he might've thought her younger if she didn't have the figure of a full-grown woman.

"Are you the man who married my friend Bailee?" She stepped up on the wagon as though she planned to sit beside him.

Carter nodded and moved toward the center of the bench.

Lacy leaned closer and whispered, "I'm Lacy. Will you take a note to her?"

He nodded again.

"I got to get word to her as fast as possible." The girl looked as if she might cry if he refused her request. "I've no way of contacting Sarah. No one seems to know where her husband took her once they married."

She fought down tears, then added, "One of the men in the print shop said this was your wagon, so I've been watching, hoping to catch you."

Lacy stopped long enough to breathe. "You'll tell Bailee I'm fine, won't you? And you'll watch over her? She's a real good person even if she does have a temper and tends to kill people."

Carter fought down a laugh. He had a hard time believing the creature curled up in the huge four-poster bed last night was a murderer.

Lacy pulled a folded paper from her pocket. "Would you give her this? It's real important or I wouldn't ask."

Carter took the paper and folded it into his shirt pocket with one hand.

"Thank you dearly." She leaned closer and kissed him on the cheek before he could think to move. "Give Bailee my love."

Then, as fast as she'd appeared, Lacy vanished.

Carter was half a mile out of town before he touched his cheek. He'd been kissed twice in one morning and had no idea why. Married life was certainly surprising.

He spent the rest of the drive trying to think of something to say to Bailee. A man's first words to his wife should be something worth remembering. But he was afraid if he started talking, he wouldn't know how to stop. Over the years he'd had long conversations in his mind about things no woman would probably be interested in hearing. He'd seen women walking the street talking, but he had no idea what the creatures talked about.

It was noon when he pulled into his small farm yard. He sensed the changes even before he pinpointed each one. Rugs hung across the clothesline. The porch had been swept. The chickens that normally wandered around the yard were missing.

Every muscle in Carter's body tightened. When the raiders had attacked years ago, they'd taken everything, including all livestock. They'd left only broken dishes and furniture too large to bother with.

As he swung down from the wagon preparing for the worst, he glanced at the windmill and relaxed a bit. The broken blade still pointed north. No one had entered the back gate or it would have moved.

Bailee stepped through the front door with an armload of quilts, and he forgot about the windmill trap he'd put into place months ago.

She smiled shyly. "Hello. I didn't think you'd be back so soon. I thought I'd air out my bedroom."

He watched her blush as she sat the blankets aside.

"I'll put your lunch on the table." She turned to step back inside.

He touched her shoulder, stopping her progress, and for a second, felt her stiffen. When she looked back at him, he thought he saw fear in her eyes.

But she didn't step away. She just stood beside him, so

close he could hear her breathe, silently telling him she planned to face whatever happened.

He reached into his pocket and handed her the note Lacy had given him without taking his eyes off her face. He liked the way she pulled her hair up on the sides so he could see her clearly.

The hint of panic drained from her as she opened Lacy's note and smiled at the bold signature. "It's from my friend," she said as she read the note to herself.

Emotions battled in her expression, and he wished he'd thought to glance at the letter earlier. The blood seemed to drain from her face as he watched her finish the note.

Worry or fear drew her mouth tight. "I . . . I . . ." A cry choked through. She fought for control. Her slender fingers pressed against her throat.

Carter caught her when she crumbled, sweeping her up as easily as one might a willow branch. He carried her into the cool house wondering what he was supposed to do with her. She made no protest as she suddenly breathed deeply as though she'd been under water, but her body stiffened once more. Whatever had been in the letter terrified her, but his nearness gave her no comfort.

He lowered her into the rocker and knelt beside her. For the first time he noticed how frail she seemed. He guessed that for the past weeks she'd been the leader, the rock on whom the other two women depended. Only whatever had been written on the note had broken her strength, if only for a few moments.

For a long while he just watched her, unsure what to do, and having no idea what to say. She closed her eyes and leaned into the chair as if the wood could cuddle her fear away.

"Lacy writes to warn me," she whispered without opening her eyes. "The man we thought we killed on the road is rumored to be alive. Since the deputies the sheriff sent to look for the body never found one, Sheriff Riley fears the rumors may be true."

Her fingers twisted together in her lap. "A drunk swears Zeb Whitaker told him we have something of his, and Lacy writes that he's sworn to kill us all if he must in order to get it."

Bailee made herself breathe. "The sheriff thinks the drunk could be lying, just to stir up trouble, but if he's not . . ."

Carter covered her fingers with his hand, and she finally opened her eyes. He saw not fear, but embarrassment in her stare. Somehow, seeing her like this was too intimate for strangers, but she was not a woman to run and hide. Even now, she faced him.

"I don't have anything of his." She leaned forward slightly. "I swear. We took nothing, not even the gold coins that spilled out of his saddlebags when he fell."

When Carter didn't answer, she rocked back in the chair. "How can I expect anyone to believe me." The words were more to herself than to him. "I'm just so tired of running."

He tightened his grip on her hands until she looked at him once more.

She smiled. "I can't allow myself to panic over a rumor, now can I? There is much to do."

The rattle of an approaching wagon drew their attention. As they both looked up, her schooner and oxen pulled into view.

"You brought my wagon and team here?"

He nodded.

"I thought you'd sell them." The fear and sadness in

her eyes were gone, replaced by excitement. "You had a right, you know. All the things I ordered from the general store must have cost quite a sum."

Carter followed her to the porch as Mosely drove close. She lowered her voice. "It does look ragged, doesn't it? You'd hardly believe how only a few months ago I thought it looked grand."

She moved closer to him as Mosely stepped down from her wagon. Carter found it little comfort that she was less afraid of him than the livery owner.

"Morning, missus." Mosely tipped his hat. "Your man paid me to bring your things out."

Bailee was so excited she hardly greeted the man. By the time Mosely stepped a foot on the porch, she had jumped into the back of the wagon and was handing out boxes to Carter along with a steady stream of orders as to where she wanted each crate placed in the house.

One box was china, one quilts, one table linen. Bailee told him about each as she watched him carefully carry it into the house. Mosely stood far enough away so that she didn't hand him a box, but close enough to offer a comment or two as she worked.

After several trips Carter returned to the back of the wagon to find her standing empty-handed. "That's all I have. The bed is ruined and everything else is just empty crates."

Carter raised his hands and she leaned forward. His fingers encircled her waist as he lifted her down.

"You'll keep the wagon?"

He nodded.

"And the oxen?"

Carter smiled as he lowered her slowly. The oxen were in such bad shape he wouldn't have been surprised to have to pay someone to take them off his hands, but she seemed to think they were somehow a part of her dowry.

"I best be getting back," Mosely interrupted. "As it is, I probably missed lunch all together, what with having to drive all the way out here. I had no idea your place was so far out."

"You're welcome to join us for lunch," Bailee said, then glanced at Carter.

He tried to hide his anger, but his fingers must have tightened slightly at her waist, for she pulled away.

"But we understand if you need to get back to your business," she added, as if knowing she'd been too quick with the invitation. She watched Carter. "Perhaps you'll join us some other time, Mr. Mosely?"

Mosely didn't take the hint. "I guess I could stay. No one will miss me for a while."

Carter wanted to stop the man from going inside. He didn't like anyone in his house. He'd let the woman in for one night, and she was already opening the door to others. He'd seen the fear in her eyes. He knew she needed to be safe. Couldn't she understand that this wasn't the way?

There was nothing to do but follow her inside. He wanted to unhitch the horses, but he wasn't about to let Mosely into his house without watching him every moment. The horses and the oxen would have to wait.

Carter glanced at the rug covering the entrance to his underground home. It was still in place. Luckily, Bailee, while cleaning, hadn't worked her way across the room. No one knew about the stairs, not even Sheriff Riley. It was only a matter of time before Bailee noticed. Another thing Carter hadn't thought about when he'd decided to put his name in the marriage hat last night. Before long she'd know his secrets.

Mosely walked around the room inspecting everything. "Mighty nice place you got here, Carter. Look at all them books." He pulled one from the shelf. "I'll bet they're your parents. Folks say your mother could read and your pa had even attended one of them colleges."

Bailee thought the comment strange, but didn't ask what he meant. True, most folks in this part of the country were lucky to get any schooling at all, but if Carter's folks came from back East, it wouldn't have seemed extraordinary that they were educated.

"Great furniture. Some of the finest I've seen made in these parts. Wouldn't want to sell any of it, would you? I know folks in town who would like having someone to buy tables and chairs from besides the undertaker."

Carter didn't bother to answer. He had no interest in going into business with Mosely.

Bailee suggested twice that Mosely wash his hands before the man took the hint. By the time he'd scrubbed off a few layers of dirt, she had lunch on the table. A simple vegetable stew Carter didn't take the time to taste as he watched Mosely.

The man ate half of Carter's monthly loaf of bread, even going so far as to use one thick slice to wipe up the last drippings in his bowl. He bragged on the food as his good eye continued to scan the room, probably trying to spot every detail to tell his friends, assuming Mosely had any.

The clank of Mosely's spoon in the empty bowl hadn't finished rattling before Carter stood at the door waiting for him to leave.

Mosely was a man used to feeling his welcome wear

thin. He said his farewell to Bailee, grunted at Carter, and hurried out, claiming it was time to get back to work.

Bailee walked to the porch, but Carter watched Mosely from the doorway. The little man untied the nag he'd brought behind the wagon and climbed up. He waved, said her cooking was mighty good and he'd have to come back some time and try it again.

Bailee glanced back at Carter before thanking the man. She didn't encourage him to make good on his promise.

They stood in silence and watched him ride away.

When he disappeared, Bailee turned to face Carter.

He was surprised to see anger in her eyes. The kind of anger that set her face afire. The woman was a kaleidoscope of emotions.

"You didn't want me to invite him to lunch, did you?" She asked the question as though *he'd* done something wrong.

He wasn't sure whether to nod or shake his head while he tried to figure out if she was angry at him, or at the fact Mosely ate so much. Surely she noticed how much bread the little man put away.

He'd taken too long to think about it by the time he realized patience wasn't one of her virtues.

Her hands rubbed up and down her skirt a few times before balling into fists at her waist. "Well, how am I supposed to know what you want if you don't tell me?"

He had a strong suspicion that she was mad at him, not upset about the bread.

"I know we're both new at marriage, but I'm trying. You have to tell me what bothers you." She moved her hands down the sides of her skirt once more as if trying to remain calm. "Then I'll try not to do it. I'll tell you what bothers me and hope you'll respect it just the same.

Trying not to get on each other's nerves seems as good a place to start as any."

When he didn't answer, she pushed past him and went into the house. As she began prying into one of her crates, she added, "I can't be a mind reader. You have to talk to me sometime, Carter McKoy. You can't go around nodding at me once in a while and expect me to know what you are thinking."

One board came off and clamored to the floor. "Patience has never been my strong suit. I'm not sure I can live here in silence. If you didn't want me around, why did you pay the fine and marry me? Maybe you just want a housekeeper. But that doesn't make sense. Except for a little dust, this place is clean."

Another board hit the floor. "It's not that I don't thank you for fetching my things. That was a kind thing to do, but you could have told me about Mosely. If I'd gotten a foot closer to him, I never would have invited him inside. He smells worse than a horse."

Fascinated, Carter watched her. He'd never seen anyone argue with herself.

She took a deep breath. "All right. If you won't tell me what bothers you, tell me what you like."

She faced him squarely, a warrior preparing to fight.

Carter swallowed, guessing she wasn't going to back down. He had to say something to her, and he had to say it now. "I like . . ." He hesitated. "I liked it when you kissed me."

She couldn't have looked more surprised if he'd slapped her. "Well, that was only proper. That is what married folks do." She no longer met his stare.

He was in over his head. He should stop talking. But he had to ask, "How often?"

"How often what?" she answered.

"Do married folks kiss?" He couldn't remember ever seeing his parents kiss, and he knew he never saw the preacher and his wife touch.

She pulled linen from her crate as if it were vital she got everything out as fast as possible. "I don't know," she answered without looking up. "As often as they like, I suppose. I can't stand around all day talking. I've work to do."

Carter walked to the door as she turned back to her boxes. He decided she was the most fascinating creature he'd ever met. She'd demanded he talk and when he'd asked one question, she'd suddenly been too busy to discuss anything.

He couldn't get her out of his mind as he unhitched the oxen and put them out to pasture, or when he brushed down the horses and backed the wagon into a corner of the barn. He pulled out his tools and began repairing the bench seat. It would take a month, maybe more, of working a few minutes at a time to get the wagon back in shape. But he could find the time. If she wanted to keep the thing, he'd see that it was in good shape.

He was hanging up the newly oiled harnesses in the tack room when he heard her enter the barn. He didn't turn around as she neared, he only listened to the swishing sounds her skirt made as she walked and wondered if she ever walked anywhere slowly.

"I thought I'd come out and say thank you once more for bringing my things back from town. Everything happened so fast, the letter, Mr. Mosely, and all. I didn't tell you how much having my things means to me. The week we were in jail, I was sure someone had taken them or that the weather would ruin them. Not that they're worth much, but some of my belongings have been with me all my life."

He could hear her shifting, waiting for him to say something.

"Well, I'll be getting back. It's almost time to start supper."

He turned to face her just as she moved to leave. He held his hand up but stopped short of catching her arm. The memory of how she'd stiffened to his touch was still too fresh.

Her eyes were bright with question, but he saw no fear.

Slowly he brushed his hand along her waist. When she didn't step away, he slid his fingers to her back and tugged slightly.

Hesitantly she took a step closer to him.

He leaned down, until his mouth was a breath from her lips. There, he waited.

All she had to do was step away, for his hand rested only feather light against her back.

But she didn't. She waited.

He moved closer, brushing his lips against hers in a kiss as light as summer lace. He wouldn't frighten her. He'd step away the moment she stiffened to his touch. He just wanted to feel what her kiss would be like on his mouth. He wanted to taste her lips.

To his surprise, she leaned closer.

EIGHT

BAILEE REMINDED HERSELF SHE'D BEEN KISSED A FEW times before by men who seemed finely polished in experience, but none compared to Carter. He barely touched her lips, yet a warmth spread through her, melting muscle and bone to butter. This wasn't an advance he made, or conquest. His kiss was simple and straightforward, an experiment in intimacy.

When she leaned closer, his body jerked slightly. She knew he was a man who'd let very few people near.

His short beard tickled her nose, but she wouldn't break the kiss. Not after she'd told him this was how married people behaved. He was doing what he thought was right, what he obviously wanted to do. Yet at the same time, his silence asked that she respond.

She rested her hand on his shoulder. His body was solid, like an oak. When she opened her lips slightly and moved them against his, she once more felt a quake rivet through him. The very core of his being reacted to her.

But he didn't step away. He stood, suddenly turning to

stone while she brushed her mouth over his, teaching him something he hadn't known to ask about.

Her fingers slid from his shoulders to his chest, testing the wall that was him, feeling heat pass through the thin layer of his cotton shirt. After a lifetime of being surrounded by people and still very much alone, she needed to know someone was close. She loved pressing her palm against the drumming of another heart. She slowly moved her hand down to his waist, sensing his reaction to her. He was newborn to the feel of her so near.

When her fingers rested at his belt, his hand moved to her shoulder. This time it was her turn to be shocked. His fingers slid down the front of her blouse.

She sighed against his lips as he brushed over her breast. Her mind told her his action was totally improper. Such advances, if they had to occur, should only happen in the bedroom. But she'd been so long without feeling anything but fear or anger that his caress warmed like a beam of paradise accidentally slicing through on a cloudy day.

He was like a child in his discovery, but there was nothing childlike in the way he made her quiver inside. No man had ever made her warm this way, not even Francis Tarleton. How could she be so wanton, so free with a man she hadn't known twenty-four hours? She'd known Francis all her life. He'd never touched her so intimately. He'd never tried.

Carter was her husband, she told herself. The man with whom she would carry out her marriage duty. But this was far more than duty. This was pure pleasure.

His hand now rested solidly at her waist. The warmth and the strength of it penetrated her clothing. His mouth opened slightly, as hers had, and the light pressure increased against her lips.

Bailee shook once more, for the warmth became a fire inside her. A fire she'd never known, sweeping through her limbs and stirring her blood. Anger also crept into paradise. Anger that she'd lived her life without ever knowing this feeling existed.

She broke the kiss and lowered her forehead against his shoulder while trying to control the emotions running wild within her. How could a man, a silent man, make her discover this huge gap in her life, especially when he knew even less about what he was doing when it came to loving than she did?

"Is something wrong?" he asked between quick breaths. His words seemed rusty, unsure.

"No," she lied, knowing something was very wrong. Not with him, or even with them, but with her. "Your beard." She grasped for something to say. "Your beard scratches my face."

He stepped away without a word. For several minutes she watched him working, putting all his tools back in order. She couldn't tell if he was angry at her or embarrassed at what they'd done. For once, he didn't stare. He didn't even look at her. He seemed to have forgotten she was in the barn with him.

"I best be getting back to the house. I think it's time to start supper if I plan to have it ready by dark. I need to stop at the garden, and I want to check the smokehouse as well." She was rambling. She knew it. All her life she'd hated people who spoke simply to fill the silence. Now she was doing just that. She hurried away before she made an even bigger fool of herself.

The sun had completely disappeared by the time Carter

joined her hours later. He looked tired. His clothes were
stained and sweaty as though he'd been working hard.
Droplets of water dotted his beard and sleeves. She
guessed he'd washed his hands and face at the stand by
the well.

Bailee wondered if his dress was unusual or if he returned to dinner every night like this. Except for a few
tobacco stains or ink spots, her father never got anything
on his clothes, and though he often looked tired, he never
looked sweaty. His dress was a ritual with him, as orderly
as his accounts.

Bailee watched Carter twist his shoulder as if trying to
work out soreness. His shirt tightened across his back,
revealing the muscles beneath. The bulk of him seemed
unnatural. Her father and Francis were both lean. Compared to Carter, they looked little more than skin over
bones. She'd seen men on the street, workingmen, with
such bulk, but never a gentleman.

She thought of telling him to change his clothes before
he sat down at her best table, but she guessed people who
lived out here isolated from all society didn't follow such
rules. She also had no idea where he kept his extra
clothes, surely not the barn or tack room. Yet there were
no dirty clothes lying around, and the ones he'd worn last
night in the rain had disappeared.

He didn't seem to notice the white linen across the table, or the napkins, or her best candlesticks. He watched
her, as though seeing only her in the room.

Bailee set the food on the table in serving bowls, not
pots. He didn't say a word as he studied her, following
her lead when she filled her plate. She thought of several
things to say, but feared the words would sound like rattling so she remained silent. His table manners were not

polished, but they were passable. Bailee wondered if he tasted his food, for his attention never left her.

When they finished, he helped her carry the dishes to the washstand and, to her shock, began washing them. Bailee dried and put everything away, thinking how strange it was for a man to do such a thing. She tried to reason that, of course, he'd done dishes thousands of times if he lived alone, but she'd never seen a man do any housework with a woman near. The few times she'd left her father for a day or two, her work had been waiting for her when she'd returned.

As she put the last of her dishes in Carter's china hutch, he slowly folded into the rocker by the fire. A book rested on his leg, but he didn't open it. For a time he watched her. Then, slowly, his eyes closed, and she knew he'd fallen asleep.

She debated waking him, but decided to let him sleep. Whatever he'd done all afternoon must have been hard work. Besides, she wasn't sure he hadn't slept in the rocker last night. Maybe this was where he planned to sleep until the month was over and he joined her in her bed.

She sat in the shadows beside the hearth and listened to the sounds beyond the house. The noises of the night in the cities she'd lived in were totally different from what she now heard. All her life she fell asleep to buggies rolling in the street below and people talking as they walked. With the night's aging, there were fewer walkers and they talked in whispers.

But tonight there were no rolling wheels, no hushed conversations. Even the mumblings of families bedding down on the wagon train were gone. Tonight there was only silence.

She scooted closer to the fire, telling herself the strange sounds she now heard were nothing to fear. The warning in Lacy's note crossed her mind as it had a hundred times today. Zeb Whitaker wasn't alive. He couldn't be. Lacy was only listening to rumors. There was nothing to fear, Bailee reminded herself. She was safe.

Carter's hand moved against the rocking chair's arm. For a moment she hoped he was awake so she could tell him how silly she was being, worrying about a dead man. But Carter's eyes were closed in sleep, his face relaxed. Yet his fingers twisted in odd movements as if making a pattern of shapes.

He had to be dreaming, trying to accomplish something in his sleep. She lay her hand gently over his. The movements continued inside the cup of her hand. Slowly his fingers relaxed as he traveled deeper into sleep, and she leaned back into the shadows.

Bailee stood and lowered the lantern's wick. Hesitantly she brushed a kiss across his forehead and lifted the book from his leg, then checked to make sure all the locks were in place. Yet, when she crawled into bed, she still didn't feel safe. If, by chance, Lacy's note was true, Zeb Whitaker might be out there somewhere planning to kill her. He seemed a ruthless man who would stop at nothing if he thought she'd taken something from him. Alone in the darkness, she wasn't sure the locks, or even Carter, would be enough to protect her.

If she were being practical, she would be safer and so would Carter if she left.

Bailee twisted deeper into the covers. Reminding herself she had married. She couldn't just announce she was leaving because someone she thought she killed might be alive.

Staring through the shadows, Bailee tried to reason. Her eyes drifted to the thin strip of brown paper she'd first taken from her pocket and placed on the dresser when she'd arrived. The room was far too dark to read the words, but she remembered what Carter's note said: "Be my wife, all my life."

It didn't matter if Zeb Whitaker was alive or dead. There was no more running. She'd agreed to Carter's terms of marriage, and she wouldn't back out.

Beneath the covers Bailee moved her fingers as Carter had done, hoping by repeating his action she too would fall sound asleep. She remembered the way his lips had touched hers, how she'd felt safe in his arms. Finally she fell asleep thinking of being wrapped safely in his embrace.

After a restless night Bailee was up and in the kitchen at dawn. The sun came through the long windows, brightening the room. Carter had disappeared from the rocker, but he'd already made a pot of coffee, which told her he was up and probably working.

She'd only had time to slice a few strips of bacon when he charged through the door and bolted to shelves over the washstand. For a moment the bright slice of sunlight made her blink, and she couldn't see what he did in the shadows.

"What . . . ?" Her question died on her lips when she saw blood staining the front of his shirt.

He didn't look at her as he searched for something amid jars lined along the top shelf.

"Are you hurt?" Bailee grabbed his arm and pulled until he turned to her. "Carter, are you hurt?"

There was no need for him to answer. She saw it on

his face. Tiny cut marks slicing into his throat and chin bubbled blood a drop at a time.

He would have pulled away and resumed his search, but she held fast to his arm. "Dear Lord, Carter, what happened?" She dabbed at the cuts with a kitchen towel.

"I was shaving." He smiled as though realizing what a fool he must look like.

Bailee moved between him and the counter. She tried to stop the bleeding at his throat by pressing each spot with her towel. "You made such a mess, you'd think it was the first time you shaved."

His blue eyes met hers. "It was," he said simply.

Bailee's hand stopped moving across his face. All she could do was stare into his eyes. He didn't say more; he didn't have to. She knew he'd attempted shaving because of her words. When she'd been embarrassed in the barn, she'd said she broke the kiss because of his beard.

When a drop of blood bubbled over the spot where she'd been blotting and ran across her finger, Bailee remembered her purpose. "Sit down," she ordered. "Let me have a look at the cuts."

He didn't move, and she realized how close they stood to each other. Another inch and the entire length of their bodies would have been pressed together. Blood from his face had dripped in crimson raindrops on her sleeves and apron front.

"Sit down," she ordered more gently, moving aside. "I know what you're looking for. I saw the yarrow leaves in a jar when I was cleaning. My grandmother always kept them for cuts. She swore they closed wounds like magic."

This time he did as she said. He pulled a chair from the table and sat.

She grabbed an old jar from the back of the cabinet.

Bailee wasn't at all sure the leaves would work. Her father ridiculed any medicine that didn't come out of a doctor's bag. She'd seen a medicine box on the bottom row of the bookshelf. If the leaves didn't work, she'd see what else Carter kept that might be helpful.

Carter waited. Bailee poured cold water into a pan and moved to the table. Standing above him, she carefully worked across his face, cleaning blood off a square at a time. He'd done a good job of removing his beard. Unfortunately, in places he'd taken several layers of skin along with the hair.

Once the cold water cleaned them, most of the tiny cuts stopped bleeding; only a few stubbornly flowed. Bailee crushed the leaves onto the cuts and waited. She tried not to meet his stare, for his eyes might make her forget what she needed to do. His jaw was strong and square, a little too square for him to be thought of as handsome, but it was a nice jaw just the same. Or at least she predicted it would be once the cuts healed.

"If you're going to take up the habit of shaving, I suggest you allow me to assist you, at least for a while. I often shaved my father. A good soap might help the blade slide easier across your face." She was rambling as she worked, but she couldn't seem to stop. "My father didn't have much of a beard, but he was fond of wearing a goatee and never seemed to be able to get it right without my help."

The cut on his throat stopped bleeding. Bailee wiped away the excess yarrow leaves and smiled down at him.

"I didn't mind so much kissing you with the beard. Honest I didn't. I could get used to it in time."

She brushed his hair back from his face and felt its dampness. "I could cut your hair as well, if you like. Not that I think it's too long or anything." She didn't want him to think she was one of those women who wanted to make a man over the minute she met him.

She moved her fingers into his hair, feeling its thickness. "I'm a fair barber."

One by one she worked on the thin cuts. It wasn't easy. The rest of his body kept getting in the way. When she stumbled over his legs and feet for the third time, he lifted her onto his lap without comment.

Bailee didn't take the time to tell him that it was most improper for a woman to sit on a man's lap. She had more important concerns. But she couldn't ignore the way his arm rested around her waist, almost casually, as if he'd done so a thousand times.

With a brushing of the towel across his collar, she finally met his gaze. "There now. You weren't as wounded as I feared. If you'll remove that shirt, I'll soak it in cold water."

She would have stood, but he held her tight. His gaze studied her closely. Pretending she didn't notice his arm about her, she began unbuttoning his shirt. "It's never good to let blood set in cotton."

His free hand moved to her neck and pulled the strings holding her apron. Slowly his fingers slipped down the front of her dress, crumpling the top of the apron to her waist. When he passed over her breast, she made a little sound of surprise.

He stopped, his hand cupping her fullness, his blue eyes searching her face.

Bailee knew she should pull away, or say something to let him know that his actions weren't proper. But she reminded herself that he was her husband, and though his touch was bold, it was not at all unpleasant.

Her silence challenged him.

This time his fingers didn't just pass over. This time he felt of her, warming her flesh even through the layers of cotton.

She closed her eyes and leaned her head back against his solid arm, telling herself she'd demand he stop in a minute. One minute couldn't matter. For a short time she wanted only the unexpected pleasure of such an intimate encounter.

He shifted her body and placed his elbow on the table, gently pushing her into the circle of his arm. She made no protest as she nestled into the warmth of his embrace, loving the way he held her as though she were fragile.

Suddenly he lowered his mouth to cover hers and tasted her cry of surprise.

His lips parted, claiming her mouth more boldly than he had in the barn. His hand moved along the side of her body in a hesitant caress.

She didn't move as his kiss turned gentle and searching. His hands migrated over her, stroking her with a caress that said he'd never touched a woman. He ended the kiss and moved his lips to her throat, tasting her skin. He buried his face into her hair and breathed deep, almost as an animal finds his mate by scent.

She moved within his arms, thinking she should pull away. But he held her securely as he raised his head and looked down at her with searching eyes.

When he returned to claim her lips once more, there was a hunger in his kiss, a need far deeper than curiosity in his touch.

Bailee felt dizzy, surrounded. Frantic, she fought for control. She shouldn't behave like this with a man she hardly knew.

With a sudden movement she broke the kiss and sat up.

For a moment there wasn't enough air in the room for her to breathe. She held the top of her apron up as though she'd been nude beneath it and not fully clothed. His blue depths held a question, but how could she explain? She'd been the one who'd started the kissing, started the touching. He'd obviously had no experience with women. He was only following her lead. Done what she'd showed him to do.

Only what he'd done was far more than a kiss, far more than a light caress. She'd only meant to show him what married people do, a light kiss that was meaningless. But what he'd begun was more. He'd begun a mating.

"I have to start your breakfast while you change your shirt." She moved off his lap. She wanted to add that she truly didn't think married people did such things before breakfast and certainly not with the sun shining in through an open door, but she couldn't bring herself to find the words. She wanted to scream that loving belonged in the dark and nowhere else.

Suddenly she needed air. She couldn't face Carter. He hadn't said a word, but the questions were in his eyes. She grabbed a bucket and hurried outside. The three mangy mutts who lived under the porch didn't bark as they had when she arrived, but they watched her from their shady retreat.

"Do these dogs have name?" Bailee snapped, trying to think of something but the way Carter had kissed her.

"No," he answered simply.

Bailee had to talk about something. Somehow she had to get the day back to normal or his touch would be the only thing on her mind all day. "Well, I think they should have royal names to make up for their mangy appearance." She pointed at one. "Henry the Eighth." Another poked his head out from under the porch. "And King Solomon."

She heard Carter moving about the kitchen and hurried on out in the sunshine. She didn't want to face him until her face had cooled.

At the well she sat the bucket down and took several deep breaths. She had to get control of herself. She wasn't some animal, and she wasn't married to one. Carter might not talk much, but he could certainly understand every word she said. She'd just have to sit down and talk to him about what was proper and what was not. Her behavior had been outrageous. Allowing him, no *encouraging* him.

When she finally got control, she filled the bucket with cool well water and turned back toward the house.

Carter stood in the doorway wearing a clean shirt and staring straight at her. His blue eyes spoke of a need so great she almost yelled for him to be quiet.

As she walked past him, he lifted the bucket from her hand and asked, "What's the third one's name?"

For a moment she had no idea what he was talking about. "The third. He's not near as royal as the other two."

Carter smiled. "How about Cromwell? Almost a king."

Bailee giggled and agreed. Her silent husband was talking, and there was far more to the man than she might have guessed.

NINE

THE SUN SPARKLED IN BAILEE'S HAIR AS IF DIAMONDS were tied into the strands. Carter decided it looked blacker in the morning light of this, their third day together.

He'd worked late the night before, getting her wagon in shape. They hadn't said more than a few words to each other over supper, but this morning he'd kissed her when he'd returned from shaving.

She'd looked surprised, but accepted his advance willingly. She was a strange woman, this wife of his. Bossy, definitely bossy. And beautiful. Not the kind of beautiful anyone would notice at first, but the kind that grew with time. With contact. He smiled. When he touched her, her cheeks reddened, and she lost that control she fought so hard to maintain.

Carter crossed his arms over his chest and leaned against the door frame. As before, she'd felt the need to fetch water when she'd stepped from his embrace. He'd followed her outside and was now in no hurry to stop watching her.

She reached the porch before looking up. The blush still

stained her face, but her forehead was lined in thought and her lips held tightly to a frown.

He didn't have time to react to the sudden storm that raged across her features.

She charged the three steps as if advancing on a hill in full battle gear. "I don't think we should be kissing like that in daylight." The words exploded from her in rapid fire.

Carter only lifted one eyebrow in question. He was rather hoping it might become a habit in their marriage.

Bailee held up her hand as if needing to fend him off. "Not that I didn't enjoy it. I won't lie about that. And not that there's anything wrong with what we did. After all, we are rightfully married. But I don't think it's proper."

Carter nodded. After all, she was setting all the rules—at least for twenty-six more days. He stepped aside. When she passed, he lifted the bucket from her hand as he had before. With the brush of his fingers against hers, she jumped away.

Without looking at him, she hurried around making breakfast. In less time than he thought possible, she placed a plate of eggs and bacon on the table. As he took his chair, he noticed the last slice of bread rested on his plate. Carefully he tore it in half and passed one piece to her.

"Oh, no, that's all right. I don't need any." She tried to hand it back, but he wouldn't take it.

The loaf he always bought once a month had lasted three days. He usually tried to eat it slowly enough to make it last and fast enough so that the final piece wouldn't go stale. Bread was the one luxury he allowed himself on his monthly trips to town.

"You like bread?" she asked. "Even this bread from the general store?"

He nodded. This "bread from the general store" was all he could remember. The preacher's wife bought loaves each week from Willard's store the year he lived in town. She claimed she would never waste the time to make her own. She allowed Carter one slice a day, never more. Vaguely he remembered his mother making biscuits. He'd tried it a few times over the years, but all he'd been able to make was a mess.

They ate in silence. He thought of telling Bailee where his rooms were below, but he wasn't sure what she'd do. When Mosely brought her wagon by, she'd invited him inside, something Carter would never have thought of doing. Underground was his sanctuary. He'd have to trust her completely to take her there. If she told anyone, he'd not only lose his privacy, but the only place in his world where he felt safe.

When he stood to leave, she said "you're welcome" as if he had just thanked her for the meal. Something that had never occurred to him. She might have cooked the bacon and eggs, but he'd slaughtered the pig and raised the chicken. He'd even bought the bread they'd shared.

Carter shoved on his hat and stepped outside, figuring she should be the one thanking him. The three yard dogs jumped to attention as he reached the end of the porch. They were smart animals who knew his first chore after breakfast was to feed them.

He found it interesting that she'd named them, along with the oxen he'd brought in with her wagon, and the two squirrels that lived in the trees that shaded the corral. He didn't mind the animals having names, but he figured he'd have to draw the line if she started on the chickens.

He walked to the barn and mixed dried strips of deer meat with a mush made of leftover milk and oats. When he handed each dog a bowl, he mumbled, "You're welcome." The dogs were as responsive as he'd been.

Next, he turned the milk cow out to graze and hitched up his buckboard. Except for rainy days, every summer morning was spent in the fruit trees. Carter's father had brought saplings from Connecticut when they'd settled along the Canadian River. Apples and pecans. When he'd crossed into south Texas and headed north, he'd picked up peach trees north of Austin to add to his collection for his farm. With the ample water and protection of the bluffs, the trees had grown. Carter's earliest memories were of following his father through the orchard, tending each tree as if it were a child.

Most of the peaches were ready to harvest, but the crop had not been huge this year. Carter would pull a few bushels tomorrow and store them until he had a wagon load. Then he'd make his third trip to town in less than a month. The apples were still weeks away from being ready, and the pecans could wait in boxes until winter.

Carter worked until past noon. It was his habit to finish tending the trees before stopping back by the house for a bite of lunch. The meal wasn't important, but he enjoyed getting out of the sun for an hour and reading. Then he'd work until dark on his ranch, always building, or fixing, or tending.

He heard one of the yard dogs clearing the brush at the creek bed. Bailee was only a step behind the animal. She looked like she'd been running.

For a moment she glanced around, letting her eyes adjust to the shade of the trees. Then she spotted him and smiled. "I brought you some lunch. I wasn't sure you'd want me to. I've never lived on a farm, but it seemed

logical that I could walk out here as easily as you could
stop your work and come in."

She held out his lunch wrapped in a napkin.

Carter climbed off a box he'd been using as a ladder
and accepted her offer. Lunch consisted of three strips of
bacon and funny little round cakes that tasted like potatoes.

She handed him a jar of tea made with cold well water
and sweetened with sugar.

Carter thought it was a fine lunch, but before he could
say anything, she apologized. "I'm still figuring out where
everything is. I found your garden out back and a small
cellar in the house with all kinds of vegetables stored, but
there was no fruit." She looked around. "Do you mind if
I take some of these peaches back to the house for a pie?"

He shook his head. He'd store apples and nuts when
they were ready, but Carter never kept any of the peaches.
When he'd been a boy, the peach crop had been the only
one to produce. Sometimes that was all he had to eat.
They never kept long, and once they were too rotten to
eat, he'd almost starved until Willard could get a shipment
to him. In the winter, that was never dependable. Many
times he'd gone hungry with the last taste of overripe
peaches lingering in his mouth.

Bailee held out her apron to take a load back with her.

From the direction of the house, two yard dogs barked.
Henry the Eighth, who'd ventured to the orchard with
Bailee, shot through the brush as though afraid he'd miss
something if he didn't hurry.

Carter listened for a moment more, then grabbed
Bailee's arm. He pulled her into the thickest part of the
trees. "Stay here!" he ordered.

He retrieved a rifle from the box beneath the buckboard

seat and ran toward the house. By the time he reached the back of the barn, his heart was pounding in his throat more from panic than exertion. Normally, when he left the house, he locked the door. Anyone wanting into his home without the key would have to use an ax.

If she left his fortress unprotected, all the precautions he'd installed over the years would be worthless.

He checked the windmill. The broken blade still pointed north. No one had entered through the back gate.

Carter moved in the shadow of the barn until he could see the house. He carried the rifle at ready, his finger on the trigger.

The front door stood wide open, but all was quiet except for the barking of the dogs.

Carter moved closer, knowing that if anyone had arrived recently, the dirt would still be settling.

Nothing.

He followed the sound of the dogs to the far side of the house. There, the three animals had a frightened mule deer cornered in front of the chicken coop.

Carter forced his muscles to relax one inch at a time. Whistling, he drew the dogs' attention for a moment, allowing the frightened animal to escape.

Resting his rifle on his shoulder, Carter turned back to the house.

There, in the shadows along the porch, stood Bailee. She hadn't waited in the safety of the trees, as he'd asked her. She stared at him with angry green eyes. He'd been wrong, her eyes weren't the color of late summer, they were fiery emeralds and would warm even the hottest day of the year.

He'd asked her to stay so that he could protect their

home and her, yet for some strange reason she looked mad at him.

When he reached the porch, the fire exploded. "Don't ever push me into a corner again. If there is trouble, I stand with you, not hidden away in the trees, or shoved into a safe place. I stay with you. Don't ever leave me again."

He knew more inspired her demand than what had just happened, but he didn't know her well enough to pry. Without answering, he turned and headed back to the orchard, knowing she wouldn't follow.

An hour later he left a box of peaches on the porch when he brought the wagon back to the barn. He didn't bother to step inside. He wasn't sure he'd be welcome. A full day's work remained to complete the corral fence. He needed to stop thinking of her and remember all his responsibilities.

But putting her out of his mind wasn't as easy as he'd thought. Carter mentally listed all the ways she would help him around the house, freeing him to improve the ranch, build up a herd, and tend the trees. To be fair, he also listed how much of a distraction she was, taking his mind off work, changing his house around, making demands. He usually had the opportunity to read the books he ordered two or three times each before the next month's shipment came into Willard's. But since he'd brought her home, he hadn't finished a page. At this rate he'd never read again.

It was almost full dark when he returned to the house. He stopped to wash at the stand by the well and changed shirts when he noticed a clean one hanging beside a clean towel. There was no sign of the blood he'd spilled on the front of the shirt yesterday morning, and it smelled of the starch his mother used years ago when she ironed. He'd forgotten how it lingered in the cottons, whispering of cleanliness.

He added another reason it was good to have Bailee around.

The aroma that greeted him a step inside the house washed over him like a flash flood. He'd smelled it before a few times. The wonderful perfume of fresh baked bread. It surrounded him so completely he felt as if he could open his mouth and bite into the very air.

Four perfectly shaped loaves rested on a cutting board in the center of the table.

Bailee's voice drifted to him as he took a deep breath. "I see you found your shirt."

She was somewhere near the stove, but he couldn't take his eyes off the bread.

"I had a little trouble getting the blood out, but it washed up nicely. If you'll leave your dirty clothes somewhere I can find them in the morning, I thought I'd wash a few tubs before it gets hot."

Carter rested his hand atop one loaf of bread, feeling the warmth.

"Those may still be too hot to cut properly." She set their plates on the table.

He fought the urge to pull a loaf in half and eat it whole.

She took her seat, and he followed. "I found your garden in good order, but there are no jars for canning. The next time you go to town, if you'll bring back the supplies I need, I'll put up enough peas and tomatoes to last the winter."

Carter didn't tell her his winter vegetables were usually beans and potatoes. Since he'd never learned to can, all extra vegetables at the end of the summer were fed to the pigs.

She continued to talk about growing up canning with her grandmother. As Bailee spoke, she sliced a thick piece of fresh bread from the first loaf and handed it to him.

Carter stared at it a moment. "Thank you," he said, interrupting her.

"You're welcome." She didn't meet his gaze. "I made butter in a jar the way my grandmother used to let me do while she used a butter churn. She'd put a little cream in the jar, and I'd shake for what seemed like forever, then she'd strain out the butter, salt it and let me make my own little butter presses with spoons."

He stared at the butter she passed him. It never occurred to him butter would be so easy to make. He remembered it from years ago, but had no idea making it would be such a simple task.

"It'll melt nicely on the bread," she added.

He tried it sparingly at first, not wanting to spoil any of his bread. It had been so long since he'd had butter, he couldn't remember if he liked it or not.

Neither one said another word. Carter ate his food fast as though inhaling it so he could get on with other things. The only time he seemed to chew was when he took a bite of the bread. Then she could see pure pleasure in his eyes. But when she offered him another slice, he refused.

As he'd done before, he helped her with the dishes before settling into the rocker. She sat at the table, near the lantern and tried to mend her only other dress. She had to make it presentable enough to wear while washing or she'd be doing laundry in her petticoats.

Bailee couldn't help but watch Carter out of the corner of her eye. He lifted a book from the table by his chair, but made no effort to read. As he rocked, he fell asleep as he had every night.

When his breathing grew long and low, his hand began to move once more, going through a pattern of movements that made no sense.

Tonight, she moved nearer and watched closely. The movements were repeated over and over. She gently cupped her hand over his and felt the pattern, trying to understand what he could be doing so diligently in his sleep. As her hand warmed over his, his movements slowed, then stopped, and she knew he finally relaxed.

She stood and moved silently through the shadowy room. She locked the door, turned down the lantern, and covered him with a blanket.

When Bailee leaned to kiss his forehead good night, sleepy blue eyes stared up at her.

"Good night, Carter," she said more formally than she intended. Her lips touched his cheek so briefly, she barely felt his day's growth of beard.

Hurrying from the room, she didn't allow herself to breathe until she was safely behind her bedroom door. Bailee closed her eyes and pressed her fingers against her lips.

He hadn't moved. Hadn't said a word. Hadn't made any advance, but she suddenly felt a danger in his presence. A pain rocked through her chest, for she knew. She was in danger of losing her heart to this man.

TEN

CARTER LEFT HIS LAUNDRY ON THE KITCHEN FLOOR
before dawn. He felt strange imagining someone else doing it. He'd developed a habit over the years of scrubbing
out his clothes the day he realized all were dirty. When
he'd been a boy, he'd often gone naked for a day so
everything could be washed. But as he'd grown, he
bought enough trousers and shirts to stay dressed on laundry day. Old Samuel, the carpenter who sometimes
stopped in, commented more than once on how he appre-
ciated Carter's wearing clothing.

Carter smiled remembering the old man's joking as he
left to do the milking and early chores. Samuel was not
a man of many words, and most of them had been spoken
to himself over the years he'd known Carter.

When Carter returned from the barn, his breakfast sat
on the table, but Bailee was already hard at work at the
washstand. Since she didn't have a huge pot to boil outside, she'd left a pot on the stove to heat so she could
change water. The smell of lye soap filled the morning
air.

Without a word Carter carried out a few loads of boiling water and refilled the pots from the well before he left.

Four hours later, when he walked from the orchard, he noticed the washtub turned upside down behind the house and all the clothes pinned on the line to dry. He stopped and stared. There were sheets and towels and a half dozen shirts and trousers. And one dress.

He entered the kitchen with more noise than usual, hoping, for once, not to startle her. Bailee wore her apron with the lace ruffles on her shoulders. It had to be her best apron, he thought, and she'd worn it to protect, or rather hide, a dress that looked to have patches on patches. She reminded him of the rag dolls he'd seen little girls carry with dresses made from scraps.

She smiled as if proud of herself. "I've finished the laundry and have your lunch almost ready."

He was glad she couldn't read his mind.

"I would have brought it out to you, but it's been a busy morning."

She seemed nervous. Almost as if she expected him to be angry at her for running late. Had she lived on such a tight schedule all her life? Had no one ever allowed her time to spare? Something bothered her now, but he had no idea what it might be.

Without thinking of why, he leaned over and lightly brushed her lips with his.

Bailee reddened. She pushed a loose strand of hair behind her ear. "Well"—she hurried away—"that was nice."

Carter had no idea if she meant it, but at least she wasn't thinking up some new rule about kissing, which seemed to be her favorite thing to do any time he got close to her. He fought the notion to do it again, figuring it would be better not to push his luck. He sat down and ate his cold lunch in silence, even forcing himself to finish half of the peach she put on his plate.

She talked of her home back in what she called "the civilized world," but she didn't make it seem too civilized. Not once did she mention a friend or relative other than her father. Carter couldn't help but wonder if Bailee hadn't been as lonely in the city, where people passed right by her windows all day, as he'd been out here without seeing a soul most months.

She liked to talk while they ate. He tried to slow down, for he liked the sound of her voice. It didn't matter that she was talking about something he knew, or cared nothing about.

He left without saying a word but returned before dark. When he banged through the door carrying a chair, he knew he startled her. She fought down her panic, trying to act as if nothing were wrong, but something definitely made her jumpy.

She followed him to the fireplace and watched him position the chair across from his rocker. Then, for once, she didn't question as he touched her shoulders and directed her to the chair. Her nervousness flickered like static between them. He'd done nothing to make her ill at ease, yet her nerves were on edge. He knelt to make sure the legs of the new chair were just the right height for her.

His hands brushed along her sides as he tested the fit. Bailee relaxed into the smell of freshly cut wood.

His fingers slid along her arms, gauged the level of the wide armrests. Then he sat back on his heels and grinned.

Bailee's chair was a perfect fit.

It took her a few seconds to realize he was giving her a gift.

"Thank you," she whispered. "I've never had a chair made just for me."

For a moment she closed her eyes and let her tired shoulders relax. The light brush of Carter's fingers along her arm reminded her she was safe.

When she opened her eyes, Carter still knelt in front of her, watching her as always. His clear blue eyes filled with the honest pleasure of having made her happy.

Bailee leaned forward until her face was only a few inches from his. "Shall we have dinner?"

He nodded once and stood, offering her his hand. He pulled her gently from the chair. They were so close, they could have been dancing.

Neither moved. The last rays of sunlight fanned golden, then red across the wooden floor.

Bailee raised her arms slowly and placed them about his neck. She wanted to curl up into the feeling of safety she experienced when he was close.

He didn't move.

She leaned against him, the softness of her body resting next to his chest. His heart pounded against her. His breath tickled her cheek.

She knew he must think he'd married a crazy woman. One minute she was pushing him away, the next stepping close boldly. But if she told him the fear of Zeb Whitaker grew in her mind like bindweed, he'd think her unbalanced. They had no proof the man was looking for her, only a note written by a frightened woman who was little more than a child.

Bailee's fingers brushed Carter's hair. If the rumors were true, she had no right to put this silent man in dan-

ger. The thought that their marriage could be broken if
Zeb Whitaker were alive had also nagged at the back of
her mind for three days now. If she wasn't a murderer,
there was no reason for the wife lottery, and therefore no
reason she had married. She knew she'd upset Carter's
world. Would he change it back to the way it was, if he
had the chance?

Then, she realized, she may have had to marry, but he
hadn't. He'd paid her fine and married her because he
wanted to.

Bailee buried her face against his shoulder. He'd chosen to marry her. He could have backed out after he'd
seen her, but he hadn't.

Carter fought the urge to sweep her up in his arms and
make her worries go away. He knew he was little more
than a stranger to her, and she had nowhere else to turn.
Whatever trouble waited for her was far worse than her
fear of being near him.

Her fingers combed through his hair making it hard for
him to think. She was so close he could breathe in all the
smells surrounding her, starch from when she'd ironed,
the bread, soap, and something that belonged only to her.
An aroma sweet and womanly that had nothing to do with
store perfumes.

"Would it be all right if you held me for a while?" she
whispered against his ear. Her body moved closer, totally
unaware of the effect she had on him.

When he didn't answer, she stepped away, gathering up
scraps of pride as she moved. "I'm sorry. I'm usually not
so in need of . . ."

Before she could retreat further, he caught her around
the waist. With a mighty tug, he lifted her off the ground
and into his arms.

Her feet dangled above the floor, her face right in front of his. There was no way for her not to look into his eyes.

She struggled for a moment as his arms hugged her so tightly she could barely breathe, then laughed. "More gently, Carter. I need to be held, not crushed."

He lowered her feet to the floor but relaxed his arms only slightly. Leaning her head against his shoulder, Bailee closed her eyes and smiled. As she rocked her face against the cotton of his shirt, his fingers moved along her sides.

His hands washed away all her worries. She melted against him, finding a safe haven at last. All day she'd watched and waited for trouble. Now she just wanted to feel safe.

His hands continued to search, warming her flesh through the layers of clothes. She kissed his throat where the pounding of his heart throbbed, and he lowered his mouth to hers.

His kiss grew familiar, and she welcomed it. The exhaustion she'd felt only moments before melted away as his kiss brought a warmth once more deep inside her.

An apple tumbled from the small shelf by the door, shattering their silent world. Carter reacted as if a cannon had been fired in the room. Before Bailee could say anything, he moved her aside and grabbed the long rifle near the fireplace. In less time than she thought possible, he slammed the door and bolted it. He leaned against the wall, raising the gun barrel to fit along one of the narrow slips by the door.

Bailee picked up the apple that had rolled almost to her feet. "It was only an apple falling, Carter. Nothing more. I keep taking it down when I clean, but you keep putting it back on that same shelf. I figured it would roll off one day."

He didn't appear to hear her.

"McKoy!" came a shout from beyond the door. "It's me, Sheriff Riley. Put down that rifle I know you got aimed at my heart. I'm coming in."

Carter lowered his rifle and relaxed against the wall. When he glanced at her, the fire of their embrace was still in his eyes, his lips still wet with her kiss.

And something more, she thought. A promise to finish what they'd started sparkled in his blue eyes.

She looked away. She didn't want to admit she felt the same. They'd had a taste of passion and both wanted more. She only hoped there would be time.

"How did you know someone was coming?" Bailee glanced first at Carter, then the apple in her hand. Carefully she set the apple back on the shelf, but it rolled into her hand before she could step away. Somehow the shelf had slanted downward. She touched the bottom of the wood and pushed it level. "It's a warning device."

Carter nodded.

"There are others?"

He nodded again as he lifted the bolt and opened the door.

Bailee smiled. "I may be safer than I thought."

When Riley's boots sounded on the porch, Bailee slipped the apple behind her, hiding away her newfound knowledge. There were secrets in this house, secrets that might save her life.

"Evening." Riley removed his hat. "How are you folks doing tonight? I hope I'm not interrupting your supper."

Bailee glanced at Carter.

He read her thoughts and nodded.

"We'd love to have you join us for dinner, Sheriff. I made a peach cobbler."

He hesitated a moment before agreeing. "I got something to talk to you about, Carter. If you don't mind me talking while we eat. There isn't much time to waste."

Bailee hurried, placing the food on the table while the two men took their seats.

Riley watched them with a frown until he saw Bailee lean against Carter's shoulder when she asked if the sheriff had heard from Lacy or Sarah. Riley didn't miss the gentle way Carter put his arm around his wife's waist, holding her a moment longer by his side. "They're doing fine," Riley answered with a grin. "As fine as the pair of you seem to be. Last I heard Sarah's new husband sent me a note that he's taking her to Dallas to see a special doctor. I'll send word if I hear more."

She wanted to ask if he knew more about Zeb, but fear kept her silent. If the sheriff had come to tell them about Whitaker, she wouldn't have long to wait.

They were halfway through the meal when the sheriff lowered his voice to an official tone. "I need your help, Carter. We've got a problem in a little whistle-stop in Childress County."

Carter steepled his hands in front of him and listened silently.

Sheriff Riley nodded as if hearing an old argument explode in the air between them. "I know you don't want to travel. I know, son. You haven't been a few miles from this farm since I've known you. But you're needed, and, to my knowledge, you may be the only one who can help." He added, "I'll go along with you even though it means leaving that worthless Wheeler in charge of my office. I promise, I'll be right by your side."

Bailee listened closely. She couldn't imagine what talent Carter might have that would make the sheriff willing to beg him to make a trip.

"We can take the six A.M. train and, with luck, be back by nightfall," Riley added. When Carter didn't answer, he continued, "There was a train wreck last night. Luckily, only one passenger car, but it was directly behind the engine. All other cars were hauling freight. Passengers weren't supposed to be on the train, but they added a carful when they pulled out of Fort Worth."

Riley looked tired. "When the train derailed, it was one hell of a mess." Riley glanced at Bailee. "Pardon me." He looked back at Carter. "Twenty-three died in the collision, a few linger still badly burned and busted up. Only one walked away, a little girl."

"That's terrible!" In her mind's eye Bailee could picture a child crawling from the wreckage.

"The terrible part is, Miss Bailee, we think the collision wasn't an accident. The train was carrying payroll money for several of the big ranches in the area, and the mail car's safe is missing. The little girl may be our only hope of clues."

"But how can Carter help?" The sheriff wasn't making any sense. Carter had been here with her. He could know nothing of the wreck or the robbery. And judging from the doctoring of his face, he could be of little help to those suffering.

Riley looked directly at Carter. "The local law, an old friend of mine named Parker Smith, is having trouble communicating with the girl." He hesitated for a minute before adding, "From the book she carried we believe she may have been heading to a school in West Hartford, Connecticut."

Carter bolted out of his chair and stomped out on the porch. He didn't need more information.

But Bailee did. "I don't understand, Sheriff."

Riley didn't meet her stare. "We think the girl, like Carter's mother, attended a special school there. Carter's father told me once his brother was one of the teachers in what he called Gallaudet's school." Riley watched Carter through the open doorway. "The full name of the place was the American School for the Deaf. A doctor named Gallaudet founded it in 1817. To my knowledge it's the only one in the country."

Suddenly Carter's world made more sense to Bailee. "His mother was deaf." Her words were a statement, not a question.

Riley nodded. "I didn't think it was important to mention because that was years ago and Carter can hear, even if he doesn't listen most of the time." Riley raised his voice slightly on the last few words.

"And his father?" Bailee wanted to know all about them.

"Carter's father could hear. He met his wife while visiting where his brother worked. He said it was love at first sight, and, to tell the truth, I don't think he ever saw it as a problem between them." Riley leaned back in his chair. "At least not until Carter was born. Some of the kids around town called him the dummy's kid and made fun of his mother like he couldn't hear every word they were saying."

Bailee could imagine how it must have been.

"She got to where, when she came to town, she would make movements with her fingers in Carter's hand hoping no one would see her. I think they used their own silent way of talking most of the time. When I found him that day, with the bodies of his parents, he kept covering his hand with his mother's and sending her some silent message no one could understand. I finally had to pull him away from her side. Tears were streaming down his face, but he didn't make a sound, he just kept moving his hands in some strange pattern." Riley lowered his voice. "It was like he was shouting to her in a language none of us could hear."

Bailee fought down her own cry. Carter's booted steps stormed back into the house. She turned her back, not wanting him to see her face.

Riley waited. "Well, son, will you help us? There isn't a person for three hundred miles who knows the language of the deaf. We have to talk to this little girl and find out what she saw. She may be the only one who can describe who took the safe after the wreck. Sheriff Smith has no way of knowing how to contact her family. It will take a few days for them to arrive even after they get word, assuming she has any relatives. With your help we can learn all she knows and keep her safe until they pick her up."

Carter spread his hands out on the table as if forcing them not to move. He hardened before their eyes as though not seeing or hearing anymore.

"I know what I'm asking." Riley leaned forward. "I remember how many years it took you to just come into town once a month. If it wasn't important, I wouldn't ask."

Bailee placed her hand on Carter's shoulder. His body felt as if it were made of iron. Not a muscle moved. "You have to go," she whispered. "The child is all alone. You have to talk to her."

Carter didn't answer.

Riley watched Carter carefully. "I talked to Miss Lacy before I left town. She said you can stay at her place tonight. The train leaves at dawn. With luck, you'll be sitting in the Childress sheriff's office by noon."

Carter covered Bailee's hand with his own. "We'll be ready in fifteen minutes."

Bailee opened her mouth to say that there was no need for her to go along. Then the realization that she'd be left alone registered. "I can be ready in ten." She hurried toward her bedroom.

Ten minutes later she stepped from the house with her small carpetbag in one hand and a basket of eggs and peaches in the other. She'd not go to Lacy's home for the first time without a gift, and the eggs and peaches were all she could think of to take.

Carter followed her out a moment later, locking the door behind him. He carried nothing but a book in one hand. He laid the book in the wagon and helped Bailee onto the bench seat while the sheriff rode out ahead of them on his horse.

She locked her arm around his and slipped her fingers into his hand. There was no need to say more.

ELEVEN

It was almost midnight by the time they stored the wagon and horses at Mosely's livery. Sheriff Riley waved good-bye, saying he'd meet them at the station at dawn. Carter carried Bailee's bag as they walked the block to Lacy's apartment above the print shop. She welcomed them at the door with a wild round of hugs and led them up a small staircase in the back of the shop.

Despite her exhaustion, Bailee couldn't help but laugh at Carter's expression. He stared at Lacy with a mixture of confusion and panic. If Lacy had tried to hug him again, Bailee wouldn't have been surprised to see Carter bolt for the door.

He hadn't said a word to Bailee since he'd agreed to go. She knew he wasn't happy about leaving his ranch, yet he came. He was a man out of his element, trying hard not to show it.

Lacy's chatter was a welcome relief from the silence for Bailee, but she guessed Carter found it bothersome. The girl rattled on about how she loved learning in the print shop and how wonderful her father-in-law was to her. The old man couldn't do much, including climb the stairs to help her get settled, but he was kind, always respecting her as if she were a lady, treating her like he'd found a treasure, not some murderer he had paid to get out of jail. He even set up a household allowance at the store.

To Bailee's surprise, Lacy's apartment was cozy, with a small living area in the front overlooking the street and a bedroom in the back. The furnishings were old and worn, but good quality. There was even a small dining table with one chair next to it. The matching chair hung on a nail on the wall.

"I put the other chair up there so I'd look at it when I ate and remember that I would take it down the day my husband comes home. Then I'll no longer eat alone."

"Don't you take meals with your father-in-law?" Bailee sat her basket on the table.

"At lunch we eat at the café, mostly. He takes breakfast and dinner at his boardinghouse. He said he'd pay for me to eat there, but I wanted to be on my own. I figure my Frank is probably sitting by himself somewhere eating his meals. I feel somehow closer to him knowing I'm doing the same."

She pulled a lean stack of mail from a box on the table. "I have all the letters he's written his father. He's a fine man, I can tell by the way he writes. He talks about doing the right thing and loving his country."

Bailee smiled. In truth, Lacy probably knew more about her man than Bailee knew about Carter. "Is there any word about when he'll be home?"

Lacy shook her head. "A year, maybe more. I'll wait. I've never had anyone to wait for before. I tell myself he's just a man, nothing more, so I won't expect too much. But if he wants me, I'll love him. My father-in-law says his Frank ain't fool enough to not want an angel like me. Imagine that, he thinks I'm an angel."

Bailee thought of Lacy's words an hour later when she lay in the darkness of the tiny apartment bedroom. She had almost the same thought when it occurred to her that Carter might be able to go back on the marriage if Zeb Whitaker were alive. That is, if he truly was alive. If he was, Carter might not have to reconsider the marriage. Zeb might make him a widower.

Lacy had insisted they take her bedroom. She had no way of knowing Carter slept in the room's one chair, his legs blocking the door.

Bailee knew he wasn't comfortable, but as always, he didn't share his thoughts. In fact, she wasn't even sure he was asleep.

If he wants me, I'll love him. She almost said the words aloud. Was she so desperate that she'd give her heart to a man, any man who would just want her? For three years she pretended Francis Tarleton wanted her. Everyone asked about him, talked about what her wedding would be like when she joined him out West. But the time never came, and eventually folks stopped asking. Like water on a stove, her dreams evaporated in mist, leaving her unwanted, unloved, and untouched.

Bailee rolled over so she could see Carter's outline. "Are you awake?" she whispered.

He leaned forward far too quickly to have been asleep.

"No," he answered.

"If you want, you could lay on top of the covers on the other side of the bed. That chair couldn't be comfortable."

Carter was silent for a moment, then she watched his shadow move. He propped the chair across the door and leaned his rifle against the nightstand. The room was too dark to see more than an outline, but she heard him remove his shirt, boots, and trousers. Carefully he lowered his weight to the other side of the bed, mindful not to touch her.

She waited, but she wasn't sure for what.

"Are you cold?" she whispered.

"No," he answered without moving.

"Good, but if you get cold, I don't mind you having one of the blankets. I'm never cold." She was rattling again.

"Can you sleep?" she asked more to hear his voice than anything else.

"No," he answered again. "It's too light in here."

Bailee thought about what he said. She could only see the outline of her hand in front of her face. Wherever he slept on the ranch, the place must be very dark.

He must have guessed what she was doing, for he closed his fingers around hers and lowered her hand to rest between them. "Go to sleep . . . Bailee."

His low voice whispered through the night, and she couldn't help but like the way her name sounded when he said it.

Closing her eyes, she tried to lie still. After what seemed like hours, she finally fell asleep listening to Carter's steady breathing and feeling the warmth of his hand resting atop hers.

Bailee slept on Carter's shoulder through most of the train ride the next morning. The people shifting like sand along the aisle didn't bother her. Carter watched every person who passed as though he expected them to pull a gun and start firing.

Sheriff Riley sat a few rows away talking with a widow lady and her old maid daughter. He didn't seem to be flirting, just passing the time.

When they reached the tiny town at Childress's county seat, Bailee was disappointed. If possible, it was dustier and shabbier than Cedar Point. There were people on either side of the platform with wares spread out on filthy blankets. One man had a pot of soup swinging over a low fire. "Stew!" he yelled to everyone getting off the train. "Fresh venison stew!"

Several people bought, others had to wait until bowls were returned to be reused on the next customer without washing. Bailee noticed that any of the soup not finished by a previous customer was scraped back into the pot to be reheated and reserved.

Carter looked as if he were lost in a nightmare. He couldn't watch all the people, but he tried. He might bolt and run at any moment. She wished they had arrived at dawn, or after dark, when the streets wouldn't have been so crowded.

Bailee slipped her arm in his. "Please, stay close," she whispered. "This many people make me nervous."

He stared down at her as if she'd read his mind. His hand closed around hers in a tight grip. A smile brushed the corner of his mouth as he nodded slightly.

She couldn't resist leaning closer and kissing his cheek.

The sheriff coughed loudly. Bailee straightened, not the least embarrassed.

Sheriff Riley led them through the crowd and down two blocks of what must be Main Street. He rattled on that he remembered when this place was nothing more than a watering stop for cattle. Bailee decided it had gone downhill since then.

At least the sheriff's office was clean. After one look at Sheriff Parker Smith, Bailee decided Riley had a twin. Oh, there were subtle differences: Most of Smith's hair had slipped off his head onto his throat, and Riley wore a few more wrinkles across his lean, weathered face. But the two men's life stories were painted in their features, and they came from the same palette.

Parker Smith, however, proved to be more direct than Riley. He wasted no time with small talk. After shaking Carter's hand and nodding at Bailee, he led them to the back cell of an empty jail. He made a point to say that he wasn't locking anyone up, but only providing quarters for a minor in need.

All the cells were as clean as his office, but the smell of vomit filtered through the air like rotten perfume. For a few moments Bailee didn't see the child curled up in a pile of blankets inside the last cell.

"Honey!" Smith shouted as he opened the cell. "Honey! I got someone who wants to talk to you."

The girl didn't raise her head.

"If she's deaf, Parker, she won't hear any better with you shouting, but you might manage to damage my hearing." Riley screwed a finger into his ear.

"She don't respond at all unless someone touches her. Then she starts crying. I tried to get some of the good ladies to take her in last night, but you'd have thought her condition was catching. They all have their hands full with normal kids; none of them wanted to be responsible for a dummy."

Bailee glanced at Carter, but he held himself in tight control. In truth, he didn't act like he heard the sheriff as he stared into the cell. His blue eyes watched the little girl carefully as if he were trying to figure out what to do.

Smith turned toward Carter. "You think you can get through to her, mister? We tried a pencil and paper, but she wouldn't touch it. My guess is she's too young to read or write. But we were hoping she could pen her name. At least that would be some help. I can't notify her people until I know who she is."

Carter removed his coat and lay it between two bars, then without a word he stepped into the unlocked cell.

He made no effort to touch the child, but knelt in front of her, slowly forcing his way into her line of vision.

She raised her head slightly as he gestured to her with his hands, signing as though he were speaking low to a frightened creature. His movements were slow, unsure.

After a few minutes the blankets slipped away. She scrubbed a tear from her cheek and nodded. She lifted her head high, a brave little soldier in a frightening world.

Bailee felt as if she watched a miracle. This man she married, who never had more than a few words to say, talked to a child in a way only the two of them understood. Bailee couldn't understand the symbols, but she sensed the meaning passing through his fingers. He was telling her that she would be all right. He was telling her not to be afraid. He was telling her he understood her.

As time passed they all watched the child talk to Carter. He listened and answered, his hands moving faster as he became more comfortable with the language.

Suddenly the girl jumped from the cot into his arms. Her arms wrapped around his neck and held on tight as though she were drowning and he were her only hope.

He stood, holding her against him, protecting her from the world, at least for a while.

"Well, I'll be damned," Riley mumbled, then with a quick glance to Bailee added, "Pardon me, ma'am."

Carter rocked the child as he walked. When Bailee saw her face, tears streamed down reddened cheeks. She cried, silently on Carter's broad shoulder. Finally she had found someone to hear her.

After a while Carter motioned for Bailee to come closer and have a seat on the cot. He pried the child from about his neck and sat her in Bailee's lap. She struggled to return to Carter, but his hands moved quickly, telling her it was all right.

The little girl nodded and looked up at Bailee with a shy smile. She ran her thumb along her tear-stained cheek.

"What does she say?" Bailee asked without taking her gaze from the girl.

"She says you're pretty," Carter answered.

When Bailee glanced at him, he smiled. His blue eyes caught her stare and held it for a moment. Then he returned to the girl.

The bookend sheriffs watched from several feet away while the man who never had three words to say to anyone communicated endlessly with a silent child.

When the girl leaned against Bailee and closed her eyes, the discussion was finally over. Bailee rocked her gently as Carter stood and moved to Smith.

The child must be about five or six, Bailee thought. Her grandmother would have called her Daddy-carrying size. So big, mother would have made her walk, but still small enough for a father to lift easily.

"She was asleep when the train derailed." Carter leaned back against the bars and folded his arms, determined to say what had to be said. "She remembers seeing her mother lying on the floor of the car. She said her mother's eyes were open wide and blood dripped from her mouth. She tried to get her mother to sit up when smoke began to fill the compartment. But her mother signed 'run' before she went to sleep with her eyes still wide."

Bailee held the child closer, as if she could guard against the memory.

Carter placed his hand on Bailee's shoulder as he continued. "She told me she grabbed her little bag, because her mother told her to always keep it close. She ran as far away from the fire as she could. Then she sat down next to her bag and waited for her mother to join her."

"That's where I found her," Smith interjected. "She was sitting there as calmly as if she were waiting for another train."

He leaned close to Carter as though he thought his questions might wake the child. "Did she see anything after the wreck?"

"Horses," Carter answers. "Men in huge black coats riding horses. She said the leader had a horse with spots on its back. They took a box from the train and loaded it onto a wagon, then rode off. She couldn't watch them long because they rode into the sun."

"That's all?" Smith looked disappointed. "I know twenty men who ride horses with spots on their backs and a hundred who own black coats. Every man in the county probably owns a wagon. Anyone robbing the train would probably ride west. East is town."

Parker Smith glanced at the child. "Wake her up! See if she remembers anything else. Over twenty people died in that wreck, another six were injured. We've got to find out who is responsible." Smith took a step toward the little girl.

Carter blocked his path. "She doesn't know more."

"She has to. We'll keep questioning her until she remembers details. She's the only lead I have."

Carter folded his arms. "Go ahead."

Frustration huffed from Smith like steam. "You know I can't do it without you. If she hadn't had that book in her bag, I would have thought her an animal incapable of relating to us."

He glanced at Riley for support. "But I remembered Harman talking about a woman in his town who couldn't hear or talk. He said she was at a special school in West Hartford, which was not too far from where I grew up."

Parker realized he wasn't making his point with Carter. "Twenty years ago I rode over to help solve her murder, but there were no witnesses, unless you count her son, who was little bigger than . . ."

Smith stopped, staring at Carter as if he just saw the man. "You're the dum. . . . You're the couple's boy. The only one who lived after the raid."

Carter didn't answer.

Smith continued. "That's why you speak the language. Your mother was one of them. She spoke with her hands."

Carter showed no sign of listening. He didn't need a review of his life; he was here to help the child. "Her name is Piper Halloway, and she has a big family in Sherman. Her mother had taken her to visit the school. Piper is worried that her father is waiting for the train still. She said her mother promised him they'd be home soon."

"I'll send a telegram to the local law down there." Riley moved toward the door, happy to find something he could do. "We should have an answer. Maybe even a relative on his way by morning."

Smith nodded. "The kid can stay here until she's picked up. I'll let her sleep a few hours." He glared at Carter.

"Then we're waking her up, and you're talking to her if I have to put you both behind bars."

Bailee glanced at Carter. He hadn't said a word to Smith, but she could see the anger building. She stood with the child in her arms. "Is there a hotel in town, Sheriff?"

"One right across the street, ma'am."

"Good. We're taking Piper Halloway with us." She stared at the sheriff, daring him to argue. "We'll let her sleep until she wakes, then have something to eat, then we'll ask more questions."

When Smith started to argue, Bailee turned on him. "What kind of monster are you, Sheriff Smith? She's been here for two days, and you haven't even cleaned the dirt from her clothes or her mother's blood from her hands."

Smith obviously didn't like being called a monster. He stepped aside and let them pass.

TWELVE

Bailee had no idea if Carter carried enough money to pay for a hotel room. He looked uncomfortable when they stepped into the lobby, but then, he'd been uncomfortable since they'd pulled away from his ranch.

The hotel lobby was small with a writing table against one wall and a few chairs by the one window. The counter looked as if it had had a former life in a bar.

Holding Piper close to her, Bailee walked up to a sleepy-eyed desk clerk. "We need two adjoining rooms and a bath delivered as soon as possible."

The clerk frowned. "With all the trouble over the train wreck, we ain't got but one room left in the place. I could bring a crib in for your child, but it'll be a few hours before I have time to heat and lug up water for a bath. We're only offering a bath for women and children. Men can go two doors down to the barbershop."

"All right." Bailee hesitated. "How much?"

"Two dollars for the room. Four bits for the bath." When Bailee frowned, he added, "There's no charge for the crib."

Carter laid a twenty-dollar gold piece on the counter, and Bailee relaxed, thankful he had the money to pay.

"Could we have lunch brought up to our room in an hour?" she asked.

The clerk grinned at the money. "Yes, ma'am. My wife serves a special plate every meal. Today she's outdone herself—chicken and dumplings. I'll bring up three bowls before it's all gone." He gave Carter back his change and the key. "First room on the right at the top of the stairs. It's the best we got. May be a little noisy, but a nice breeze blows through it in the afternoon."

Bailee carefully handed Piper to Carter and climbed the stairs. When they reached the landing, she unlocked the door and held it for him to pass.

The room was small, but clean and furnished with a bed, one straight-backed chair, and a washstand. The clerk followed them upstairs with a small bed that was more like a child's cot than a crib. When he set up the bed, half the walking space in the room was eliminated.

Carter gently placed Piper on the cot, and Bailee covered her with the light quilt from the end of the bed.

"We'll let her sleep until the bath gets here." Bailee opened Piper's small bag and smiled. "She travels with nothing but a book and a rag doll."

Bailee glanced at Carter, thinking he'd comment on why Piper's mother might have insisted her child always carry her bag since there was so little in it. But Carter wasn't listening.

She almost swore aloud. The man had the ability to turn off his hearing at will. He moved slowly across the room letting his fingers touch the faded wallpaper as if he expected one of the flowers to stand out from the others.

When he reached the ladderbacked chair, he tested it for strength and frowned.

"Carter." Bailee moved to his side and waited until he looked at her before continuing. "Do we have enough money to buy her another dress and maybe a nightgown? I could go get them while she sleeps."

Carter fished in his pocket. "Maybe the mother just wanted her to look like everyone else on the train." He handed her two twenty-dollar gold pieces.

"Oh, no. That's far too much. The dress and gown together shouldn't cost more than a few dollars." She tried to give back half the money.

Carter pulled a book from his coat pocket and sat down on the chair, ignoring her offering. "Buy what the child needs," he whispered as though slightly embarrassed by his words, "and what you need as well. I'll stay here with her."

Heat climbed her cheeks. He must have noticed she'd worn the same dress every day except on wash day. She'd lived with nothing new for so long, the thought of buying anything for herself was a little frightening.

Her father had given her a household allowance that never seemed to last the month. She never remembered there being a dime left over for anything but what she had to have. Even when he'd bought her wagon and paid for her to travel west with the wagon train, he'd figured how much she'd need to the penny.

"How much should I spend?" She hated asking. The thought that she must now account to a husband left a sour taste in her mouth.

He didn't look at her. "All of it. I have more if you need it."

Bailee closed her fingers around the money. "All of it?"

She knew Carter couldn't be a rich man, yet he'd given her so much.

He finally met her gaze, and she knew the money meant little to him, but his blue eyes warmed as they watched her. He wanted her to have all the money she needed, and she wouldn't insult him by insisting he take part back. When she returned home, she'd put what was left over in a jar in the china cabinet. No matter how little it was, it would be her money.

Bailee fought the urge to hug him, settling instead for placing her hand lightly on his forearm. "I'll return as soon as I can."

He stared at her fingers resting on his shirt, then looked up at her without saying a word.

She almost ran from the room. What she saw in Carter's eyes frightened her far more than Zeb Whitaker ever could. For in Carter's gaze she saw a promise that might stand forever.

Bailee walked the street trying to figure out how she felt about this strange man she'd married. He was good. She'd seen that in everything he did. And kind, at least to her and Piper. There was so much about him she didn't understand, might never understand. Like, why had he married her? He hardly noticed her cooking. He didn't seem to need her conversation or housekeeping. He might never have touched her if she hadn't shown him how. So, why did he put his name in the hat with all the others?

Bailee almost bumped into Sheriff Riley before she noticed him standing in the center of the walk, as active as a lamp pole. He had that look about him, like he was thinking hard trying to remember what it was he'd forgotten yesterday.

"I'm sorry," she said, stepping aside and hoping he'd

pass her. She didn't want to talk to him, or anyone really. She just wanted to buy what she needed and get back to Carter.

Riley paced nervously, taking a step, then backtracking. He looked worried, like a man about to lie, she thought.

"I was just coming to check on you. Make sure you got the girl settled down."

"She's still asleep." Bailee stepped around the sheriff. "Carter's with her. I'm just going to pick up a few things while she sleeps."

Riley circled like a slow-moving carousel and fell into step at her side. "I'll just tag along." He seemed to be looking more behind her than at her. "I need to stretch my legs."

Another lie, Bailee thought. He wasn't the kind of man who would enjoy shopping just to "stretch his legs," but what could she say?

She tried to accept his presence and go about her mission, but for once the man made her feel on edge. Maybe it was the way he kept brushing the butt of his Colt, making sure it was in place. Or the way he glanced around, watching people. This might not be his town, but it looked no meaner than Cedar Point.

"You know," he mumbled from a few steps behind her, "the three of you might be just as comfortable in the jail as over in that hotel. It ain't much for what they charge and, being it's full, there'll probably be noise till midnight. Unless we have trouble in town tonight, you would have the whole jail to yourselves." He grinned. "It would be just like old times having you there."

"The hotel's fine," she answered, trying to ignore his poor attempt at a joke. A noisy room was better than a cell with bars for walls. She knew from experience.

Bailee bought a nightgown for Piper and one for herself, trying not to notice Riley pacing up and down between her and the store windows. When she moved to the small dress shop next door, he relaxed a little, probably because no other customers were in the store.

"The jail would be free," he mumbled. "Sure you don't want to reconsider? After all, first Carter's out the train ride, then room, then all these clothes."

"No," she answered. "We're staying in the hotel, and Carter wanted me to buy the clothes."

He didn't look happy when she excused herself to try on two dresses the dressmaker had ready-made. Bailee decided to ignore Riley as much as possible.

Both dresses fit as if they'd been made just for her, and the dressmaker suggested she buy new underthings as well. When they began looking at camisoles, Riley moved to the door and became engrossed in watching the people pass outside.

She knew she needed to hurry, but she couldn't help but spend a little time picking out new underthings. For once she didn't buy cotton. After all, she was a married lady now. It was no longer scandalous to buy silk with a touch of lace.

Bailee kept expecting the old sheriff to say he had somewhere else to be, but he didn't. When they left the dress shop, they passed a barbershop.

Bailee loaded her packages on Riley. "I'll only be a moment," she announced as she disappeared into the shop.

True to her word, she returned in a short time with another package under her arm.

Riley wrestled with what she'd bought. "Maybe it's time you got back," he mumbled beneath his breath "The kid might wake up."

Bailee looked at him and slowed her pace. He had no choice but to do the same.

"I'm not going back to the hotel, Sheriff, until you tell me what is going on."

"Nothing," he said too quickly. "I was just thinking we got about all we can carry now. I think there may be some kind of law about a woman buying more than she can carry."

Bailee slowed more.

Riley took a few steps ahead, realized she was no longer at his side, and turned to her in frustration.

"What has you worried?" She stood in the middle of the walk, refusing to budge.

The sheriff swore but didn't try another lie.

"Is it Zeb Whitaker? Is he somehow still alive and looking for me?"

He almost laughed with relief. "So you've heard the rumors. I've already had Lacy in my office crying with fright, and Sarah's husband sent word that if Zeb shows up on his land, there'll no longer be a question about his death. He'll be glad to provide the body."

"So it's true?"

Riley shook his head. "Rumors always get started when a body's missing. If he is alive, he'll show up in town and I'll have a talk with him. My guess is, some animal dragged the carcass off in the brush, and, not knowing exactly where you left him, we got about a hundred miles to cover before we find the bones."

"If he's alive . . . ?" She couldn't make herself finish the question.

Riley shrugged and grinned. "Then I give the money back to all three husbands, and you ladies are free to go."

"You mean if Zeb's alive, I'm not married?" He

couldn't be serious. He had to be lying again.

"Seems to me the fair way to do it. 'Course, if he's alive, he's probably coming to kill you. When he does, I'll have to arrest him and hang him, so he better stay dead." Riley smiled tolerantly. "Stop worrying about Zeb."

"Aren't you?" Bailee watched him closely. "And don't tell me you just like to shop. You've been guarding me for the past hour as though you feared someone might shoot me or kidnap me right off the street."

Bailee's blood froze as she saw the truth show for an instant in Riley's face. Then, just as quickly, he covered his reaction with a fatherly frown. "Of course not. No one is going to shoot you."

"But someone might kidnap me?"

Riley caved in at her question. "Smith seems to think whoever robbed the train will try to get the kid. Her being the only witness and all. We tried to keep it quiet about Carter coming in, but someone in town is bound to know. If one person knows, there's not any telling who else might know. The robbers might all be from here and watching our every move. Waiting for a chance to get to the child."

"Carter would never let anyone kidnap her."

Riley agreed with a nod. "But if they can't reach her, they might try snatching you and bargaining." He took a deep breath. "Smith's right. All three of you would be safer at the jail."

Bailee didn't answer. She held the packages tightly against her and ran toward the hotel. The sheriff did his best to keep up.

When they reached the room, she stopped long enough to take a deep breath and slowly turned the knob.

Carter sat in the chair, holding Piper on one knee. His arms circled her as his hands moved in a swaying motion in front of her.

"What's going on?" Riley asked between breaths.

Carter smiled. "I'm singing her a song."

The old sheriff looked as if he were about to pull his gun and shoot Carter for going completely mad. On a good day he didn't understand most folks, and today didn't seem a good day.

Bailee quickly stepped between them and dumped her packages on the bed. "I bought her a dress and a night-gown. Would you tell her?"

Carter's hands moved in front of Piper once more. This time there was no swaying action.

The little girl nodded.

"The gown has pink bows and lace along the cuffs." Bailee rummaged through the packages without stopping her chatter. "I'm sure she'll like them, and I hope I guessed the right size. I'm not used to buying things for children. I tried to remember how tall Piper was by where she came to when she stood beside me."

Riley turned his stare to Bailee, as if reconsidering using a bullet on the insane Carter and putting Bailee out of her misery from terminal chattiness. The woman had driven him loco while she was in his jail with her endless statements and planning. Maybe he should just let the train robbers capture her. They were sure to give her back within the hour. He glared at Carter for help, but Carter didn't appear to be listening. The man seemed to think hearing, as well as talking, was an option he controlled.

Riley finally interrupted Bailee. "Would you two re-consider moving back to the jail?" True, his plea was not as demanding as it might have been, but after all, he'd been shopping for over an hour, and that could take a great deal of the determination out of a man.

"No," Bailee answered for the third time.

Riley's shoulders dropped an inch. "Well, I'll go tell Sheriff Smith. We'll give the kid another hour or so to have her bath and eat something, then we'll be back to ask a few more questions." He spotted Bailee's mouth opening and quickly added, "And I'll have no discussion about it, miss. As it is, we could put you both in jail for interfering with the gathering of important information."

"And how much information would you have gathered without Carter, Sheriff?" Bailee spliced in the question while he took a breath.

Riley frowned at her. "I'll be back," he stated quickly and hurried into the hall before he lost a fight.

True to his word, Riley and Smith returned in an hour. Carter had given Piper and Bailee time alone while they bathed. He'd spent ten minutes taking a bath at the barbershop and the rest of the time watching their hotel window from across the street. When Bailee opened the curtain, he knew it was safe to return.

The three had barely had time to eat lunch before Carter let the sheriffs in. Carter knew he had to do all he could to help them catch the robbers. Men who were willing to kill everyone on the train to commit a robbery wouldn't stop at killing a child if they thought she could identify them.

Carter worked with Piper the rest of the afternoon, talking of every detail before the robbery and afterward. It was after dark when the two lawmen left with little more information than they had that morning.

Carter was relieved when Piper let Bailee help her into her new nightgown. The little girl played with her rag doll in the center of the bed. Carter pulled his chair as close as he could to the window and tried to read, but Bailee was like a butterfly, fluttering about the room as though there was something to do. She used the damp towels from Piper's bath to scrub dirt from the child's carpetbag, then replaced everything inside three times before she was satisfied.

Carter watched her movements from the corner of his vision. He forgot what he'd been reading and had to flip back a few pages and start again. The day had been end-less and talking through Piper's tragedy had been like reliving his own parents' deaths over again. But, true to her word, his wife has stood by his side, helping wherever she could. Now there was a peace in watching her that surprised him.

She continued to walk about the room as the street be-low clamored into evening. Businesses closed their doors. Strolling couples replaced shoppers. The wind increased, promising a storm as it whistled between the buildings.

Bailee took down her hair. The dark richness of it sur-prised him as she let it tumble to her waist.

Carter turned back three more pages and tried to focus on the words in his book once more.

About the time a piano's music drifted from somewhere on a side street, Piper curled around her rag doll and fell asleep. Voices wafted up like smoke through a chimney, mingling, changing from courting whispers to good-time joking.

Bailee tied back her hair with a ribbon and began loos-ening the buttons along the back of her dress.

Closing his book, Carter tried to stare out the window. At this rate, he'd unread the entire book if he didn't stop.

She stood with her back to him, her dress loosening as

it opened to reveal a slim sliver of skin trailing from her neck to her waist. Her black hair swayed across the space as she worked.

He tried not to look, but his eyes saw nothing out the window no matter how hard he pretended to be looking in that direction. All that registered in his mind came from the corner of his vision where she stood.

While he studied her without appearing to watch, she did the strangest thing. With her clothes still covering her, she slipped her nightgown over her head.

Carter gave up pretending and stared. Like a turtle slowly moving from one shell to another, Bailee slipped an arm out from her dress and moved it into the sleeve of the nightgown. Next the other arm. The gown glided into place at the same time the dress worked its way to the floor.

He'd never seen such an action in his life. In the entire process, very little flesh was revealed. Not that he wanted to see her bare, he lied to himself. But her action was practiced to perfection. He wouldn't have been surprised to learn she did such a performance at the circus side-show. Everything was so proper . . . and yet.

And yet, what? he scolded himself. What had he wanted her to do? If he'd been any kind of a gentleman, he would've excused himself for a few minutes to allow her some privacy. She might be his wife, but she probably didn't want to be gawked at.

Carter stared out the window watching lamplight flicker in the wind as the air grew colder with the promise of rain. Why couldn't he ever think of what to do before something happened and he'd already done the wrong thing? He could have walked down to the lobby and sat in one of the uncomfortable chairs as easily as he sat in this one upstairs.

The thought occurred to him that she was already ready for bed, and he was sitting by the window fully dressed.

THIRTEEN

CARTER OPENED HIS BOOK AND TRIED TO LOOK LIKE he was reading. He wore his good trousers and the white shirt Bailee had washed and pressed for him. If he slept in his clothes, they'd be wrinkled come morning. If he didn't, at some point he'd have to climb out of his uncomfortable ladder-back chair and take them off. There would be no nightshirt to hide inside of as Bailee had. He hadn't worn a nightshirt since he ran away from the preacher's. Never saw any need for them, at least not until tonight.

Last night, in Lacy's tiny apartment, it had been so dark Carter figured Bailee didn't even notice he removed his clothes before lying on top of the bed. He was up before dawn and dressed. He spent most of his life dressing and undressing in total darkness. But tonight was different. The lamplight from across the street shone through the windows so brightly he'd never get to sleep even if he found the nerve to take off his clothes and lie down.

Bailee lifted sleeping Piper from the center of the bed and tucked her beneath the blanket on the cot. Carter watched as she leaned over and kissed the child's cheek. He couldn't help but wonder if his mother had once done the same thing to him. The memory of her death had polluted all other memories. He'd never told anyone the details, he never would, but no matter how hard he tried to remember her living, her dying always trumped on his thoughts.

Bailee lifted the bedcover and crawled beneath.

Carter tried to guess how long he could sit there acting like he was reading. An hour? Two? All night? His body already ached to stretch out. He'd slept little last night, and the day had seemed endless. He felt as if his nerves had been running double time for hours.

Carter stood. He'd never considered himself a coward, and he wouldn't start now. This wasn't some strange woman he was spending the night with. This was his wife. A wife that he would be sleeping beside often in the years to come. If she panicked at the sight of him undressing, he might as well find out now.

He pulled his shirt from his trousers, unbuttoned it, and hung it on the chair. His underwear was made of unbleached cotton. Carter cut the cuffs off the undershirt when he bought it so the sleeves only went to his elbow. Since he had no idea how to sew a seam, the sleeves were frayed and the cotton thin from washing. But until this moment, he'd never cared about how they looked, only that his clothes were relatively clean. Summer underwear was just something he ordered four for a dollar every spring, then tossed in the rag bin come fall when it was time to order four winter pair.

He debated taking off his socks, but decided against it. He wasn't sure why, but it seemed indecent to sleep in the same bed with a woman and be barefooted.

Carter reached for the thin blanket and sheet. He slipped into bed before he did any more thinking. If he wasn't careful, he'd think himself back in the ladder-back chair and out of any sleep.

Bailee didn't move. For a moment he thought she might be asleep. But before he could get his body to relax, she rolled over to face him. Carter tried to act like he didn't notice she was two inches away, staring at him.

"Will you sing the silent song to me?" she whispered.

"What?" Carter closed his eyes and swore. Why'd he say that? She must know he heard her. She was only two inches away.

But she was kind. "Would you sing to me with your hands like you did to Piper?"

The request was so foolish, he almost refused. Why would anyone who could hear want to *feel* a song?

Carter didn't say anything. He'd already said one word and that was a dumb one. He thought for a minute, then opened his arm.

When she didn't move, he gently placed his hand on her shoulder and rolled her against him. Her back pressed against his chest as he circled her with his arms and took her hands in his.

He formed her fingers just above his hands so that when he moved she could feel the words he signed. It wasn't a comfortable position, but he wasn't about to sit up in bed and have her sit on his knee.

Slowly he began to move his hands, swaying back and forth as if his fingers were directing a melody as they moved. He could only remember parts of songs his mother used to sign to him. Phrases, some of which made little or no sense, but they lingered in his memory.

After a while, she turned her face so that her cheek

brushed his. "Would you tell me the words?" she asked. "Help me understand?"

Resting lightly against her hair, Carter whispered the words he could remember into her ear. "Rock-a-bye, rock-a-bye, don't you cry."

Her body was warm against his and somehow comfortable in a way he'd never expected. Her fingers lightly caressed his hands as he repeated the movements for each word.

She laughed when her fingers got tangled up in his hands. He liked the sound of her laughter and the feel of her as she wiggled, trying to get back into place so he could continue.

He slowed his signing so that her slender fingers could brush along his hands, touching the silent words. When her palm pressed against his, he stopped completely and their fingers slowly intertwined.

Bailee turned in his arms and faced him. They were now so close her breath mingled with his.

"I'm afraid," she whispered as she touched his lips with her fingers. "Afraid I'll never feel for the rest of my life the way I feel when I'm close to you." She brushed her lips lightly against his.

He wrapped his arms tightly around her and molded her against him. His unbleached underwear or her new nightgown no longer mattered. All that mattered was Bailee wanting to be in his arms.

He kissed her gently, learning how she liked to be kissed by the way her body moved against him. She was a woman afraid of never feeling, and he was a man afraid of feeling too much. But tonight he couldn't have pulled away if a gun had been pointed at his head.

Their kisses grew longer and deeper. At some indefinable point he knew he'd reached her knowledge of what they were doing. He plunged onward, exploring into waters neither had ever charted.

When he was capable of having a thought, he remembered he was supposed to touch her also, not just kiss. Only this time when he moved his hand over her chest, there were no layers of undergarments binding her breasts. The softness filled his hand and molded inside his grasp.

Bailee sighed and leaned away a few inches to allow him to touch her more completely.

Carter's mind exploded. Her mouth was warm, soft as velvet and inviting. He moved his hand to her other breast not believing it could also feel so good.

She opened her mouth wider in response to his touch as though rewarding him. He knew, without doubt, that he was bringing her pleasure with his caress. The kiss deepened. His stroking became bolder, moving over the cotton of her gown in gentle caresses.

Tugging at the buttons of her gown, he tried to free them.

She placed her hand over his as if to stop him.

He didn't move, unsure what she wanted. His mouth brushed her ear. "Bailee," he whispered.

She turned her face slightly and kissed him softly. As he deepened the kiss, he felt her hand slip from over his fingers.

With a sudden longing, he pulled at her gown. The buttons gave way to his encouragement. The front of her nightgown opened to the waist, and he slipped his fingers between the cotton and her skin.

Her body tightened in surprise, but she made no protest as he hesitantly spread his hand across her chest. At first he explored, but with each slight caress a need for more grew. A need deep in the pit of his stomach that told him no matter how long or how completely he touched this woman, he'd never get enough of the feel of her. He was like a blind man touching heaven for the first time and knowing all the wonder and beauty of it without seeing anything.

He moved his hand into her hair, pulling the ribbon free as his fingers curled around the dark mass of silk. Their kiss changed from tenderness to liquid passion, and suddenly he couldn't get enough of the taste of her.

He wanted to kiss her like no man had ever kissed a woman. He wanted to twist his fingers into her hair and feel her breasts and pull her closer all at the same time. He wanted to bury himself so deep inside of her they'd become one.

Rolling over her, he pressed his body to her, letting her know how much he wanted her.

Suddenly she jerked her face away and fought to crawl from beneath his weight.

For a moment he held her, not believing that she wasn't feeling everything he was. Why would she want to leave? How could she think to end this paradise between them?

But she pushed away, clawing her way from the bed. He watched her stand in the pale light of the windows, shaking and frightened. She held her gown together in one tightly clenched fist and brushed the fingertips of her other hand across her lips as though silencing a cry.

Carter collapsed into the pillows praying he'd smother in the folds and not have to ever look at her, so beautiful and so afraid. He wasn't even sure what he'd done wrong, but whatever it was must have been terrible, judging from her expression.

But the gods didn't cooperate. He lived. After he managed to get his body under control, he rocked to his side and took a breath. He wasn't sure he was brave enough to face her. He wouldn't lie to himself and pretend he didn't know what happened, but he never thought he'd lose control. Or that it would frighten her so.

When he thought he'd do his duty as a husband, he never thought it would be like this. His blood still boiled and the need to pull her back to him was so strong, still rocking his senses with the smell of her, the feel of her, the taste of her.

"Carter," she said, her voice breaking just a hint.

He forced himself to open one eye. She was still there, as desirable as ever. Her left hand continued to hold her nightgown together in the front, her right gripped the bed frame so tightly he could see her knuckles whiten even in the shadows.

"I . . . I . . ." She couldn't seem to get her thoughts together, either. "We . . . we . . ."

He had to help her out. "I'm sorry I ripped your gown."

She glanced down as if she hadn't noticed. "The buttons only fell off. That happens all the time with ready-made clothes." Her fingers moved along the aisle that had once been lined with tiny buttons. "I usually sew them on myself before I ever wear anything that isn't made by hand."

Carter figured his mouth had taken to the road without his brain when he asked, "May I see you?"

She gripped the opening tightly closed. "No. Of course not." She hesitated, dragging a shaking hand through her hair. "Give me time. When I'm more wife then stranger. Maybe."

That's how it is, he thought with a frown. I can touch

her, but I'll never see her. We'll spend the rest of our married life dressing in the dark, or she'll go through that ritual of changing clothes without revealing so much as an ankle. He'd know the feel of her, but never the sight.

In the midst of his depression, he realized she wasn't angry at him. Sure, she'd jumped from the bed like a flea on wash day, but she hadn't said an angry word at him. She wasn't even issuing orders like she usually did.

Carter studied her. Her cheeks were flushed. Her hair wild about her shoulders. Her eyes still shinny with passion. Suddenly he knew, she was as confused about what had just happened as he was.

He rolled to the far side of the bed and turned a pillow sideways.

She relaxed a bit as he patted the pillow into a feather wall.

"One month," he finally said, looking deep into her green eyes. Hoping she'd understand.

Bailee nodded and crawled back into what was now her side of the bed. "One month," she whispered, accepting his truce.

FOURTEEN

Watery dawn spread across the room through the thin hotel curtains, bringing a promise of rain. Carter lay sound asleep on the other side of their pillowed wall. His beard was several days old now and in great need of shaving, yet Bailee couldn't help but think he was handsome. Asleep, he looked younger. No more worry lines across his forehead. She wasn't met with the silent strength in his stare, as if he faced the world alone and had all his life.

She closed her eyes and remembered the night they'd shared. She'd wanted him to be near, needed to feel him next to her. She'd loved the way he kissed her and the way he made her tremble inside with his touch. But he frightened her, as well. She wanted him to want her, but when he kissed her that last time, she had the feeling he didn't just desire her, rather, he'd die without her. She wasn't just something he craved, but an essential in his life.

The feeling was overwhelming. Bailee had always been useful, but no one had ever needed her, truly needed her.

Fancis Tarleton had talked about marriage in terms of how she'd be a great help to him, never about how his life would be hollow and incomplete without her by his side. But Carter made her feel just that way. It frightened her to think she could ever mean so much to someone.

If the time came and Sheriff Riley declared her not a murderer, offered Carter his money back, then allowed her to go on her way, could she? And even if she could, would Carter let her go? They were married, and in less then a month they'd be married in every way. There would be no turning back then, no matter what happened.

Even if Riley told her it was all over, Bailee wasn't sure she could leave Carter. But what if she wanted the marriage still and Carter turned his back? What if all she thought she saw was no more real than it had been with Francis Tarleton?

A tear bubbled from the corner of her eye. It would be far worse to think you were passionately wanted and loved and find out that you never were, than to learn a halfway love like Tarleton's wasn't real.

Francis had made promise after promise of undying love and left her. What made her think Carter would stay in a marriage when he'd never said one promise aloud?

Carter shifted on the other side of the bed. Bailee kept her eyes closed. She heard him dressing, but she didn't move. She wasn't sure how she'd answer him if he asked about last night.

When he slipped from the room, closing the door gently, Bailee finally let the tears fall. Not because she was trapped in a marriage to a husband whose name had been pulled from a hat. Or because the man she'd thought she killed might be alive and coming after her. Or even because Francis was a rat for never letting her know about passion. She cried because . . . because she felt like crying.

A tiny hand slipped into hers. Bailee turned to see the angel face of Piper watching her from the edge of the bed. The child's dark eyes held a silent question.

Bailee lifted the covers, and the little girl crawled in beside her. She hugged Piper against her and willed herself to stop crying.

By the time Carter returned, they were both dressed. He seemed uncomfortable, not meeting her gaze when he told her he'd ordered breakfast and that it would be up within the hour. The only one he seemed comfortable talking with was Piper.

After several minutes Bailee could stand no more. She moved around the corner of the bed and stood directly in front of him. "Is it all right between us?" she asked, not knowing what else to say.

He looked at her as if searching for the answer in her eyes.

"Is it?" he asked.

She smiled. "I think so." How could she explain that she needed time? And with each hour she needed him more. There was something about the way he looked at her that made her feel as if she belonged by his side. It was as if they were in the middle of a forest fire and all she could think to do was light a match.

Bailee reached for his hand. He closed his fingers gently around hers. His smile reached his eyes. "I think so," he repeated her words.

She led him to the chair she'd placed beside the washstand. "I have a surprise for you."

Carter didn't look like he enjoyed surprises. He was reluctant to turn loose of her hand.

Bailee pulled the small package she'd bought at the barbershop from her things and handed it to Piper. She motioned with her head for Piper to take it to Carter.

The child understood.

When Carter opened the gift of shaving equipment, he frowned. "I thought I'd give up shaving for a while."

"Nonsense." Bailee moved behind him. "You just need the right things." She winked at him boldly. "And me to help."

Carter slowly handed over the gift.

Piper tugged on his shoulder and spoke to him with her hands as Bailee wrapped a towel around his neck.

"What does she say?" Bailee asked as she prepared the soap and mug.

"She tells me to be very brave." He made a face at Piper and the child smiled.

Bailee dropped the razor as she pulled it from the package. The blade fell open on the floor between Carter's feet. When she picked it up, she noticed Piper frantically signing.

"What did she say now?" Bailee glanced at Carter as she tried to hold the razor correctly.

He grinned at her. "Piper told me to run like hell."

"She shouldn't talk like that."

"She didn't say a word." He showed no inclination of following the child's advice as he leaned back in the chair. When Bailee stepped closer, he moved his hand along her waist as though he'd touched her a hundred times just so.

"All right?" he asked.

"All right," she answered, brushing his hand with her own.

His grip tightened slightly, reminding her of how close they'd been only a few hours before.

Bailee smoothed the towel at his neck, then lathered the soap. When she finally looked down at Carter, their eyes met. Without saying a word, he watched her work.

A warmth spread through her as she worked, touching him with great care. She liked the feel of his beard against her fingers and the way the smell of soap blended in the air between them. As she worked, their bodies brushed and each contact made her heart beat a little faster.

Bailee was cleaning the last bit of soap from his face when a knock sounded at the door. She froze.

Carter gently moved her aside and stood. Within a few steps, he'd reached the door.

Sheriff Riley sprang into the room like a tattered jack-in-the-box. "Good news!" he shouted, probably waking anyone on the floor who might still be asleep. "We got a telegram late last night that says the kid's relative will be in this morning to claim her." He paced the tiny space between the bed and Piper's cot. "Only sighed the telegram with initials, but said he's coming on the first train to make it from Down South since the wreck. I offered to make sure the body of Piper's mother was ready to transport as well, but there was no reply."

Riley sat on the corner of the bed as if he'd been invited to do so. He crossed his legs and used his knee as a hat rack. "Smith's given up on the kid adding any more to what she saw, so he said she could go back home. The sooner we get her away from this town the better for us all. Before we got the telegram, Smith and I were racking our brains trying to think of some way to get her into hiding."

Lifting his hat, Riley slapped his knee. "I can't believe our luck. We figured it would take a day, maybe two to find any relative of the girl even if she's from a big family around Sherman. To get an answer this morning the law must have searched all night."

Sadness spilled over Bailee's heart. She'd grown close to Piper and didn't want to think she'd never see the child again. She thought of asking Carter if Piper could visit them sometime but wasn't sure how long she'd be around to call Carter's home hers.

"Be packed and at the station at ten," Riley ordered when neither one of them was interested in talking to him. "We'll hand the kid over, wait for a freight car to run through, then catch the passenger train about one. I'm ready to get home. There ain't no tellin' what that deputy of mine will get into before I return. Wheeler's good at mopping, but anything else is stretching his brain. I'll probably find him and that worthless Mosely passed out in my office."

Carter opened the door for the sheriff.

They could hear Riley still mumbling to himself as he walked down the hallway.

Bailee stared over Piper's head at Carter. She couldn't help but wonder if he felt as she did. She wanted them to be alone with Piper for a few hours. Maybe, in some way, they could prepare the child for what might prove a very long day.

Bailee combed her hair while Carter talked to Piper in their silent language.

Once, when Bailee was standing above the child and knew Piper couldn't read her lips, she whispered to Carter, "I know she's going back to her family, but part of me wishes she could come with us."

Carter circled behind Piper. "You don't know what you ask. She'd break your heart. How would you explain to her that some of the town's folks will call her 'dummy' or think her a freak? How many times does a mother yell at her child to 'watch out' or 'step back'? Only if she stayed with us, she wouldn't hear. You'd scream and scream, but one day she'd walk right into danger."

Bailee had never heard him say so much, and each question tore at her heart. He wasn't just telling her facts, the questions were obviously echoes from his own childhood. The vision of a small boy screaming to warn his mother drifted through her mind. Had he tried and failed the day his mother died?

She faced him, but Carter turned his back to her, closed inside his silent world once more. She wanted to hold him, but she wasn't sure he'd understand. He might push her away if he thought she offered pity.

"It's time we left," he finally mumbled without making a move.

Bailee nodded and collected her things. Piper insisted on carrying her little bag that now was rounded with her old dress and new nightgown. She took Carter's hand, trusting wherever they were going would be all right, if he were near.

They didn't say a word as they walked to the station with the child between them. The sky looked as dreary as Bailee's mood. The streets were Sunday morning empty.

Carter's words rolled through her mind. He was right. She'd seen how cruel folks could be to someone who was different. How many times had she watched the crippled boy down the block from her old home? He'd walk home every day with kids following behind him, imitating his limp. Carter was right. Piper had relatives and a fine school to attend. She belonged there, not with them.

Both sheriffs were waiting at the deserted station house. Riley ushered Piper and Bailee into a small room to the left of the ticket window while Smith talked with Carter at the door.

"I'd like you to meet Piper's grandmother." Riley pointed with his hand toward a woman in her fifties perched on a bench. "She came as soon as she heard. Said her son wanted to stay in Sherman to make arrangements for his wife's funeral."

Bailee moved toward the woman in black, but Piper didn't budge. For a moment, Bailee thought the child either didn't understand or didn't recognize her own grandmother, though such a huge woman would be hard to forget.

"Come here, child, and give your grandmother a big hug." The woman stretched her arms, but didn't stand.

Piper only stared.

When Bailee leaned down, she was startled by the fear in the child's eyes.

"I haven't got much time." The grandmother puffed as she stood and built steam. She dropped her arms, forgetting all about the hug. "I'm Mildred Tyler Halloway. The mother of Piper's father." She didn't offer her hand to Bailee or reach to comfort the child.

Her widow's brooch clanked against the watch dangling from it, a reminder of Southern dead. The piece of jewelry was common, designed to be worn by a war widow until she remarried. Since the war had ended almost twenty years ago, Bailee guessed Mildred Tyler Halloway would carry the brooch to her grave.

"I understand you looked after my son's child." She looked up at Bailee. "I thank you for that. I know it couldn't have been easy."

Before Bailee could answer, the woman turned to Riley. "Where's that train? I thought you said it would be here before eleven. I've been waiting over an hour as it is."

"It must be running a little late." He lowered his voice, trying to be patient. "I know you're ready to be gone. This must be a hard journey for you to make."

Carter joined the group, but didn't speak to Mrs. Halloway. He stood behind Bailee listening.

Bailee searched her brain for something, anything, to say to the woman. "I'm very sorry about your loss," she finally managed to whisper.

"A great loss," Mildred agreed. "One of many I've suffered in my lifetime. One of many." She brushed her brooch, her badge of mourning. "I was surprised to learn my son's offspring survived. She's been nothing but pampered from the day she was born, and now with my son overcome with grief, she's left on my doorstep."

Bailee opened her mouth to speak, but Carter's hand on her shoulder held her back. He didn't need to tell her anything, she knew he wanted her to remain silent. Bailee reminded herself that Mrs. Halloway was in grief. She surely didn't mean to sound so cruel.

The widow reached to pat Piper's head, but the child stepped away and faced Carter, her hands flying frantically.

Carter folded to one knee as the grandmother lunged, silencing the child with one hand over both hers.

"Tell her to stop that crazy signing!" Mildred snapped. "We'll have no more of that. My daughter-in-law might have thought it wonderful, but I think not."

When Carter didn't move, she raised her voice. "Tell her no more signing. I don't want to see her hands moving like that ever again."

Bailee opened her mouth, determined to give the woman a piece of her mind in language she could clearly understand. But Carter's gaze caught hers, holding her with his plea for silence.

Mildred was impatient with Carter's hesitance. She grabbed Piper's chin and turned the girl's face up. "They tell me you can read lips. That's all you need to do for now. When you learn to write, I'll read your notes. Until then, you'll be silent with both your mouth and your hands."

She squeezed Piper's hand and dragged the child in her wake. "I hear the train coming. We've no time to delay. Come along little one."

She glanced over her shoulder. "Thank you, Sheriff Smith and Sheriff Riley, for your help. If one of you will see the body's loaded, I'll get the child on the train."

The old woman glared at Carter as if she thought him silently challenging her. "It's my understanding that until a few generations ago, no one tried to train children who can't speak or hear. They just let them be the animals they were meant to be. Wasting good money on school for her is no better than trying to talk to a horse."

Riley, who followed behind her, mumbled, "What's wrong with talking to a horse?"

The sour taste of panic filled Bailee's mouth. She didn't want this woman to take Piper. She could guess what the child's life would be like from this point on with a grandmother who didn't understand and a father sick with grief. Yet, the woman was her grandmother, maybe Piper's only relative besides her father. Bailee had no right to the child or to stop her from leaving.

Carter said nothing as he followed them onto the train. Bailee wanted to take the child from the old woman, if only for a few moments, but the grandmother wasn't turning loose of Piper's hand.

They made sure Mrs. Halloway was seated. Piper wouldn't turn loose of her bag when her grandmother demanded she put it on the overhead rack. Mildred might have ripped it from the child's arms, but she suddenly became aware of all the people on the train watching her. Carter and Bailee were of no importance to her, but she didn't seem to want to make a scene.

Bailee fought down tears as she kissed a frightened Piper good-bye. "I'm sure she's afraid." Bailee tried to keep her voice calm. "What with the wreck and all. Maybe putting her on a train again so soon isn't a good idea?"

Mildred nodded. "I suppose so, but there's no other way to get home, so she'll just have to get over any fear." She patted Piper's knee, more a warning than comfort, then clamped her hand over both of the child's.

Carter knelt, blocking the aisle. "I'd like to say good-bye to her in sign."

Mildred looked like she might object, but too many other people watched.

Carter waited until Piper looked at him. Without any emotion, he signed only a few movements, then stood and left.

Bailee had no choice but to follow. She wanted him to fight for the child. Tell her grandmother she didn't deserve to raise such a precious little girl. If he fought, Bailee would stand beside him. She'd do all she could, even if it meant the sheriffs had to drag them both off to jail.

But Carter hadn't said a word. In fact, he'd kept her from saying anything.

Bailee stopped cold halfway down the aisle. She turned to retrace her steps to the grandmother as the train shifted and began to roll out.

There was no time and nothing she could do. She whirled, running to catch up with Carter and Riley. They only had a few minutes to get off the train safely. She couldn't look back. She couldn't have the memory of a frightened Piper forever in her mind.

They pushed their way from the train as the last passengers climbed aboard.

"Well, that's done!" Riley yelled above the noise as he headed back to the station. "Can't say as I liked the grandmother much, but kin is kin."

Bailee agreed with him and turned to take Carter's arm.

Her husband wasn't at her side. She glanced back to see him running after the train like a madman. It was moving too fast for him to jump back on safely. A thought flickered across her mind that if he planned to say something, he should have done it on the train.

The truth slapped her in the face. He had! He had said something before he left. Only he'd said it to Piper.

She bolted after him just as a tiny body clutching a small carpetbag jumped from the steps of the train right into his arms.

Carter swung her, carpetbag and all, around like a human windmill as he fought to slow his pace and the last of the train sped past them.

"What the hell!" Riley yelled.

"No." Bailee smiled, remembering the pattern of hand signals she'd seen earlier that morning when Piper had signed to Carter. The same sign Carter had knelt and said farewell with. "Run like hell."

FIFTEEN

"Wait!" rain began to splatter in huge drops as Sheriff Riley ran toward Bailee and Carter. "Stop!" he yelled in anger and panic. "The child has to go!"

The train paid no heed to his cry as it picked up speed with each revolution of the wheels. The engine's hollow cry echoed across the stormy sky, whitewashing all other sounds.

A few feet from Carter, Riley realized Piper's escape was lost. He folded forward, his words coming between jagged breaths. "Even if her grandmother turns around at the first stop and comes back"—he gulped in air before continuing—"it will take her hours to return. What are we going to do with the kid until then? How can we keep her safe?"

Carter said nothing. Piper held to him as if to life. Bailee stood solid at his side. She wasn't sure what would happen, but she'd promised to stand beside him and, right or wrong, that was what she planned to do.

Smith finally reached them. He was slower than Riley, but no less angry. He pointed a thin finger at Carter like a weapon. "She's not safe with any of us. Everyone in town knows we were keeping an eye on her. Even if you leave, it wouldn't be hard to track you down, Carter. I had every deputy in town riding on that train to see her safely home. Now I'll have to send a telegram and get them back as fast as possible."

Riley agreed. "All three of you could be dead before the grandmother gets back. The men who robbed the train know they'll be hanged if caught. They can't afford to leave a witness."

Smith paced out a square, nodding at Riley's words as if keeping time to music. "She would have been better off with her grandmother. In a few hours she would have been home with her father." He sang Riley's chorus one more time.

Bailee had no argument to defend against the lawmen's rage. The sheriffs were right, but somehow it hadn't been fair to send Piper with that horrible woman. Yet, by saving her, Carter may have put the child's life in great danger. At least with the grandmother, she'd be away from this place and hopefully out of the outlaws' range.

Carter showed no sign of turning loose of Piper. He faced the two lawmen and let them yell until their steam vanished like that of the train's, then he said calmly, "That wasn't Piper's grandmother."

"What?" both men chimed at once. "How do you know?"

"Piper told me, or tried to before the woman stopped her hands. It took me a while to guess what she'd been about to sign."

"And you figured it would be your word against the old woman's, so you risked the child's neck letting her jump from the train?" Riley reasoned.

"No," Carter answered. "It would have been Piper's word against the old woman's. Who would you have believed?"

The lawmen looked at each other.

"Mrs. Tyler Halloway had no reason to lie," Smith ventured.

"Unless she was paid by the outlaws." Riley's head bobbed so fast it could have been on springs. "We both commented on how fast she got here. The woman would have to have been standing at the station in Sherman when she got our telegram to have made it so fast."

Bailee followed his logic. "If Piper had stayed on that train, no one would've ever seen her again. Ever." The last word chilled them all into silence.

Carter walked back to the deserted station. When he reached the corner of the platform, he sat Piper on it so that she was at eye level with the others. They were all soaked by the drizzle. Carter placed his coat around her to keep her warm.

"That doesn't solve our problem." Smith paid little mind to the child watching his lips. "If the old woman wasn't the grandmother, she'll never show her face again. She knows by now that you've had time to talk to the girl."

Smith swore. "Grandmother or not, we're still stuck with the kid with nowhere to hide her."

"I'll keep her at my place." Carter glanced at Bailee.

She nodded. It wasn't the best of plans, but it seemed the only answer.

"No." Smith shook his head. "You'd be out there all alone. Any gang organized enough to pull off a train robbery would have no trouble picking you off while you went about your work, then moving in on Bailee and the child."

Riley scratched a layer of hide off his chin while he thought. "Town's not safe. Too many people around. At least your farm would be isolated. As many times as I've been out there, I've never come up on you unaware."

"She'd be safe with us." Bailee said the words like she believed them.

"Maybe." Riley glanced at Smith. "If I go along as guard." He shifted his stare to Carter. "I'm sure the McKoys could put me up for a few days until this problem is solved. We could be back here in a matter of hours if needed."

A freight train whistled in the distance announcing its arrival. Riley moved closer and stared directly at Carter. "What's it to be, son? If you take the child, I go along as part of the bargain. We can catch this cattle train when it slows to take on water and be home before anyone in town knows we're gone."

Bailee knew without asking that Carter had never offered the sheriff a night's lodging.

"You'll sleep in the bunkhouse," she prompted.

The sheriff nodded as Carter swung up on the platform to retrieve Bailee's bag from the station.

Bailee put her hand over Piper's cold fingers and looked around. The drizzle seemed to close the world in around them. She couldn't see beyond the station house. The town vanished in the gray light.

The train grew closer, signaling again with a longer whistle, then a short blast.

The sound hadn't died on the air, when a popping noise made Bailee jump. It took her a heartbeat to register the sound. Gunfire!

Riley jerked his pistol from its holster with far more speed than she'd thought him capable.

Smith ordered, "Everybody down!"

Bailee glanced at the platform and saw Carter fall forward as more shots rattled the air like rapid-fire thunder.

She had no time to get to him. Grabbing Piper, Bailee knelt beneath the platform, holding the child close.

Riley was on the move. Running through the silent morning like a man dodging invisible bullets, he made it to the edge of the platform, then beyond. Smith followed, both Colts at ready.

For a moment, before they disappeared into the rain, Bailee saw them as young men once more, in their prime, in their element. Neither lawman slowed until they'd circled the area twice.

"If we can't see them," Smith yelled at Riley, "how the hell can they see us?"

"Maybe they're shooting at sounds?" Riley answered, his voice high with excitement.

Several shots splattered off the wood of the platform, proving his point. The noise of the train grew louder, drowning out more shots.

Bailee backed into the blackness beneath the loading stage and waited. The platform smelled newly built, but sturdy. Piper was wrapped warmly in Carter's coat, with her little carpetbag dangling from her hand.

When Riley came close, Bailee ventured a quick look above the wood and whispered, "Carter? Is he all right?"

Riley didn't look in her direction as he backed near the opening and answered. "He's fine. Keeping his head down. Don't you move. There ain't no telling who's shooting at us. Might be one, might be more."

For once, Bailee didn't argue with the man.

Smith had disappeared into the fog, but she knew he was still circling, searching. She could hear the tapping of his boots along the edges of the platform. Riley stayed close, putting himself between her and the shooter.

Bailee felt Piper crying on her shoulder, but there was little she could do to comfort her. She tried not to jerk when the next round of gunfire came, knowing the child wouldn't hear anything. If Bailee could keep still, maybe Piper wouldn't know the shooting continued.

Rain ran off the wood above and splattered, forming a curtain between her hiding place and the world beyond. The thin liquid barrier might save her life.

A thud sounded suddenly against the wood above her. Someone had fallen.

Bailee fought down a scream.

Smith's voice cracked over the noise of the train. "Riley! Riley!"

She heard footsteps running across the wood, then the scraping sound of a body being moved. Then nothing but the rain and the release of steam as the train pulled close to the platform. Unlike the new passenger train that had left minutes ago, this train hauled freight. It rattled and groaned and spit.

Carter dropped down so suddenly in front of her, Bailee felt her heart jump. He carried Riley's limp body over one shoulder as he stepped through the thin waterfall coming off the platform.

"Bailee?" he whispered.

"Yes," she answered without moving out of the blackness.

"When I run toward town with Riley, can you get Piper on the train?"

"Yes," she answered, seeing only the bottom half of slowly moving cattle cars before her.

"Stay hidden until then." His tone was low, solid, worried. "We have to time it just right. I'll distract them, you run. With luck they'll be watching me and won't see you climb aboard."

"Is Riley still alive?"

"I think so." The train sounded impatient to be on its way. "Head toward home. I'll find you."

He moved away before she could say more. She waited in the steamy wooden cave for his signal. She wanted to beg him not to go. Riley was already shot. When Carter moved into the open, the ambusher would try again. He was putting his life in great danger to give her a chance to run for a train she wasn't even sure she could board.

The train shuddered and began to move as Bailee heard Carter's boots hit wood above her. The sound of the train muffled his steps, but she listened. Solid, strong steps ran away from her.

There was no time to make certain he made it. Even if she could lift Piper up and look over the platform, the fog would prevent her from seeing more then a few yards.

The air rumbled once more, and she wasn't sure if it was thunder or gunfire.

Holding the child tightly against her, Bailee did as Carter told her. She bolted for the train.

At the last possible second she grabbed a boxcar door handle and jumped for the opening. Piper's little bag banged against the outside of the train, but the child gripped it tightly.

Bailee held on to the opening with one hand and tried to pull them both inside.

Her wet skirts and the weight of the child drew her

back. Her fingers slipped an inch down the handle. Just when she thought she could no longer hold, a solid grip closed around her wrist and pulled. Suddenly several hands touched her and tugged at once, drawing her to the darkness of the car.

She felt as if the tugging on her arm ripped her muscles apart, but she couldn't turn loose. There was no going back. If she fell from the train now, she and Piper might both be killed.

Then, suddenly, she was inside the car. The wind no longer whistled in her ears, the rain didn't sting her face.

For a long moment she knelt just beyond the doorway, not caring that her new dress was getting filthy on the car's muddy floor. All she could think was that she'd left Carter to face trouble, maybe even death, alone.

With muscles near frozen in fear, Bailee lifted herself enough to scoot backward, pulling Piper out of the opening. The sudden freedom from the wind and rain blanketed over her. She leaned her back against the door and took a deep breath for the first time since she'd heard a shot.

"It's all right," she whispered as she stroked Piper's hair. "We're safe. We made it. Everything's going to be all right."

Tears fell from her eyes as she realized Piper couldn't hear her. The child had to know she was in danger, but did she realize she was safe?

Bailee touched Piper's shoulder, pushing her an inch away. "It's all right," she said again, hoping Piper could understand when she watched her lips move.

Piper's eyes stayed tightly closed.

Bailee increased the pressure on the girl's shoulder, planning to shake her slightly to get her to look up.

Warm blood streaming between Bailee's fingers stopped her.

"Oh, my Lord!" Bailee cried as she saw blood covering half the child's chest. She looked closer: Blood soaked the front of Piper's dress and the lining of Carter's coat. The child was wounded, must have been all the while they'd hidden in the darkness. Yet she hadn't made a sound.

Panic shattered the last ounce of sanity she'd clung to. Bailee felt herself slipping into a cool darkness where all the problems of the world disappeared and nothing mattered.

"No!" she screamed. Anger ran through her blood. The same anger that had made her hit Zeb. The anger that had made her act before she thought when she saw someone robbing her father's office. The anger that had gotten her into trouble must now somehow save her life. And Piper's.

Bailee fought the dizziness and stood to her knees. "I'll get help. Don't worry." She pulled Piper close as she moved farther into the boxcar hoping to find something, anything to help the child.

She took one step, tripped over her muddy skirt, and fell. Twisting as she tumbled, she let her shoulder hit the floor a moment before Piper fell atop her.

Bailee's head hit the floor of the car so hard the thud echoed around her.

She cried in pain and looked up, praying she hadn't hurt Piper more.

Just beyond the child, almost invisible in the shadows, strange faces watched. Suddenly Bailee remembered the hands pulling her in. But had they pulled her to safety, or into their lair?

Bailee drew in a breath to scream as the faces moved forward. The light inside her mind faded.

SIXTEEN

THE RAIN FOUGHT CARTER AS HE RAN, BLINDING HIM, tripping him in knee-deep puddles, thundering in his ears until he could hear nothing else. He longed for the luxury of one look back, of knowing Bailee got on the train safely with Piper in her arms. But he couldn't risk it. Riley bled from several bullet wounds. If Carter didn't get him out of the rain and to help quickly, the sheriff would be dead.

Gunfire sounded behind him. He couldn't tell if it echoed or if someone fired back. The train's whistle muted the noise. *Bailee is pulling away from the station with Piper,* he told himself. *Bailee has to be on the train.*

Carter stepped onto packed, slippery earth. He'd reached the main road that led to town. He slowed enough to try to make out any place where he'd find help.

The stores were closed for Sunday. Even the saloon had been locked when he passed it on the way to the station. Their hotel was two blocks away, and he doubted he'd be able to find much help there. Nothing ahead invited him to enter.

He glanced to his left at a two-story house standing apart from Main Street, closer to the tracks than any residence would want to be. A lone woman, still in her nightclothes, sat in a porch swing watching the rain, watching him.

Plowing through the mud, Carter headed toward her.

She stood as he neared and leaned forward. "You need help?" she yelled over the storm. "Hey, mister, what happened?"

Carter drew closer. "A man's been shot!" he shouted as he tumbled onto the porch, without bothering to use the steps. "Can you help me?" Carter forced the words out as he asked another for help for the first time. But this time he had no choice; the sheriff's life was at stake.

"I'll do my best." The woman wasted no time asking more questions. She helped Carter carry the sheriff into the house and yelled for someone called Fat Alice. Several women answered her call.

"I thought I heard shots between the train's noise and the thunder," a huge woman said as she barreled into the room. "I figured trouble was riding in with this storm."

Carter stood a few feet inside the door as a swarm of women, some who must have just gotten out of bed and hadn't taken the time to put their clothes on, clamored around the sheriff. The one who owned the name Fat Alice shouted orders like a general in full charge as they took Riley from Carter.

They spread Riley on a gaming table in the center of the main room and began stripping clothes off the poor man. Carter thought of throwing the sheriff over his shoulder and heading back out into the rain. But he felt sure these women would fight for the wounded prey they seemed to have caught. They chattered so rapidly as they worked, Carter couldn't make out individual words.

A young girl, who still looked like she had a head to grow before she could call herself grown, handed Carter a towel.

"Thanks," he managed to say without taking his eyes off the flock of women working on Riley. Fat Alice lifted her gown above her knee and pulled a thin knife from where it was strapped to her leg.

The girl watched him with open curiosity for a minute before saying, "Don't worry. They know what they're doing. They'll get your friend patched up. He ain't the first fellow who stumbled in here full of lead."

"I got one!" squealed a woman with the strangest color of hair Carter had ever seen. It reminded him of autumn leaves left damp in a pile to rot.

The woman plunked a tiny piece of lead into a bowl as if she were panning for gold.

"I got the one out of his leg," another bragged as she added her metal to the bowl.

The girl beside Carter stood straight and proud. "Some of these girls weren't more than my age when they was with Colonel Hooker's troops during the war. On good days, they'd do laundry and make a little extra on their backs. On bad days, they'd help keep their paying customers alive to fight, and love, another day."

Carter didn't comment, so she continued. "See those brandy snifters on the mantel? One's full of tails from rattlesnakes we've killed around the place, and the other is bullets we've dug out of folks. One day this town will get a doc, and we'll lose half our collection. Before then, both glasses will probably be full."

Carter looked down at her. "How old are you?"

"Fourteen, but I been a working girl for so long I can't

remember when I started. I even got beat up one night by a low-down bedbug who goes by the name of Amos Ally." She stopped long enough to look like she might spit. "Broke my nose, the bum. You want to feel the knot it left?"

"No," Carter answered. The girl spoke some foreign language he couldn't quite understand. The words seemed normal, but she put them together all wrong.

She didn't take offense. "My name's Nellie, Nellie Jean Desire." She said her last name real slow and low almost as if it were part of a song. "I thought that sounded good for a name. You ever heard of me?"

Carter shook his head.

"Fat Alice says I'm gonna be something. Pretty soon men will be coming from all over the state to wrestle me. Miss Nellie Jean Desire." The name slid off her tongue like warm molasses. "I should be something when my chest comes in."

Definitely a foreign language, he thought. Or maybe the child was mad. Maybe this was some kind of insane asylum like he'd read about in a paper from Austin. That would explain the house being set off from the others and the clothes. But there didn't seem to be any bars or guards. Surely the mad didn't just stay here of their own accord.

The place was obviously decorated by the insane. Colors of reds and unnatural greens fought for space on a battlefield littered with feathers and fringe.

Carter moved closer to the table, fearing what they might have done to the sheriff. He wouldn't have been surprised to see the old man cut up like a turkey.

There was blood everywhere. On the sheriff. The table. The hands of several of the women.

"I got the last one!" the large woman yelled. She wore a dress that had been washed so thin he could see through it. The sight was not one he was thankful for viewing.

She must have bought her dress when she was fifty pounds leaner, for it no longer seemed to come completely closed in the front. "Bandage all the wounds and get him upstairs." She stepped back and grinned.

The woman turned her attention to Carter. "Got any idea who he is, handsome?"

Carter looked behind him trying to figure out to whom the strange woman was talking.

"Two Bits! Has this guy got a voice?" Fat Alice yelled at the girl who'd called herself Nellie Jean.

The girl beside Carter stormed like a barn cat caught in the house. "I ain't answering to that name no more, Fat Alice. I told you my name's Nellie Jean. How am I ever gonna make top money with a name like Two Bits?"

"You don't worry about making top money until I let you start working. I'm not one to let fruit be picked before it's ripe no matter how much it wants to jump off the tree." The large woman slapped the girl out of the way as easily as if she'd been made of spiderwebs. "Now listen up, deary." She gave her full attention to Carter. "We don't mind helping out, but we like to know anyone's name who goes upstairs. We may be cheap, but nothing here, not even the doctoring, is free."

Carter fished in his pocket. He'd happily pay the ladies. From the looks of their clothes, they could really use the money. "How much?"

"Three bucks a bullet. Luckily, we didn't have to use whiskey to get him still. So it'll only be twelve dollars." She saw the color of his money. Gold. "And I'll throw in the bed rest for free, providing all he does in it is rest."

Carter glanced up, noticing the other women had Riley halfway up the stairs. They were trying to turn him at the landing without getting his legs entangled in the railing, but the long-legged sheriff wasn't cooperating. "I'm much obliged, ma'am," Carter continued. "Twenty should cover his expenses. His names Riley. Sheriff Harman Riley."

The caravan climbing the stairs suddenly turned around as if someone had yelled "retreat" and started back down.

Fat Alice huffed a quick breath of air, pulled her dress together, and took Carter's twenty-dollar gold coin. "He can stay down here on the sofa. I run a respectable board-inghouse for mature ladies. We don't allow no men up the stairs. Not even a sheriff."

Carter had no idea what to do. He needed to find Smith and tell him what had happened to Riley, but he didn't want to leave the old sheriff alone with these strange women. They reminded him of the saloon girl who'd tried to get him to go upstairs, but they were all cleaner, better fed, and older by ten years. Except for Nellie Jean, who, unfortunately, was still at his side.

"Are you a lawman?" she asked when the huge woman hurried off.

"No," he answered.

"Good. I didn't want to think of a prime cut like you being wasted behind a badge. You know, I'm willing to offer a deal for the right price. Think of you as part of my advertising discount."

Carter didn't even try to figure out what she meant. He covered Riley with a blanket he found on the back of the sofa and pulled a chair up close. "Nellie Jean," he said slowly so she could understand him. "Would you sit with my friend until I get back? I would be grateful."

To his surprise, Nellie seemed to understand. She

plopped down in the chair and smiled. "Sure whatever you want. You will be back?"

"I promise."

"And I'll be your dancing partner when the music stops? I'm not near as young as Fat Alice thinks." She wiggled her eyebrows as if he were supposed to fill in the blanks.

He saw no harm in humoring her. "Of course."

To his shock, she winked as if he'd just signed over his soul to the devil. Carter couldn't get out of the house fast enough.

He ran straight into the rain, wanting to wash clean of the place. He wished he could breathe in water and wash his lungs free of the odor of it. The women looked like they bathed regularly, but they smelled strange. Fat Alice had an aroma that reminded him of the peach barrel when the crop had turned bad.

The rain shifted from a whirling assault on the earth, to a steady downpour. Carter retraced his steps to the station. Bailee's bag sat on the corner of the platform where he'd dropped it when the shooting started, but nothing else remained to tell what had happened less than an hour before.

He picked up the bag and continued his search.

A thought gnawed at the back of his mind. If a gang of robbers had wrecked the train, why had only one gunman tried to ambush them? Carter didn't know much about battle strategy, but it made sense that if there had been two men firing at them from different angles, they would have all been shot, maybe dead.

He stared down the tracks, wishing Bailee safe. She was more than just the wife he'd won in a lottery. She mattered to him. Women are strange creatures, he thought.

A man doesn't even care if he has one until she's missing, then he feels the loss like something's been cut out from inside of him. Carter wanted her back with him ten times more than he ever wanted her in the first place.

With the bag in one hand he began circling the station as he'd seen the sheriffs do. He half expected to trip over the body of Smith, or maybe even the shooter.

Nothing.

When he came to the edge of the tracks, he looked north as far as the rain would allow, wishing he knew about Bailee. She made it to the train, he told himself. She had to have climbed aboard, though it couldn't have been easy for her carrying a child in her arms. But his wife was strong. She was one of those people who did what must be done. No matter what.

Carter walked back across the tracks and headed toward town. He'd check there for Smith. As he walked, he thought of Bailee and couldn't help but wonder if sleeping with him was one of the things that "had to be done" in her life.

He plowed through the rain, hoping he wasn't just a duty to her, but guessing he was. She hadn't married him because she wanted to. Marriage had been the only choice other than jail. She was trying. From the very first day, the first kiss, she had tried. Doing what she had to do. What she knew was right to do. Last night, when he'd gotten too close, she must have found out just how difficult her duty would be.

The image of her frightened, clenching her gown that he'd ripped open, flashed in his mind like lightning.

Carter's free hand began to jerk at his side spelling out words he wanted no one to hear.

If she was safe. If she'd gotten away alive, he promised

never to frighten her like that again. If it meant not touching . . . never touching her . . . then so be it.

Carter hit the door to the sheriff's office at a full run. It took him three steps into the room before he was able to stop.

The sight before him drained all other thoughts from his mind.

Sheriff Smith sat atop a man almost twice his size. The old sheriff was bleeding from his left side, his few hairs stringing wet in his face, and his Colt pointed at the man's forehead.

Smith barely glanced at Carter. "Thank God you're here, Carter. I'm having a little trouble cuffing my new prisoner."

The man on the floor struggled, slinging water from his buffalo-hide coat. "Get off me, old man. You're bleeding all over me. Shoot me or holster the gun, because it'll take more than you and this dummy's brat to put me in this town's jail."

The outlaw suddenly shoved the sheriff toward Carter.

Smith yelped in pain as Carter tumbled to the floor, trying to break the old man's fall. The sheriff's gun fired as it hit the floor. The explosion rattled the room, but the bullet missed his prisoner.

Carter jumped for the stranger, catching him by the arm and trying to pull him back. The mountain of a man turned on Carter with the fury of a seasoned soldier fighting for his life.

Carter was tall and strong, but the stranger outweighed him by more than fifty pounds and must have cut his teeth on frontier fights. Carter took blow after blow before landing a few of his own. The battle was like some kind of tortured lesson. Carter was learning from a master, but it was costing him dearly.

The outlaw roared and shoved against Carter with his entire body weight. Both men flew through the window, rolled across the porch, and landed in the mud. Glass cut into Carter's shoulder and sliced down one leg but there was little time to notice as the stranger pounded against first his side, then his back.

Finally, Carter raised to his knees, pooling all his energy so he could stand. A fist slammed against the side of his face sending him backward. For a moment he lay in the mud in too much pain to open his eyes.

When he finally fought through the agony and raised his head, the stranger was gone.

SEVENTEEN

"LITTLE MOTHER? LITTLE MOTHER, YOU WAKE UP now?"

Bailee tried to open her eyes at the sound of someone talking, but they were glued closed with fear. She rocked to the movements of the train. The air was thick with smoke and the smells of a barn. Slowly memory returned, but when she forced her eyes open, all she could see were shadows moving above her.

A wrinkled hand patted her shoulder. "You all right, Little Mother? We take good care of your child."

Bailee pulled herself up to a sitting position and tried to see through the darkness. Pale, watery moonlight squeezed between the wood that formed the walls of the smelly freight car. A light flickered at the far end. Hazy forms huddled along the fringes, unclear, unidentified. "Piper?" she whispered, feeling as if her mouth were as full of straw as her clothing. The odor of damp hay and cow manure thickened the air.

"She is fine." A thin man, wearing a hat almost as wide as his shoulders, answered. "Bullet only skid across her shoulder and arm. Bled a great deal, but she will live with only a scar and her memories."

The old man helped Bailee to her feet, and they walked slowly across the car to where Piper rested in the lap of a woman layered in rags. The child's arm was in a sling made from a multicolored scarf. White bandages replaced the top part of her dress over one shoulder and arm.

"She not say a word," he whispered as Piper turned her pale face toward Bailee and smiled. "We use the nightgown in her little bag to make the wrap for her wounds. Even as we work, she never cry out."

"She can't hear or speak," Bailee whispered as she brushed her hand over the dressing. "And she's not my daughter; she lost her mother in a train wreck a few days ago." Bailee knew she shouldn't be telling the little man so much, but she had to trust him. She owed these people her life. If one of them hadn't grabbed her from inside the car when she jumped toward the opening, she never would have made it.

The man spoke to the woman in a language Bailee couldn't understand.

Bailee closed her fingers around Piper's hand, wishing her words true as she told Piper they were safe now. No one would be shooting at them again, Bailee mouthed slowly.

"My wife says"—the man in the hat smiled—"the child has the gift of silence. A rare gift indeed. Think of all she must hear with the world stepping back."

Bailee thought labeling Piper's lack of hearing a gift was a strange way to look at it. As her eyes adjusted, she saw the other faces lined along the walls of the car. They were clustered in families, holding to one another for warmth. Fathers trying to block the rain seeping through the cracks from their wives and children. Mothers cuddling their little ones close, using their skirts to blanket them. All were dressed in an odd mixture of rags and brightly colored scarves. And jewelry, Bailee noticed. Rings, bracelets, necklaces. Beggars wearing gold.

The old man appeared nervous. "We meant no harm. We only wanted to help you and the child. When we reach the next town, you will not tell anyone we are here, please?"

Bailee stared at him. "You . . . all of you are running also? Like Piper and me."

The man nodded but still looked fearful. "Not like you. You are running to safety. We only run away. For us there is no place named safety."

Bailee wanted to ease his fears. "We were being shot at by someone who wants Piper dead. If I hadn't jumped on the train, I'm not sure what might have happened to us."

"But why would anyone want to kill such a fine little girl?" he asked. "Or a lady?"

"Outlaws who think she might be able to identify them. Men who wrecked a train and killed everyone but her."

He nodded and she noticed several of the others who were listening also nodded. The fear she'd seen in all their eyes faded as they saw a glimpse of her trouble.

Bailee lowered her voice, suddenly wanting to share. "We hoped to get her to her father, but a shooter opened fire at the station. Now we have no idea when her family will pick her up, and I left my husband behind to face the outlaw alone. There was a sheriff with us, but he was shot. I don't know if he's alive or not. It all happened so fast, and with the rain I could see little."

The people in their strange layered rags moved closer

and asked questions, first shyly, then more boldly. Their problems were forgotten as they worried about the child who was now unprotected and unable to communicate.

Bailee relaxed, relating every detail of the past few days. She even showed everyone how Carter moved his hands and sang a silent song to Piper.

They all commented about how this Carter McKoy must be a good husband. Bailee agreed. She'd been lucky in the drawing. She had picked a good man, a brave man. Today had proved it.

As the train sped through the rainy shadows toward Cedar Bend, one by one the people relaxed. Each one told his story in tiny parts that fit together like a puzzle. They were all of the same family, uncles, cousins, brothers.

They had no home in Europe so thought to find one in America. But no matter where they went, it was the same story. Someone's cow died, or a wagon was stolen, or a barn caught fire. They were always blamed. Finally they made it to Galveston, thinking they'd be safe, but three nights ago a drunken mob shoved them onto the train without even allowing them to gather all their belongings. Now they traveled, just traveled, hoping to outrun trouble.

Bailee watched them closely. She saw the hollowness in their cheeks, the thin hands, the dark circles beneath their even darker eyes. They never mentioned the word, but she knew who they were. She'd heard stories of a people, dark and wild, who caused trouble wherever they went. Gypsies.

Lacy crossed Bailee's thoughts. She remembered how the people on the wagon train had considered it grand that she had a gift of nursing. But when the sick wife she'd been hired to tend while they traveled across country died, the women of the train began to talk. They mentioned the strange way Lacy talked of luck and blessings and curses. They told of hearing her chant when she brewed a mixture of herbs by a campfire late one night. One of the older women even swore she saw Lacy dancing beneath the moon.

The days on the trail were boring, and speculating about Lacy became first a game, then a plot the women played. She went from being valued nurse to an extra without a wagon, or a family. Extra baggage.

When Lacy offered to try to nurse Sarah back to health, the others turned on her. They saw Sarah as a poison in the group. Lacy must have been a witch or a simpleton not to be afraid of her. Though they disliked Bailee for offering Sarah a ride, they resented Lacy for trying to stop what they all believed should happen. Sarah should die, if for no other reason than all her family had. Sarah had somehow sinned by living when her husband and child died.

These people huddled around Bailee now were no different than Lacy. They were looking for somewhere to belong. They helped Piper, and for that Bailee owed them her loyalty. Yet they seemed afraid their good deed would be punished.

The whistle blew—one long, one short blast.

"We're coming into Cedar Bend." Bailee took action. "It's only a little town, and my home is two hour's ride away on dry roads. In this rain it may take us most of the night, but once we're there, we'll be safe." She stood and raised her voice. "Come home with me. All of you."

The men shook their heads. The fear in their eyes returned. "It is better to keep going," one mumbled.

"We know not this place," another whispered. "We must travel farther."

"We know no place," came an answer from the back of the car.

"You can rest," Bailee pleaded. "We have a ranch with plenty of stores of food. I know my husband would want you to at least rest for a few days with us." Bailee knew no such thing, but she said it so strongly, she almost believed it herself. "I was told once that Cedar Bend was named after a lone cedar tree that the Apache tied so that it would bend and point toward their winter camp. Let it point you toward a resting place now."

No one moved. Fear settled once more over the boxcar.

Bailee closed her eyes. She couldn't bear to think of these people who'd just saved her life, starving as they rode half frozen on a train to nowhere. "Come home with me, please. I need you to so badly. I have no one to protect Piper and me. I can't get her to the safety of my land alone. I need your help. You helped us once. You may be all that stands between us and death tonight."

When she opened her eyes, they'd stopped shaking their heads. The old man stood in front of her. His gaze circled the room. "We will consider. If we are needed."

"Piper's already been shot once. The outlaws may try again. I left my husband behind to face a shooter. He may already be dead. I'm not sure I can keep her alive by myself."

Slowly one by one, the people nodded.

Bailee began doing what she did best, organizing. "First, we have to get off the train without anyone in town seeing us. I spent a week in town watching this train go by my cell . . . I mean room. It only stops for a few minutes. We'll have to hurry to get everyone out of the back of the car and into the breaks beyond the tracks. There's not enough cover to hide this many people in daylight, but at night, with the rain, we might just make it."

The people collected their few belongings.

"I have to get to my friend without anyone seeing me. She lives in the center of town. She can help me get my husband's wagon and maybe one other."

A boy of about fifteen stepped forward. "My name is Rom. I can be a shadow in the rain. I will take you to your friend."

"Good." Bailee put together a plan in her head faster than she'd ever been able to organize a dinner party at her father's house. "All of you stay hidden until I come back. I promise I won't be long. Rom and I will be back with wagons. In the meantime, I know you will keep Piper safe among you."

She looked at the child resting in the old woman's arms. Piper trusted the woman, Bailee could see it in the child's eyes.

The first part of the plan worked. Ten minutes after the train stopped, everyone was lying on the buffalo grass to the east of the tracks. The rain acted as a curtain, protecting them from anyone in town who happened to be glancing in their direction.

Bailee moved in the shadows with her guide until they reached the side stairs that led to Lacy's apartment over the print shop. The boy stayed behind, hidden beneath the stairs as Bailee hurried up the steps. She noticed he kept his hand at his belt and knew, without asking, that he carried a knife and was prepared to use it, if needed.

The knowledge frightened her a little. These people might not all be the gentle angels of mercy she thought them.

"Lacy," she called softly as she knocked. "Lacy, it's Bailee."

The door flew open. Lacy hugged her friend tight. "I was so worried. We got word a few hours ago that a sheriff was shot in Childress in a gun battle. I knew you were there and was so afraid. Was it Riley shot or another? If there was trouble, it's just like him to be in the middle of it. Where's Carter? Did he see the child? Could he talk with her?"

"I'm all right, but I don't know about Riley, or even Carter."

Lacy pulled Bailee into her little apartment. "I went over to the sheriff's office, but that nitwit Deputy Wheeler said he didn't know anything more than what I heard. Riley is going to be plenty mad when he gets back and finds out the buzzards have been nesting in his place." Lacy covered her wet friend with a towel. "Riley is coming back? He can't be hurt bad."

Bailee shivered as she told Lacy all that had happened while Lacy got dressed and collected all the blankets and towels she owned.

"We have to get these people and Piper to the ranch without anyone seeing," Lacy agreed. "From what you tell me, half of them will catch a fever if they don't get warm and dry."

"If you'll help with the wagon, I can drive them."

Lacy stopped her packing. "Are you joking! I'm going with you. You're not having an adventure without me. I got nursing skills, too, remember. I'll have a look at this little Piper's wound."

"It could be dangerous."

Lacy laughed. "Like traveling alone across country without even a gun or killing a guy who planned to kill us. I've been nothing but bored around here waiting for my Frank. It's time I got my heart pumping again. Come on along, we've got work to do tonight."

Lacy pushed Bailee out the side door and down the stairs. "I'd do anything to help you. We're sisters of the soul. You know, bound by something stronger than blood. If somebody's shooting at you, I'm not leaving your side."

With the light of a small lantern, they locked arms and moved into the alley. "There would be too many questions if we rented a wagon from Mosely," Lacy whispered, her voice high with excitement, "but I know someone who will not only loan you his wagon, he'll drive you to your place."

Without another word, they hurried through the back alley.

Pulled up beside the livery, protected from most of the rain, was a lone wagon covered with a thick tarp. "I met this fellow last night. In a town this size, you tend to notice when someone new comes in. My father-in-law tried to get him to sleep inside our shop for the night, but he said he'd be heading out to Carter's place as soon as the rain slowed." She leaned close and whispered, "He reminds me of a badger and seems just about as friendly. He can't see much without his glasses, and you have to almost yell to get him to hear."

Lacy patted on the canvas as though it were the front door. "Mr. Samuel! You in there?"

A gray-haired man with a mustache that went from ear to ear poked his head out of the wagon. "I'm not bothering anyone. Leave me be." He tried to put on thick glasses in the rain.

"Mr. Samuel!" Lacy jumped up, grabbing his shirt so he couldn't pull back inside the wagon. "This is Carter's wife and she needs your help. So get out here and listen for a minute."

The grumpy man crawled from the wagon and stepped into the lantern light. His face still carried a frown, but he nodded politely. "Why didn't you say so, Miss Lacy?" He slicked his hair back with a wide hand. "I'm Samuel Dodge, ma'am. I'm sure your husband's mentioned me."

Bailee didn't want to appear impolite. She had heard Sheriff Riley mention that Carter had a handyman help him out every year with carpentry. This had to be the man. "Of course," Bailee took a guess. "He says you taught him everything he knows about building."

Samuel stood a little straighter. "That I did. The boy would be living in a hole like a rabbit if it weren't for me. I stop by twice a year at his place and stay as long as I'm needed." His pale gray eyes flickered in the lantern's light as his glasses slipped to the tip of his nose. "How may I be of service, Mrs. McKoy?"

There was no time to explain. "I need your wagon and the one belonging to Carter that's stored inside Mosely's barn if we can get it without the man knowing. I have a load to pick up near the station that must get to my place as soon as possible."

Samuel laughed. "That'll be no problem. Mosely has been drinking like he came into an inheritance and can't wait to spend it. He won't be stumbling back to the livery for at least another hour, maybe more. We'll have time to take the wagon and have the rain erase our tracks before he notices."

Bailee leaned closer. "Aren't you going to ask any questions?"

"Don't need to, Mrs. McKoy." He shook his head. "I wouldn't have worked for your husband for years if I was a questioning man. I can drive my own wagon, if you can drive Carter's."

Bailee looked at Lacy. They'd fought their way across hundreds of miles; surely they could handle Texas mud. "I can handle it," Bailee answered. "But I don't know if I can manage to harness the team in the dark."

"I will help."

The voice came from nowhere through the darkness. Samuel jumped and Lacy let out a little scream.

Bailee laughed. "Everyone, meet my shadow, Rom."

The boy stepped into the circle of light.

Samuel offered his hand. "Glad to have your help." He looked around. "Any more of you standing around?"

"Just me," Rom said shyly.

"Well, help me with the wagons, Rom." Samuel glanced over his shoulder at Bailee. "If you'll stand out of the rain, we'll bring them around directly."

Bailee and Lacy huddled together beneath the overhang of the barn.

"I'll run leave a note that I've gone with Samuel to visit you," Lacy whispered. "My father-in-law won't know if I left it tonight or in the morning. I'll tell him to say nothing to anyone, just in case."

"Tell him to watch the trains for Carter." Bailee tried to keep her voice calm. "I don't even know if my husband is alive."

Lacy hugged her tightly. "Neither do I," she whispered. "Just do like I do. Think of him alive until you know different."

Bailee tried, but the only vision she could bring to mind was Carter standing in the pouring rain with Riley's bloody body draped over his wide shoulder.

Then, lightly, almost like the tickle of wind in her hand, she felt Carter's finger moving. She closed her eyes and cupped her palm as if he were there, wishing more than feeling him whispering to her in his silent words.

EIGHTEEN

"I SWEAR TO MOSES, YOU'VE BROUGHT ME ANOTHER one!" Fat Alice shouted as Carter plowed his way through her front door.

Smith was blood-covered, dripping wet, and unconscious, just as Riley had been earlier. Carter stood on the worn rug, waiting for orders as the huge woman circled him like a raiding party of one. She'd put on war paint, but must have not had time to add additional clothing.

Fat Alice grabbed Smith's scalp and turned him so she could see his face, then looked back toward Carter with a frown. "I don't know who you are, mister, but I'm running out of sofas."

She motioned to the same table Sheriff Riley had been operated on, then turned her head up as if about to break into song. "More bandages, girls!" she yelled. "Sheriff Parker Smith's come to call."

Without a sign of modesty, she raised her gown and slipped the thin knife from its hiding place just above her fat knee.

Before Carter turned loose of the sheriff, women

flocked around Smith as they had Sheriff Riley, pulling off his clothes and feeling for wounds like they might overlook one if they weren't careful. Carter couldn't help but notice that several of the ladies seemed very familiar with the old sheriff's body.

As before, Fat Alice led the crusade. "He's been shot once, but it's on the left side. If it didn't get any of his vitals, he'll only have to worry about fever. But"—she watched the small hole in Smith's side pump blood out in a steady rhythm—"gut shots are hard to patch and tricky. It'll take time for him to recover."

Carter touched the last twenty dollar gold piece in his pocket. It had taken him a year to save up the money he'd spent in the past twenty-four hours. He pulled the coin out, hoping there would be enough left to get him home.

Fat Alice never missed the shine of money twinkling in the light of her place, but to his surprise, she shook her head when he offered to pay.

"I'll put it on Smith's account." Her smile outgrew the red on her painted lips.

Carter could think of no reason why Smith would have an account in a women's boardinghouse, but he thought it might be impolite to ask.

Not wanting to watch the women dig the bullet out of Smith, he walked to the side of the room where Riley still lay on the couch with Nellie Jean sitting next to him. Riley was breathing steady, but his coloring was as gray as his hair.

"Any change?" Carter asked, knowing there probably wouldn't be since he hadn't been gone long.

"No." Nellie Jean looked at Carter suspiciously. "You some kind of collector, like the Angel of Death, roaming around picking up near-dead sheriffs who got left out in the rain?"

Carter shook his head. "I'm just trying to get home, but I keep falling over bodies."

Nellie raised one eyebrow. "You got a wife?"

Nodding, he suddenly wished he were back on his farm with Bailee. He liked rainy days because he could spend all day in the barn or small bunkhouse making furniture. Sometimes he'd get so many projects going, there would barely be a place for Samuel to sleep. He liked the smell of sawdust blending in the damp air and the way fresh-cut wood felt in his hands.

"You love her, mister? Your wife?"

Carter didn't answer. The question had never crossed his mind. He'd been thinking of making furniture, not about something like love. It would be nice to think of her there with him. Maybe, just before dark on rainy days, he'd wrap her in his coat and carry her across the yard to the bunkhouse so she could see what he'd done. It would be nice to show someone.

"Course you do," Nellie Jean answered for him. "You wouldn't have married her if you didn't. Fat Alice says she can always tell a man in love with his wife. They come in now and then window-shopping, but they go home without going upstairs, if you know what I mean."

He didn't, but that wasn't unusual, so he made no comment.

"I figured you were one of those men in love with his wife, but I was hoping. Is your woman pretty?"

"Yes," Carter answered without hesitation. He remembered how he hadn't thought her pretty that first night, but now thought of her as beautiful. He liked the color of her hair and the way her eyes filled with fire when she was mad at him, which was most of the time. He liked the way she looked and smelled and felt.

"I might get married." Nellie broke into his thoughts. "When I'm too old to dance a few rounds ever' night. We had a girl here last year by the name of Pammy who married a sodbuster. In three months she was back begging for her old job. Said life out there on the spread with no one to talk to and only him to look at about drove her mad. He didn't believe in bathing and took to slapping her around for something to do when he got bored."

Carter watched Fat Alice lift the bullet high in the air and toss it in the brandy snifter as Nellie Jean continued to talk.

"Alice wouldn't take her back, though. She don't take no married women in the place. Says she don't want a husband showing up making trouble. So, for Pammy there weren't no choice. She borrowed a gun and rode back to the farm determined to change his ways or make herself a widow so she could work again."

Glancing at Nellie, Carter waited for the end of the story.

Nellie grinned, enjoying the spotlight. "We didn't see her for a month, and I'm telling you we were more than a mite worried. Then one day they come to town. He was all washed and shaved and wearing a bandage on his arm like he'd collided with a bullet recently. She didn't have a bruise on her. Appears he fell in love."

Carter smiled, wondering how much of the story was true.

Moaning loudly, Riley managed to open one eye. A few of the women hurried over to him, bending low to check his wounds. They seemed far too worried about his condition to notice their gowns were coming open even more than usual.

Riley managed to open the other eye.

After a long look around he mumbled, "I've died and gone to heaven."

Carter moved in front of Sheriff Riley, worried that the old fellow might be talking out of his head. The women stood and moved aside.

Riley frowned, then looked around as reality settled heavy on his shoulders. "Where's your wife and the child, Piper?" He moved a few inches, trying to sit up, then reconsidered.

"On the train to Cedar Point, I hope," Carter answered. "Your friend Smith was shot, also. The ladies are working on him now."

Nodding slowly, Riley closed his eyes in pain.

Carter waited, not sure what to do.

"Did Smith find the shooter?" Riley finally whispered between clenched teeth.

"Yes." Carter knelt on one knee and lowered his voice. "He got the man all the way back to his office, but the prisoner escaped, shooting Smith. He was a huge bearded man dressed in hides."

Carter hoped Riley was listening. He had no doubt all the women in the room were. "I never remember seeing the shooter before, but he called me 'the dummy's kid.'"

Riley's face wrinkled into a thousand lines. "He's from Cedar Point, son. Huge man in hides that haven't been clean since they were on the original animal. His hair is so matted birds wouldn't nest in it."

"You know him," Carter stated without any question in his tone. Riley had just described the shooter down to the smell.

Riley nodded. "Zeb Whitaker," he whispered. "I'd swear on my own grave. He never was much of a shot with anything but a buffalo gun. I heard word he was still alive and looking for the three women who tried to kill him. Half the town probably knew we left yesterday on the dawn train. He must have figured Bailee would be the easiest to get to once she was off your place."

Carter felt like someone had stepped on his heart. Zeb Whitaker. The man Bailee was fined for killing. The man whose body was never found. The one Lacy had warned Bailee about in the note.

Gripping Carter's arm, Riley whispered, "If it's Zeb, the shooter was after Bailee, not little Piper like we thought, and he knows just where they'll be going. I'll stay here with Smith. You've got to get to your wife, son, as fast as you can."

Carter stood, trying to think of how he could get home. He'd never been so far from his place. Yesterday was his first train ride, his first night in a hotel. Bailee said she and the sheriff would stay by his side until they were back on his land. But she hadn't. Riley couldn't. And now he had to find her.

Nellie Jean must have seen his confusion. "There ain't no more trains today, but I could show you the livery."

Riley agreed. "Take Smith's horse. If I know Smith, it'll be the best one there and have a saddle and pack all ready to go. I'll see it gets back to him later." Fear cleared the pain from the sheriff's eyes. "Go! Hurry. There may not be much time. If it's Zeb, he knows this country well and already has a jump on you."

Nellie Jean wrapped a shawl around her shoulders and led the way out the door.

Carter glanced back at the two wounded men. Both

sheriffs had bothered him most of the time he'd known them, but in the end they'd been brave. He and Bailee might not be alive if it hadn't been for their efforts.

"Don't worry." Fat Alice pushed him out the door with hands still bloody. "We'll take care of them. You get back to your wife."

Carter rushed into the rain, following the thin frame of Nellie Jean as she jumped puddles. When they got to the livery, she helped him saddle Smith's horse. As Riley had predicted, the saddlebags were full of supplies and ready.

"Thanks," Carter said as he swung onto the saddle. "You've been a good friend, Nellie Jean Desire, and I won't forget it."

She straightened with pride. "Does that mean I can come to Sunday dinner sometime?"

"Any time," he answered and turned his horse into the rain.

"And you'll always call me Nellie Jean!" she yelled after him.

"Promise!" he answered without turning around.

He figured his safest course, since he didn't know the terrain, was to follow the railroad tracks. When the country started looking familiar, he'd veer off and ride along the breaks of the Canadian River to his place without having to go all the way to Cedar Point first. On horseback was far slower than by train, but without having to backtrack, he might make good time.

Carter had no idea how long it would take, but he hoped to spot land he recognized before dark.

The tracks were easy to follow, even in the downpour. Sometimes Carter thought of the man Riley was sure was Zeb Whitaker. If it was Zeb, he might be heading in the same direction. In this rain they could pass within ten feet of each other and not even be aware of it.

Carter shivered, wishing he had a coat, but glad he'd put it around Piper. If she were on the train, they might have reached Cedar Bend by now. Bailee would have retrieved his wagon from the livery, and they might be on their way back to the farm. His coat would keep the child warm. He thought that Bailee might have spent the night with her friend Lacy, but doubted it.

He rode on. Endless hours passed. With the storm he couldn't judge the time. His father had taught him to ride almost as soon as he could walk, but he'd never felt comfortable in a saddle. Maybe that was why he'd always be more farmer than rancher. He'd read a few serial novels about men who lived in the saddle, but in truth, Carter found a team and wagon far more useful than a horse. Most places on his land could be driven to, then he'd have a wagon bed to haul tools.

To forget the rain, he thought of the trees that ran along the northern side of his land, beyond the orchard. Live oak, cottonwood, and even a few bur oak. The bur oak were his favorites. They had a heavy bark that would protect the tree against the cold in winter and the grass fires in spring that sometimes swept across the plains. That's how he thought of himself, hardened with a shell around him so thick no one could reach him.

But Bailee had.

The thought that the man he'd fought in town was planning to kill his wife made Carter forget all about the rain and cold. He pushed on. He stored a dozen guns in the house and barn to protect his property, but when Zeb had opened fire he hadn't a single one to protect Bailee. It was an oversight he never planned to repeat.

He'd strap a Colt on if he ever left home again. He had always thought of himself as safe on his land. He'd made sure to protect it carefully. But would Bailee be safe? He wished he'd told her of all the traps he'd made and of his underground rooms. If he had, she could be tucked away in them now, safe from Zeb.

The sky turned from gray to muddy blue about the time he spotted the breaks running east. He was within hours of home.

Pulling his horse beneath a twenty-foot-wide overhang, he swung off the saddle. Carter wanted to push on, but the horse had to rest. Riley was right about Smith having the best horse in the livery.

Behind the saddle, he found a thin blanket and used it to rub the animal down so that one of them could be dry for a few hours before they continued. Carter felt guilty pushing the horse so hard, but he had to know where he was before he stopped. Now, even if night fell once more before he reached home, he could find his way.

Matches were in the saddlebags, along with jerky, a small pot, and coffee. Carter risked a fire, figuring the rain would blanket any smoke. He boiled coffee, but could hardly drink it. With Bailee cooking the past week, he'd forgotten how bad his own coffee tasted.

While the horse grazed on wet short grass at the edge of the opening, Carter huddled out of the wind and rain near the back of the rock wall.

He thought of the foolish question Nellie Jean had asked him about loving his wife. Love was something for poets to write about, and Carter had no time in his life for such nonsense.

In truth he hadn't even heard the word in so many years he wasn't sure what it meant. The preacher's wife said they took him in out of love, but they never shared any of it with him. He guessed his father and mother loved each other, for he'd found a note in one of his mother's books written in his father's hand that had been signed, "With love."

But did he love Bailee? If love meant he'd risk his life for her, he guessed he must, for he hadn't hesitated. He could never tell her such a thing, though.

He stretched his legs toward the fire, his fingers silently signing the words he swore he'd never say aloud.

NINETEEN

BAILEE'S ARMS ACHED FROM DRIVING CARTER'S wagon through the mud. Within a mile from town the men had climbed out of her and Samuel's wagons. They'd walked alongside the wheels, ready to help push the wagons from the mud.

Samuel's eyes were poor, and he ventured off the road several times in the rain and darkness. Finally Lacy had talked him into allowing Bailee to lead, knowing he could follow easier.

Piper slept wrapped in blankets in the old woman's arms. Through the darkness Bailee heard her singing to the child in a language Piper couldn't have understood even if she could have heard.

An hour before dawn they finally reached Carter's place. All were so tired they could hardly move. The men took care of the wagons while the women crowded into Bailee's kitchen. She made coffee and a soup of boiled tomatoes with cream added. By the time the men returned, the women were warm and mostly dry. With little talking, they all sat around the room on the floor.

Bailee dipped the soup in bowls and cups. The women passed each serving carefully around the room. No one ate until all held a bowl, then the old man thanked first Bailee, then God, before nodding that they all should eat.

Too tired to eat, Bailee refilled coffee cups for the men and milk for the children. Dawn spread across the horizon by the time they finished.

Lacy rocked Piper to sleep while Bailee stepped out on the porch. The air was still thick with the smell of rain, but the downpour had slowed to a drizzle. She realized Samuel hadn't come back from the barn with the men and worried if the old man was all right. Hurrying across to the barn, she found him.

"Mr. Samuel . . ." She stepped in front of him as he carried a board from the bunkhouse to the barn. "What are you doing?"

"Once those folks are fed, they're going to need a place to sleep. The loft will be dry, but I don't want any of them rolling off and scaring the horses. I thought I'd put some boards up along the edge."

Bailee fell into step wondering if the old man cared about the people or his horses.

By midafternoon the sky had turned dark once more, and thunder rumbled a promise of more rain. The women helped Bailee make a thick soup of potatoes and carrots. As before, everyone sat on the floor of her kitchen and ate in silence. Slowly, a few at a time, they said their farewells and ran across to the barn, finally leaving only Lacy, Piper, and Bailee in the house.

Lacy yawned and held her hand out to Piper. The child nodded and followed her to Bailee's bedroom. As Lacy helped Piper removed her dress, she called through the open doorway. "Want to sleep with us tonight?"

"No," Bailee answered. "I'll stay out here and wait for Carter."

Lacy mumbled good night and closed the door, leaving Bailee to her thoughts.

Bailee sat in her kitchen alone, unable to sleep. Too many thoughts haunted her, teasing her with possibilities of what might be. If Carter's distraction hadn't worked, the man who shot Piper might already be on his way to finish the job he started. Maybe he stayed long enough to murder Carter and the sheriffs. Maybe another was sent ahead and had somehow watched her climb from the train.

Bailee relived each step since she left town. Clouds kept them from seeing if anyone followed, but she'd listened for sounds and heard none.

Samuel was the only one who didn't seem to sense danger; she could see it in all the other's eyes. He'd helped everyone get settled, then disappeared into the small building Carter called the bunkhouse. Bailee peeked inside it once and found the long room looked more like a workshop than a bunkhouse, but Samuel seemed to know his way around. He hadn't commented on all the half-finished furniture and tools, so they must have been a common sight. He also rolled his wagon into a space in the barn as if the slot were marked with his name.

Fear kept Bailee awake like strong coffee pumping through her veins. She wanted this night to be over.

The old woman from the train that everyone referred to as "Madra" gave Piper a mixture of herbs to help her sleep and heal. Bailee wasn't sure about the concoction, but Lacy swore it smelled exactly like a brew her grandmother used to make.

Bailee was so weary she wasn't sure she had the energy to make a bed on the floor by the fire, so she curled into the chair Carter made for her. The day seemed a month long. Every bone in her body ached as she listed the reasons she was safe and shouldn't be afraid. The men took shifts on guard, the door was locked and she was home in the solid little house that had become home. For the first time she was thankful for the narrow windows no man could crash through. No one would enter until she removed the bolt after dawn.

She'd put Carter's supper on the back of the stove, wishing him home. Slowly she relaxed into the arms of the wood. She imagined him holding her. Closing her eyes, she prayed that he was all right. He'd run, not only to save Riley, but to distract the shooter from her and Piper. Maybe most of what he'd done had been for others, but maybe some had been for her. And that knowledge comforted her.

The practical side of Bailee said she didn't care why Carter had fought so hard, but another part of her wanted to believe someone cared for her, cherished her, valued her. She might have been a throwaway daughter, but she was a valued wife.

The fire flickered low, sending stray shoots of light across the room. Rain slowed to a steady plopping off the roof as Carter slipped beneath a raised board running between the top of the back wall of his home and the roof. He rolled into a room where ceiling beams crisscrossed with shadows. The beams kept him from falling as he reached behind him and closed the vent he'd discovered as a child.

He'd shown it to Samuel once, and the old carpenter declared Carter's father a genius for thinking of it.

Warm air now pressed against Carter, thawing his frozen skin. For a long moment he lay perfectly still, enjoying the feel of heat and the smells of home.

He'd thought of nailing the board closed a few years ago. His father had designed it to allow air to circulate on hot days through the door, across the room, and out the slot at the ceiling. Carter never thought to open the space. Usually by the time he returned from working, the house was cool enough to put up with at least until he could move underground. Now, with Bailee here, he'd have to consider opening the slot before he left for work.

Shifting, Carter looked down. Bailee was sleeping in her chair by the fire. He was afraid he would frighten her riding in after dark, so he tied the horse in the shelter of the trees and walked through a black night to reach the back of the house.

One of the dogs, the one Bailee called Henry the Eighth, met Carter when he came out of the trees and followed along behind him until he reached the house. The other two royalty lay stretched out on the porch without so much of a greeting or a raise of their heads. In the week she'd been here she'd turned them from guard dogs into worthless pets.

Carter half expected Bailee to be in bed but guessed she must have tried to wait up for him. Then he decided Piper must be in her bed. For the little girl, the past two days must have been terrifying. He'd told her that her family would be arriving soon to get her, then with no time to explain during the shooting, Bailee had to run with her and jump on a train.

He slowly lowered to the floor in the blackened back corner of the large room. He wished he could prevent the thud his boots and Bailee's bag made as he dropped the last few inches. Kneeling, he pulled them off hoping not to awaken Bailee with footsteps across the floor. He'd look in on the child, check the locks, then disappear until morning.

But when he stood, Bailee was gone from the chair. He searched the shadowy room looking for her, wondering if his vision had played tricks on him. She had been his only thought for hours. She'd been in the chair when he'd looked down, he'd swear to it.

Her name was on his lips a second before he saw the butt of a rifle swinging toward his head.

Carter ducked, diving toward the shadow attacking him.

They tumbled across the floor into the fire's light. She fought wildly as he rolled atop her and clamped his hand across her mouth.

Bailee struggled beneath him for a moment longer, fighting blindly.

He raised an inch above her, but didn't loosen his grip. "Bailee," he whispered. "It's me."

Her body turned to stone and her eyes were round in surprise.

He raised up and sat beside her on the floor while he tried to slow his heart. She'd reacted to a shadow and he'd done the same. He could've hurt her, knocking her to the floor like that. Hell! If she'd used the other end of the gun, she could've killed him.

Carter forced words out. "I'm sorry I frightened you."

She didn't move. The firelight flickered across her. He couldn't tell if she was breathing. He wanted to touch her, but since he'd already knocked the breath out of her and probably frightened her near to death, he figured he'd done enough.

"I'm sorry," he repeated as he plowed his fingers through his wet hair. All he'd meant to do was come in quietly. Knocking on the door couldn't have scared her worse than hearing him drop from the rafters must have. He didn't want to face her. She'd probably been through a worse two days than he had, and now he'd knocked her flat on her back.

A timid hand touched his arm, and he raised his head to meet her eyes. Suddenly there was no room for even words between them. She moved into his open arms, and he held her tightly.

All the horror of the days melted away as he felt her body against him. Her arms wrapped around his neck and pulled him closer. The need to be near her washed over him like a flood drowning all other thought. She'd been the one reason he'd fought the night and the storm all day to get home. Not the place or the land, but her.

She trembled at the coldness of his wet clothes against her, but she didn't pull away.

Her heart beat next to his, and he warmed from the inside out.

For a long while he just held her, afraid to let go for fear she'd never return to his arms. Finally her soft crying against his shoulder registered in his tired mind.

"Bailee?" he whispered as he leaned her back against his knee. "What is it? What's happened?"

"I could have killed you." She refused to look at him. "I've got to stop killing people before I think. This time it could have been you."

"I'm not that easy to do away with." Carter laughed, amazed at how good it felt to do so.

Bailee finally met his stare. "I'm glad. But I swear I'll fight the urge to murder from now on."

She touched the side of his face. "You're cold and soaking wet. I'll make a pot of coffee while you change. I have to know what happened after I left with Piper."

He stood, pulling her up with him without letting her from the circle of his arms. "I'll be needing the medicine box as well." He tried to say the words calmly, so they wouldn't frighten her.

To his surprise, she nodded and he saw it again. That brave face she put on when she knew something had to be done.

She stepped out of his embrace and crossed to the kitchen. By the time he got his shirt and trousers off, Bailee was back with clean towels and the medicine box his mother had made years ago. The names of each mixture, pill, and ointment were written on the lid of the box for quick reference. Over the years, the list had been his guide to keeping it well stocked.

Without a word Bailee cut his longhandle underwear away from his leg where the glass from the sheriff's office had sliced along his skin. The flannel was soaked in rain and blood.

The cut wasn't deep, and he'd been too cold even to feel it until now. He didn't move as she cleaned, doctored, and wrapped it with a clean strip of cotton that looked remarkably like his old tablecloth.

"You going to tell me how you got this?" she finally asked as she tied the bandage and slid her hand along his leg, making sure the dressing was smooth.

"I got knocked out of a window," he answered, debating whether he should tell her about the man Riley thought had to be Zeb Whitaker.

"And the sheriffs?"

"Both alive. Both wounded. A woman named Fat Alice is looking after them."

Bailee raised an eyebrow. He figured he'd said something wrong so he added, "She runs a boardinghouse for mature ladies and is too poor even to afford enough clothes to keep herself properly covered." He'd thought his description would make Bailee feel sorry for Alice, but instead she looked at him in a way that made him think he'd be better off to say no more.

She brought him a cup of hot coffee and a bowl of soup before she started on the cut running along his shoulder.

"Your face is bruised," she mentioned, touching it lightly with the tips of her fingers.

Since it wasn't a question, he didn't think he needed to comment. The warm soup tasted better than any meal he'd ever had, and the coffee flowed down his throat, warming him all the way to his toes. She'd set a loaf of bread on the table, and for the first time he allowed himself to take more than one slice. He wondered how long it would be before he thought he didn't have to ration bread. Even a few days old, her bread was still better than anything he'd ever bought.

She finished painting him with ointment and cleaning mud off several spots. He knew they should talk, but it felt so good sitting in his warm house with her near that he didn't break the silence. He liked the feel of her hands sliding along his back as if it were nothing unusual for her to be touching him. He liked the slight sound her skirt made as she moved, and as always, he liked the way she smelled.

He was so tired he didn't want to talk or even think. He only wanted to be near her.

Finally she faced him, and he knew it was time for the world to slip in.

"Piper's all right." Bailee laid her hand atop his. "A bullet brushed her arm and shoulder, but the wound wasn't deep. She's sleeping in my bed with Lacy, who insisted on coming home with us to protect us, though she admitted she's never fired a gun."

He waited, knowing there was more. He turned his hand over and closed his fingers around hers. He never thought much of holding hands with a woman, unless maybe if a man was afraid she might wander off, so it surprised him how good it felt just to be connected to her now.

"Lacy helped me find Samuel, who came home with me in case there was more trouble. Samuel was planning to stop by in a day or two anyway. Lacy is just afraid she'll miss an adventure."

Carter knew it was time for Samuel's visit. The man was like a bird, flying south in fall and north in the spring. It was good to know he was in the bunkhouse. If company called, he might be helpful watching from across the yard. He was not a man to get involved in others' problems, but he'd cover Carter if need be.

Bailee took a deep breath and hurried on. "And I brought home a family who helped Piper and me while we were on the train. They didn't have anywhere else to stay, so I told them they could use your barn for a few days. We need to feed them. You should see how thin they are."

Frowning, Carter fought down the panic that threatened to climb up his spine. He didn't mind Samuel. The man was the only person who'd ever stayed at his place since his parents had been killed. And Piper needed to be here where they could watch over her until her family could pick her up. And he could almost understand Lacy coming along. She might not know it, but she was in as much danger as his wife, so they should try to help her. After all, Bailee had said more than once that the girl was like a sister to her.

But a whole family . . .

"How many?" he asked, thinking he'd have another four or five mouths to feed.

"Nine," she whispered, as if trying to make the number smaller, "if you don't count the children."

"And if I do count the children?"

"Seventeen." She tried to pull her hand away, but he didn't release his hold.

Carter said nothing.

He never dreamed getting one wife would open his place up so. His front gate was becoming as wide as the Grand Canyon. If she'd known about the rooms below, would she have put people in them as well? She wasn't even apologizing for what she'd done, but simply explaining it as if it were nothing.

"I'll stack the rugs by the fire so we can sleep there tonight. If we wear our clothes, we should be warm enough. I'm afraid I gave all the blankets away."

Carter wanted to go downstairs and crawl into his own bed, but he hesitated. He should show Bailee the rooms below. They might protect her. But at the rate she was going, if she knew about them, she'd have them rented out by morning.

"Carter?"

He met her stare.

"Are you angry?" She squared her shoulders and fire danced in her eyes. "Because whether you are or not doesn't change a thing. These people had to have a place to stay. They saved our lives. I did what had to be done."

What could he say? If he argued she'd probably threaten to club him again. She was a fighter, this wife of his, and she was willing to do what had to be done to fight for these people.

He stood and lifted a clean shirt from the stack she'd washed. He could still smell the freshness of clean cotton. He took a few deep breaths before turning around to face her once more.

"I'm not angry," he said as he buttoned the shirt. "You did what you thought you had to do." Now was not the time to bring up what had been gnawing at him all day, but there might never be another time.

He had to get it said before the words died forever inside him. "But when you sleep beside me"—he couldn't look at her as he said what he'd rehearsed—"do so because you want to or not at all. I don't want you thinking it's part of your duty, even when the month is out. I don't want you near me if you see it as just something you have to do."

He wanted to add that he didn't want her letting him touch her unless she wanted to, but he figured by the surprise on her face he'd said enough and maybe he should leave any questions about touching for another time.

Bailee couldn't have looked more shocked than if he had slapped her. She'd been firing up for an argument about the people she'd invited, and he'd changed the game entirely.

"Good night," he said as he stepped around her and moved to the fire. He lifted his coat off the peg to use as cover. It didn't look like much of a bed, but he was so tired he could have slept on a box of half-penny nails.

He curled up using his arm as his pillow and turned his back to the fire. He heard her moving around in the kitchen and guessed she was banking the fire in the stove and cleaning his cup and bowl. He thought he heard her open her bag. Her clothes inside must be soaked, for the bag had been in the rain for two days. He didn't even want to make a guess as to what she might be thinking.

They were both tired, but at least he'd said what had been bothering him all day. When he'd married her, he expected to do his duty and to have her do hers, but now that he knew more about the act, he knew it was not something to be done without feeling toward the partner.

He was almost asleep when she stepped over him and curled up on the same rug between him and the fire. She wiggled until she rested against his back.

He didn't move.

She didn't say a word.

There would be no pillow wall between them tonight.

TWENTY

SOMETIME IN THE NIGHT CARTER ROLLED OVER, AND Bailee cuddled into his arms. He used his coat to cover them both as he let the dream of her and the reality melt together. Moving his face against her hair, he drifted deep into sleep with the fragrance of her dissolving into his lungs as though returning home to a place he'd never known, but always dreamed about.

Hours later, when the fire had almost died and he knew dawn was close, he lay very still, absorbing the nearness of her. He didn't need the light to tell him his mate lay at his side. There had been no doubt since the rainy night she'd looked at him through the crowd just before she drew his name. The problem wasn't that she was his; the problem lay in what he was to do with her. For the moment he wanted to kiss her, but was afraid of frightening her again.

Telling himself he'd be satisfied just to be near, he kept his eyes closed and savored the feel of her resting against him, their bodies warming each other.

His words might not have seemed much in the way of

a speech last night, but at least he now knew that she was at his side because she wanted to be. He'd given her a way out. There would have been no explaining if she'd chosen to sleep in the chair.

But she hadn't. She'd slept next to him.

When she stirred, he didn't move. She shifted an inch away from him and raised her head. Her hair brushed across his face.

"Carter?" She rolled closer placing her hand atop his heart.

He didn't breath.

"Carter?" Her hand trailed lightly up to his throat.

He was sure she felt his pulse pounding. He rolled his head toward her and opened his eyes.

"The people can stay?" Her words tickled across his face.

This time she was asking, no demanding, but he had a strong feeling she still hadn't changed her mind. He wanted to pull her closer, but he worried that she'd think he was bargaining. Whether the family in the barn stayed or left couldn't be connected with her sleeping beside him.

He finally nodded and rolled away, knowing that if he stayed next to her a moment longer he would have tasted her lips.

Dawn flickered through the slits of windows along the east wall. He liked the way she looked in the morning with her hair all a mess and dreams still in her eyes. The silhouette of her body was perfection as she stretched in the early light. Her movements were more poetry than any words he'd ever read.

Silently he walked to where he'd left his boots and finished dressing. There was much to do if he planned to make sure the place was safe and feed a few dozen more people today. He told himself twice that there was no time for foolish thoughts.

By full light he'd walked a circle around his home, making sure all the fences were up, and milked the cow. When he passed the barn, he saw the people Bailee seemed to have adopted as her own kin. She was right, they were thin and frightened. The men held their hats in their hands as he walked by. The women drew their children close.

Carter managed a nod. The thought that he frightened them bothered him more than he wanted to admit. He wasn't far from the time when every stranger made him want to run and hide.

He walked to the orchard and retrieved the horse he'd borrowed. When he returned, Samuel and a few of the men were setting up a long table and dragging every chair and stool from the house and bunkhouse that looked like it might hold the weight of a person.

Carter nodded once more at them, but he still couldn't bring himself to say anything. He wasn't sure how to start a conversation.

When he reached the porch, Lacy stormed out the front door with a tablecloth over one arm. She hadn't grown in the few days since he'd seen her, she was still part child, part woman.

"Carter!" she yelled as though seeing him on his own property came as a great surprise to her. Her childlike face lit up with joy.

Before he could react, she ran to him and hugged him as if he were kin.

"We were so worried about you, Carter. Bailee went on and on about how you risked your life so that they could run for the train." She kept hugging him as if he were a favorite toy she'd lost. "I told her you were all right. I told her you'd come back. Oh, Carter, I'm so glad you did. I had a feeling you were fine, 'cause I'd have sensed it if you were dead, you being like family and all."

He patted her shoulder, hoping she'd let go of him while there was still daylight left.

When Lacy finally moved away, Piper appeared from the folds of her skirts. The child stared up at Carter for a moment as though trying to remember, then ran toward him, stepping off the porch into his hug.

Piper didn't need to say a word. Carter could see it in her eyes, the questions, the fear, the longing to know what was going on. She'd been trapped, alone and silent among kind people, since she'd left him.

He folded to the porch step, sat her on his knee, and talked with her, using his hands.

As she answered, he smiled, realizing he couldn't think of anything to say to Lacy in words, but he had no trouble talking to Piper. He told the child that the sheriffs were being well taken care of and they'd be riding up to see her soon. She asked about the bruise across his jawline, and Carter didn't lie in his answer. Suddenly her hands flew, telling him all about her shoulder and how it hurt. She signed faster than he could keep up and he had to beg her to slow down.

The strange people gathered closer, watching, whispering.

The old uneasiness inside of Carter returned. He remembered how he'd hated people watching his mother talk to him. How he'd sometimes covered her hands, wanting her to stop. Suddenly he realized it hadn't been her shame, but his that had made her sign words within his hands. He'd been too little to understand that he'd gagged her when he'd worried about what others thought. She'd never corrected him, but it must have hurt her that her only son was ashamed of her.

Carter looked up at the people, prepared to fight not only for today and Piper, but for twenty years ago and a mother who'd been too kind to discipline a child for being embarrassed when he should have been proud.

But he saw no ridicule in these strange people's dark eyes. Only interest.

A boy of about twelve stepped forward. "Mister, sir, will you teach me to say the words with my hands? I want to tell the little girl not to be afraid. I want to tell her I can be her friend if she needs one."

Carter waited for the laughter, the joking, the name-calling. None came. Several in the group nodded and stepped a little closer. They held their hands before them, offering to learn.

Twenty minutes later Lacy pulled Bailee away from the oven where she'd been making biscuits. "You've got to see this." Lacy giggled with excitement. "You're not going to believe it."

Bailee resisted. "I've got bread in the oven and three dozen eggs to cook."

Lacy kept tugging until Bailee relented and followed to the doorway.

Bailee stepped out onto the front porch. For a moment the morning sun blocked her vision, then she saw Carter, sitting on one of the steps with Piper standing at his side. Most of the people from the barn had formed a circle around him. They were moving their hands, following each of the patterns he made.

"Water," Carter said moving his hands as he spoke.

"Rain." His fingers drifted down in slight movements like drops sliding down a windowpane.

They all repeated his action.

Bailee closed her mouth, holding back a gasp.

"Teach me *run* and *hide* in case I ever need to tell Piper that," Rom said, and several of the other agreed.

The boy glanced at Bailee. "And *pass the biscuits*, which I hope aren't burning."

Bailee took the hint and ran back to the kitchen.

The rest of the morning she watched Carter as he taught. By the time breakfast was half over, everyone at the table was asking for certain foods in sign language and signing *thank you* in return. These people who spoke English with a thick accent were having no problem understanding Carter's words. He'd teach one, who'd teach another, who'd teach another. By the end of the meal they were beginning to put words together to form simple sentences.

Piper watched for a long while until Rom signed *good morning* to her. She laughed and with Carter's help joined in the game. She remembered words he'd long forgotten and showed the others when Carter couldn't.

Samuel was the only one who showed little interest as he ate. He didn't like to talk period and saw better uses for his hands. He was not a man to play games. He moved to the edge of the porch and began whittling a spoon for Bailee.

Finally, long after the meal should have been finished and cleaned away, Carter stood. "Thank you for helping my wife and Piper. You are welcome here."

He said the words as he signed them, and Bailee couldn't help but notice the hesitance was gone from his voice.

"Stay as long as you like and rest." His eyes met hers, and she knew he meant what he said.

When Carter paused, the old man stood. "I am Farrow, the head of my small band. Everyone calls me Papa Farrow. We thank you. We do not wish to be any trouble, but it would be good to stop for a few days. My sons and I would like to help you with the guarding of your place and the work you do."

Carter didn't dishonor them by denying the request. "I would be grateful for any help. I've peaches to get to market as soon as possible even though trouble may come to call. You're much needed."

Everyone smiled and stood. The men kissed their wives good-bye. The old man assigned three of his sons to take the first shift as guards. The rest of the men must have already talked about what needed doing, for they collected boxes from the barn.

Carter stood behind Bailee. She didn't have to turn around. She knew he was there, probably trying to figure out what to say.

"I'll be fine," she answered over her shoulder. "I'll be safe. There is a gun on the bookshelf and a rifle by the front door. If I need you, I'll fire one shot."

He didn't move.

"Lacy will help me take care of Piper. Don't worry about the girl. Between us, we won't let her out of our sight."

He still didn't step away. He stood so close the heat of his body warmed her back.

"I know you have to work the orchard." She turned to face him and, as always, was startled by the blue of his eyes.

He was waiting, she realized, for her to kiss him good-bye.

Bailee almost laughed as she stood on her toes and kissed his cheek. The kiss hardly connected, but he turned and headed for the barn.

He was waiting—she grinned—*for my kiss.*

A few minutes later she saw Carter and four of the men and older boys head toward the orchard. The old man pulled a chair to the shady side of the porch, obviously seeing his job as one of watching the work.

Rom and two of the other children tagged along after Samuel, offering to help him. Samuel growled and tried to sidestep them, but they followed like pups.

At noon all the men except Carter returned and sat at the long makeshift table in the yard. They talked of the trees heavy with fruit and the fine place they'd been planted so that they were sheltered from the wind and had plenty of water. One of the men had brought each of his children a peach. He handed it to them as if giving a grand gift. When the other children stared, the father cut the peaches in slices and shared his gift with all.

Bailee set the food out, thinking how easy the meal was to prepare with so many hands helping her. Most of the women had made use of her washtub, but one or more was always at Bailee's side willing to help.

She'd cut a wide slice of beef taken from the smoke-house out back and baked it all morning with the last of the vegetables from the storage cellar beneath the floor of the kitchen. Vegetables would be coming in daily from the garden now, and she'd be able to refill the larder fast. Her first job after lunch, she'd decided, would be to clean the small storage cellar out and make room for all she planned to can and store.

Bailee watched the Gypsies fill their plates, and still Carter hadn't returned. It was not like these people to eat until all were served. Could they have forgotten about Carter?

"My husband?" she asked one of the men she'd seen leave with him that morning.

The man stood and laid his napkin down before he spoke. "Mister, Sir said his wife will bring his meal out to the trees. He tell us all to come in and rest for a few hours while the day is hot. Then we will finish later."

Bailee started to argue that she was far too busy to take Carter lunch, then realized Carter must still be working and knew she'd bring the food if truly needed. She quickly wrapped a meal and headed for the orchard.

Henry the Eighth trailed along behind her as far as the wet sand of the creek bed where he stopped for a nap. Bailee moved into the shadows of the trees. The air was rich with the smell of peaches and a dampness from the rain that still hung in the shady stillness.

She saw Carter standing by a wagon loaded with boxes full of fruit. He was on the far side of the wagon, close to where the tall pecan trees far outstretched the wide peach trees. He didn't turn as she neared, but she knew he must hear her moving through the low branches.

"I brought your lunch," she said when she was a few feet away.

He turned and thanked her for the meal, then set it down unopened on the wagon gate. Gently his hands surrounded her waist and lifted her onto the gate as well, putting her at eye level with him as he stood on the uneven ground beside the wagon.

Bailee took a deep breath, enjoying the stillness of this place. She liked the way the tall trees rustled slightly in the wind while the smaller branches swished in answer. Lacy would have thought the place enchanted if she were here. A place where fairies danced.

"There's something I must tell you." Carter broke into her daydreaming and leaned his arms on either side of her as if he feared she might bolt with the news. "I didn't want Lacy to hear. You tell her if you feel the need."

Bailee nodded and the peace she'd known for a moment vanished. "All right," she whispered, already fearing what he had to say. She could always tell when his words were practiced, rehearsed.

"The man who threw me out Sheriff Smith's window yesterday was huge, built like a buffalo and smelling much the same. Smith had tried to arrest him because he thought this fellow was the one shooting at us. He wore hides and had a beard that hid half his chest." Carter paused as if giving her time to put the pieces together.

He leaned forward, allowing his leg to rest against her knee. Bailee didn't move away.

"After the man shot Smith and got away from me, I took the sheriff over to a woman named Fat Alice so she could fix him up like she did Riley. By the time she finished with Smith, Riley was awake and asking questions. He seemed to think the huge man wasn't shooting at Piper at all, but at you. He thinks the man was—"

"Zeb Whitaker," Bailee finished the sentence. She pushed at Carter, pushing away the news.

He didn't budge. His shoulder took the blow as if made of iron. He wasn't holding her, only surrounding her.

"No." She swung at Carter's arms, hoping he would move aside and let her leave. "It can't be. Zeb's dead. I killed him myself." She wanted to run as far away as she could and hide, but Carter wouldn't let her down from the wagon. "The man at the station wasn't shooting at me. He was shooting at Piper."

Panic climbed her spine as she shoved again at Carter, angry that he wouldn't let her go. "He couldn't have been shooting at me. If he was, then Piper would have been hit because of me. We all could have been killed because of me." Her last words cracked in the air like invisible crystal.

Carter folded her in his arms and held her tight.

"I have to leave," she said between sobs. "I'll take Lacy and we'll disappear. If he's alive, he won't let anyone stop him. He's capable of killing us all."

"No," Carter whispered against her ear. "You're staying with me."

Bailee held his head in her hands and stared into his eyes. "Don't you see that I'm putting everyone in danger? Last time my father was only in danger of losing his job, and he made me leave, but now you all might lose your lives. Piper, the sheriffs, you. Zeb didn't strike me as a forgiving man. We made him angry. He'll come after Lacy, Sarah . . . and me. I have to keep running."

She knew she wasn't making sense. Carter had no way of knowing she'd killed a man back home. The banker's son, her father's boss's only child. If she hadn't left, her father said she would be tried for murder, and he'd be out of a job. It hadn't mattered that he'd lost a daughter; his job was more important. So he'd shipped her off forever rather than stand beside her when she told her side of the story.

"I have to go," she said. "Zeb Whitaker is dangerous. Maybe the meanest man alive. If he wants to kill me, he won't stop until he does."

Carter held her so tightly she could hardly breathe. "No!" he answered. "You're not leaving."

Tears filled her eyes. She wasn't being pushed away this time. He wanted to stand beside her. Not only wanted, he was determined to do so.

She wasn't sure how it happened, if he kissed her first, or if she reached toward him, but all at once they were kissing with a hunger that bolted through them both.

Maybe it was needing to belong, needing to be wanted. Maybe it was knowing she was. But suddenly she couldn't get enough of the taste of his mouth over hers.

She kissed him as if there would be no tomorrow, and he kissed her back as if he believed they'd be together forever.

TWENTY-ONE

H<small>ENRY THE EIGHTH'S BARK SOUNDED FROM DOWN BY</small> the river, and Carter knew they were no longer alone. He forced himself to move back an inch from Bailee. Her rapid breathing blended with his own.

"I want to be with you," she whispered, "like we will be when we've been married a month."

Carter didn't pretend he didn't understand. "I want it, too," he said the words low in her ear, surprised to feel her tremble as he spoke.

Someone tracked through the brush at the creek's edge, and Carter knew they only had moments.

He slid his hands to her waist and slowly moved upward, feeling her body through her clothes as he parted her knees with his thigh and closed any distance left between them. "I want to feel your skin against mine. Soon."

He said the last word so low she wasn't sure if he'd said it or she'd thought it.

Bailee brushed her cheek against his. His daring statement made her blush, not from shyness but because he spoke her thought. "Hold me a little longer." She pressed her body against the wall of his chest, wanting to be as close as she could to him. The terror of the train station and the storm had left them both raw with need.

His heart thundered against hers. His hands traveled along her to where her hips rested on the wagon, and he pulled her even closer to him as his mouth found hers once more, his kiss hungry with desire.

"Mister, sir?" Rom's voice sounded from just beyond the clearing. "Mister, sir?"

Carter broke the kiss with a groan. "Over here," he said as he moved away from Bailee. His hand lingered at her waist as though he couldn't bear to break the connection completely.

The boy called Rom stepped into the clearing. "I am sorry to bother you at lunch, but three men, one saying he is the deputy from a town, named Wheeler, are at your gate. Samuel is holding them there with a rifle until you say it is all right to let them in."

"It's all right." Carter didn't take his eyes from Bailee. "Let them in and tell them I'll be there in a minute."

"Yes, Mister, sir." Rom saluted and crashed back into the brush, Henry the Eighth dancing at his side.

Bailee tried to jump off the wagon, but Carter was still in her way. "We have to hurry. Maybe they have word from the sheriffs or Piper's father."

Carter didn't move. If anything, he leaned closer blocking her path.

"They can wait," he finally said. "I want it clear between us first."

Bailee met his gaze as he leaned closer. "You want what clear?"

He moved his hand up the side of her leg, shoving her

dress to her knee. The heat of his fingers burned a hunger through the layers of her skirt.

"You'll not run," he whispered as he leaned close, moving his cheek against her hair. "You'll not leave me because you're afraid of Zeb Whitaker?"

He wasn't making a demand or giving an order. He was asking a question, and all at once Bailee saw the boy in the man. The frightened little boy who trusted no one. The orphan who must have sworn never to care for anyone cared for her.

"I'll not leave," she answered, wanting to prove to him that he could believe her. She saw the doubt in his eyes. The fear. The worry. Somehow, in the past few days they'd gone from being trapped in a marriage to caring about each other. She wasn't sure how or when it happened: Maybe it was his little kindnesses, maybe all they'd been through, maybe just something as simple as the way he touched her.

He straightened, frowning, but he said nothing. His fingers moved slowly along her leg as though still afraid to step back and let her jump down from the wagon lest she run away from him forever.

Bailee tilted her head to one side, knowing what she had to do. Without hesitating further, she lifted shaking hands to the buttons at her collar. One by one the buttons gave to her touch.

Carter watched, a question wrinkling his brow.

She smiled as she moved down her blouse, freeing the material across her bustline. Cool air kissed her skin as she continued to her waist until all the buttons were undone.

Then, slowly, she pulled the material wide, revealing her thin camisole clinging against her damp skin.

Carter raised his fingers and touched the material. Desire replaced the question in his stare. He no longer had to ask what she was doing. He knew.

Bailee watched passion spark in his eyes as she pulled free the ribbon of her undergarment. "When I'm more wife than stranger," she whispered the words she'd said to him days before when he'd asked if he could see her body.

The material slipped away from her breasts.

For a long moment she closed her eyes and just breathed, thinking of what she was doing. With this one act she'd made a commitment to a man she'd known only days.

She'd expected him to touch her, but when she opened her eyes, he was merely staring. She couldn't help but wonder if she were the first woman he'd ever seen. Suddenly she felt very old and wise . . . and cold.

Awkwardly she lifted his hand and placed it over one of her breasts. "It's all right, I think, if you touch me. We're alone. You are my husband."

She could feel the roughness of his palms, the warmth of his fingers, and a hesitance that was so tender it split her heart in two.

"It's all right," she whispered, but he didn't move. She couldn't help but laugh. She was talking to him as if he had few brains.

He pulled his hand away. "I don't think we have time to go upstairs," he mumbled nervously.

Had she rattled his brain off the hinges? He was making no sense at all. They didn't have an upstairs anywhere on the place.

She pulled the sides of her camisole together and tied the ribbon. "I'm sorry," she said, unsure of what she was sorry about. Maybe she should be sorry for being so bold, but she didn't feel as if she'd done anything wrong. In fact, she enjoyed the fact that he'd seen her; it was somehow wild and crazy and made her feel warm deep down inside.

When she finished tying her camisole, she placed her hands on her knees and looked up at him, wishing he'd talk to her. "No, I'm not sorry," she corrected. "I know we have little time, for there are people waiting, but I wanted you to know how I feel about being with you."

Any words she'd been about to say vanished from her mind as he reached up and pulled free the bow she'd just tied in place.

The thin material fell dangerously low across her breasts, barely covering the tip of each.

She didn't move.

He tugged at the ribbons, pulling the material lower until it slipped beneath her mounds, once more leaving her bare.

The fire in his stare made her breath come rapidly as though she'd been running for miles.

He watched every rise and fall.

She waited once more for him to touch her, but he only stared. He watched her so closely she could almost feel him against her. He was making love to her with only a look.

Finally, without a word, she tied the ribbon once more. He didn't stop her as she buttoned her blouse slowly, all the way to the collar.

When she'd finished, he placed his hands around her waist, lifted her from the wagon gate, and lowered her to the ground an inch in front of him.

"Tonight," he whispered as they stood almost touching, "our month is over?"

Bailee smiled, knowing what he asked. "Tonight, our month is over."

His lips lowered over hers in a tender kiss. When she opened her mouth, he drank deep of the taste of her. As he kissed her, his hands moved over her, following the lines of her body through her clothes.

He broke the kiss so suddenly she leaned against him for support. "We have to go." His words were tight with control.

Bailee nodded and forced herself to step away. They'd have tonight. They'd have a lifetime. Now it was time to see what Deputy Wheeler wanted. Good news or bad, the deputy had waited long enough.

They moved through the trees and along the stream without saying a word. She thought about mentioning that he'd left his lunch behind, but decided maybe he'd been hungry for her and not a meal when he'd remained in the orchard.

He didn't take her hand as they moved across the open land between the orchard and the house, but she was aware of him walking closer to her. She matched her steps to his, liking the way her skirt brushed slightly against his leg.

Tonight there would be nothing between them. The thought excited her and frightened her a little. But this was her man. Her husband. And it was time to start loving him.

As they neared the house, several of the men who'd helped him that morning came out. One stepped ahead of the rest. "Mister, sir," he asked politely, "we would like to show our wives and children the trees. If you do not mind?"

"Of course. The best place to relax after lunch is among the trees. Take as long as you like," Carter answered. "Bring the wagon back when you return."

"And extra peaches for pies tonight," Bailee added, smiling at how easily he talked with these people once he'd decided to trust them. She guessed they did not want to be around the deputy and wondered if they'd had trouble with the law in other towns.

The man smiled, signed a thank-you, and signaled the others to follow.

While the band headed for the trees, Bailee and Carter circled the house. Three broken-down cow ponies were tied out front with their owners standing in the shade of the porch. Samuel blocked the door of the house, his gun still cradled on his arm. With his eyesight he'd be lucky to hit the barn if he fired, but the three strangers weren't coming close enough to test that theory. They'd tried demanding the old man put the gun down, but Samuel seemed more deaf than usual.

Tension vibrated in the air. If Sheriff Riley had made the visit, he would have been talking with everyone, probably sitting by now in a chair with a cool drink of well water in his hand. But these three were different from the sheriff. They wore badges on their vests and guns on their hips, but something about them was twisted.

Bailee had watched them come in and out of the sheriff's office the week she'd been in jail. She, Sarah, and Lacy had sworn daily that if any one of the three won the lottery to become a husband, the other two women would help their friend become a widow as fast as possible.

August Wheeler, Riley's deputy, straightened when he saw her and Carter coming, but his left shoulder still drooped as if he wanted that hand closer to his gun at all times.

Riley had told Bailee that August was a deputy for three years simply because no one else would apply. He was good at sweeping up and bringing drunks in for the night, Riley had said, but he would never make a sheriff. He was missing any sense of right and wrong.

Riley had spent a half hour one night while Bailee was behind bars telling her about how August wasn't a bad man, he just couldn't help that a part was missing. Like some folks don't have a sense of right and left, or north and south. For August, there was no degree of a crime. He'd as soon kill a man for spitting on the walk as committing murder. The sheriff saw him more as a sad joke, but Bailee saw him as dangerous.

August now looked at Bailee with the same muddy green eyes, as if he didn't really see her at all. If eyes were windows to the soul, August Wheeler's soul was in dead winter.

"Carter McKoy!" he yelled as if he wasn't sure who Carter was and hadn't known him for years.

"Yes." Carter didn't get too close to the three men.

Bailee hung back near the porch. If August was questionable, the other two looked downright mean. They were drifters who fancied themselves gamblers. Men too lazy to work, who'd lucked into being the deputy's henchmen because the sheriff was out of town. Bailee guessed the job must have come with free liquor, for she could smell it on both of them from several feet away.

August introduced them with a wave of his hand as Ludlow and Ray. He didn't bother with last names, and

Bailee couldn't help but wonder if the men even had them. Ludlow was tall and dark with a cream scar that dripped from his hairline almost to his eye. Ray didn't have his friend's height, but made up for it in width.

"I'd like to talk to you in private. Official business." August patted his gun as if he expected Carter to argue with the simple request.

Carter glanced at Samuel waiting near the front door. Papa Farrow sat a few feet away. Carter nodded at both men but offered no invitation for the deputies to step inside. Bailee was glad.

Carter pointed toward the barn, then didn't wait for an answer before walking toward it.

Bailee fell into step behind him. She hadn't gone three feet when one of the men with August blocked her path. She looked up, trying not to stare at Ludlow's scar.

Ludlow wasn't even looking in her direction. It was as if he stepped in her path without noticing her at all.

She couldn't help but think that whatever had hit his head must have also damaged his brain.

August hardly glanced at her as he passed. "This talk is between me and your man. Stay out of it, Miss Bailee." He mumbled his order, then spat a long stream of tobacco. The way he said her name seemed to be a reminder that he'd known her when she was a prisoner and still didn't consider her respectable.

Bailee started to argue, but Ludlow took a step toward her as if he planned to make sure she followed orders. His stare was dull, and she knew logic would be wasted on the tall man.

Bailee heard Samuel's heavy boots hit the dirt as he jumped off the porch behind her. She moved backward, seeking the safety of the carpenter's side. If she couldn't go with Carter, Samuel would help to make her feel less alone.

The scarred man hesitated a moment, then turned to follow August, dismissing her as though she'd been no more than a garden slug he'd noticed crossing his path.

Out of the corner of her eye Bailee saw Rom move in the shadows between the buildings toward the barn. She nodded slightly, giving her blessing to his quest.

Carter didn't like following the men to have a private talk with them, but he decided whatever they had to say might not need saying in front of Piper and the women. He'd been able to sign a few simple words to the old Gypsy about staying with the women and protecting them. He wasn't sure the old man understood the signs, but Farrow nodded, for he knew what Carter wanted done. The few of his sons who hadn't gone to the orchard moved closer to the house, as if the old man had communicated with them.

The Gypsies might be little help if facing down armed men, but they would at least give Bailee time to think. Carter glanced back toward the house, looking for her. He wanted to tell her all would be fine, but the arrival of Wheeler indicated there might be trouble. In truth, he wanted everyone to go away and leave him alone with his wife.

He couldn't help but watch her a second longer, wondering how he'd ever thought for one moment that she wasn't beautiful. When she'd unbuttoned her blouse, she'd taken his breath away with her beauty.

Carter forced the thought to a corner of his mind. He had to concentrate on the here and now, at least until Piper and Bailee were out of danger. Whatever Wheeler had to say couldn't be so bad he couldn't handle it with Bailee at his side.

The barn was dark when he entered. All the horses were outside in the corral, but he could hear August or one of his men moving around in one of the stalls. Carter had been the last to step inside, dreading what August Wheeler had to tell him, but now he wanted to get the talk over with. Whatever the news, not knowing seemed worse.

As Carter closed the side door and turned to face the three men, a fist slammed against his jaw with such sudden force it almost knocked him off his feet. Pain, along with questions, shot into his brain.

Carter balanced and swung around prepared to fight. He was no longer a newcomer to the game; he'd had a lesson a few nights before. Though his muscles were sore, he'd hold his own in a fair fight this time.

He took a swing at Ray and connected just as a shovel rang against the back of his head. Carter fought to stay standing as another blow struck his back. He crumbled to one knee. A double-fisted swing connected at his jaw and toppled him backward. There was to be no fair fight.

He made himself stand as they circled him, each taking a turn before he could recover from the last blow. Vaguely it registered that they weren't trying to kill him, only inflict pain. They were skilled at the task. When he hit the floor for the second time, the barn filled with starlight and standing became an impossibility.

"Tie him up," August ordered. "He's no longer in any shape to cause us trouble." August kicked Carter's ribs with his boot. "Just getting you in a mind to talk. Zeb did half the job for us the other night in Childress. We just needed to make a believer out of you today."

Carter tried to clear his mind as a rope cut into his wrists.

"Stand him up. I got a few questions for him before I take him in." August slapped the shovel against Carter's side while the other two lifted him off the floor.

Carter's head cleared enough to focus, but the men were making no sense. Why would they be tying him up and attacking him? He didn't have long to wait for the answer.

August fished in his pocket and pulled out two twenty-dollar gold pieces. "You've been passing these around town lately. Mosely said you used them to pay off your wife's debt at the stable, and you bought train tickets with gold yesterday. In a country where most folks are dirt poor and you, being one to always trade at the mercantile, having coins does seem strange."

Carter saw no reason to answer. Where he got his money was no business of August or anyone else.

"I noticed you used a few to buy your wife that night the sheriff had that fool lottery." August chuckled. "I didn't put it all together then. Not until I saw Zeb step back from the dead and swearing to high heaven that he'd been robbed."

August circled Carter, proud as a lawyer making a final summation on a case he knew he'd won. "He had a hundred twenty-dollar gold pieces with him the day the women tried to kill him. They claim they didn't take it. If they had, they'd have paid their own fine and never married up with the likes of you."

August laughed and shoved Carter, almost knocking him down. "You found Zeb, didn't you, dummy's son? You found him when he was out cold and stole his money."

Carter didn't answer. The question was too insane to deserve a reply.

August didn't seem to notice the silence. He was a man tone deaf to every sound but that of his own voice. "We figure you've spent a few of the coins, but you probably got the rest stashed out here somewhere. Trouble is, my partners and I don't have the time to look. Zeb will be out sometime after dark doing his own looking, and, since he's not the type to share, we'll be left without any gold if we don't hurry."

He grinned. "So we thought we'd come out first and ask you real nice to hand over the saddlebags full of coins. It's your only choice. We're even willing to forget you stole the gold from Zeb, since he stole it from a big sheep rancher over near Santa Fe."

Carter's head pounded.

"So, how about it, dummy? Do we take you in for robbery and leave that wife of yours out here to face Zeb, or do you hand over the gold and we call it square?"

When Carter didn't answer, August stormed to within an inch of his face. "Don't go thinking these drifters you got nesting at your place will help you. Zeb will squash them like they was a bed of baby rattlers. In his prime he could down a hundred buffalo in one day and still have time to skin them before dark."

No one but August laughed at his joke so he continued. "Samuel may be good with a hammer and saw, but he's not a fighter. Folks in town never had much to do with him because they say he ran when he was called to fight for the South. A man like that's not going to risk his life to save a woman he don't hardly know."

August moved his finger across the blood on Carter's

cheek and wiped it on Carter's shirt. "Talking is over. Where's the gold?"

Carter didn't say a word. He braced himself for another blow as he heard the side door of the barn open. August and his men didn't notice. They were too busy trying to beat an answer out of the dummy's son.

TWENTY-TWO

Bailee listened to the blow-by-blow story Rom told. First, he rattled off words in his own language, then he slowed down and tried to tell her what was happening in the barn. Though the words were jumbled, she pieced Rom's story together. Wheeler was looking for gold, the gold Zeb had the day she tried to kill him. Somehow, they thought Carter had it.

When Rom finished, Bailee was silent for a long moment, listening as she stared at the closed door just beyond the corral. Without a word she began pacing the porch. She wanted to storm the outbuilding and rescue Carter, but there were three armed men inside. Her army consisted of Samuel, who couldn't see, Rom with a knife, an old man with two unarmed sons, and Lacy.

Someone, maybe several, would be hurt, and Deputy Wheeler wouldn't be among the first. Wheeler was a dull blade, and his two helpers were worse. If they were rushed, there was no telling what they'd do.

She looked around her. These men were not warriors. Except for Samuel, they had wives and children to worry about. A man in a barn getting beat up wasn't worth risking their lives for.

"Rom said Carter didn't deny stealing the money!" Lacy joined Bailee as she paced. "If he took the money, he knew Zeb was still alive. He could have stepped forward and saved us a week in jail and the fine."

Bailee nodded. She tried to tell herself that Carter wasn't the kind of man to take money off an unconscious man, even one as evil as everyone claimed Zeb Whitaker to be. Carter was honest. He wouldn't let three women face a crime when he knew they didn't kill anyone. Yes, he hated talking, and, as far as she knew, he'd only been in town the day of the lottery. It might have been possible that he didn't even know anyone thought Zeb dead.

But facts kept gnawing at her logic. Carter did have gold. The same kind of gold that had spilled from Zeb's bag the day they'd clubbed him. He also didn't know how to use it, always holding it out to her as if he wasn't sure. A man who earned gold would know more about it, wouldn't he? A farmer who traded for supplies wouldn't have any use for handling gold. Unless he found it? Unless he stole it?

Another fact crossed her mind. When she'd first heard Zeb might be alive, Carter hadn't seemed surprised. Maybe Carter didn't believe she killed him in the first place? Maybe Carter knew the truth?

"What do we do?" Lacy's huge eyes were filled with excitement. "I say we go in after Carter. We got to hang on to our husbands no matter what they do. Can't let them be snatched away." She punched the air as if fighting an invisible man five foot tall in front of her.

"We do nothing," Bailee answered, realizing Lacy was too young to know the danger. "Those are armed lawmen in the barn talking to Carter. They may be going about it in the wrong way, but they are just trying to find out the truth." She didn't believe her own words, but she had to calm Lacy. Panic wouldn't solve anything; she'd learned that the hard way back in Independence.

Lacy didn't look convinced. "Carter wouldn't commit a crime, not even stealing from a man he thought was dead. We have to believe that, he's your husband. We'll stand and fight with him, if trouble comes."

Bailee's cheeks reddened. Lacy was right. He was her husband, a man who'd risked his life to save her. A man who cared about her. A man who'd been willing to stand beside her no matter what trouble came. How could she do less?

She felt ashamed. The blood of her father must run inside her. A part of her no longer hated her only parent so completely for not believing in her. A part wanted to slice her wrist and let her father's blood drain out forever.

Bailee grabbed the handgun from the bookshelf and placed it in her pocket. "I'll go talk to them." She glanced up at her troops waiting for orders. "Get Piper to the orchard. Carter says it's safe there. The rest of you stay here, by the house. I'm only going to talk to them, but if there is trouble, I don't want them thinking I'm all alone."

With Lacy at her side, Bailee stepped off the porch and walked toward the barn. "There's no need for you to come," she tried to reassure her friend.

"You're not going in there without me. I can feel trouble, and I plan to be with you," Lacy insisted.

They were within ten feet of the barn door when August Wheeler stepped out. He glared at Bailee and Lacy for a moment as if debating even bothering with them.

"Where's Carter?" Bailee's hands molded around the handle of the gun in her pocket.

"He's all right. We're taking him to town to ask him a few questions. He may have information on a recent robbery."

"Does Sheriff Riley know about this?" Lacy placed her hands on her hips and stood her ground, just behind Bailee.

"Riley doesn't need to know anything." August growled. "I'm in charge while he's gone, and, from his telegram this morning, it may be days before he returns."

"Well, you've got the wrong man." Lacy moved an inch farther behind Bailee as she shouted. "Carter McKoy is a good man. I know, he's married to my sister. He didn't commit any crime, so you've no business taking him anywhere."

Wheeler mumbled, "Children should be seen and not heard. Besides, she's not your sister, little witch."

Bailee wasn't sure which of his statements made Lacy more angry.

The short woman-child fired back, "I'm not a child. I'm a woman, fully grown and rightly married. And Bailee is my sister in my heart, and that's the only place that matters. You'd know that if you weren't dumber than a box of muddy river rocks, August Wheeler."

August reminded Bailee of a bully on a school yard. He wasn't about to back down. "Well, if you're so smart, maybe you know where two saddlebags of gold are stashed. Maybe you'll be the next one we bring in for questioning, witch."

Lacy wasn't frightened by his threat. "My father-in-law would have a paper out within the hour if you tried something like that. The whole town would come after you.

And stop calling me a witch, or I'll cast a spell on you that'll turn your toes so green, they'll all fall off and roll around in your boots."

August hesitated. Threatening men, even beating them, was one thing, but bothering the wife of a local hero whose father ran the newspaper was another. He frowned. "Well, you'd better be careful, Miss Married Lady." It was an empty threat, and they all knew it. "And I don't believe in spells and hexes."

Lacy leaned around Bailee and whispered just loud enough for him to hear. "Remember that tonight when you can feel your hair falling out, Deputy."

Bailee was almost enjoying the exchange. She smiled a moment before Carter stepped from the barn.

For a second she was frozen, standing there in the hot sun with her hand wrapped around the gun in her pocket and the silly smile still on her lips. Then Carter's appearance washed over her. His shirt ripped to rags and stained. Blood dripped from two cuts along his face. His hands were tied in front of him as though he were a common criminal.

Bailee rushed to him, fighting back sobs. "What have you done!" She glared at August.

"Nothing, ma'am. He fell over a shovel left on the barn floor," Ludlow answered in an almost believable whine. "We're just taking him in to ask a few questions—right, Wheeler?" Ludlow glanced at his boss, making sure his words were right. "If he cooperates, he should be home by dark."

Bailee drew the corner of her apron up and blotted it against Carter's cuts. He watched her with a worried stare.

August grabbed one of Carter's arms while Ludlow held the other. "Don't no one get in our way or try to stop us, or someone will die this day, and I can promise you it won't be me."

"Carter . . ." Bailee brushed his hair away from the blood still on his forehead.

"Stay here," he whispered. "You'll find safety in the house. No matter what, stay safe."

His eyes told her so much more, but they were words he couldn't say now, couldn't let anyone else hear.

"Did he say something to you?" August jerked at Carter's arm. "Has the dummy decided to talk?"

Carter didn't answer.

"He's guilty of stealing. All he has to do is give the gold back, and I'll let him go." August put his arm around Carter as though they had suddenly become friends. "What do you say? Hand over what you stole, and I'll ride off your land. You can stay here with your wife. We'd stay around and help you remember where you put it, but there are reasons I don't want to stay long. Someone else might make a visit."

Carter wasn't even looking at August. He stared at Bailee.

August turned away to get the horses while Ludlow pulled his gun. He waved the old Walker Colt as if daring anyone to question their actions as he pulled Carter toward the horses.

Lacy tried to comfort Bailee. "Don't worry. I'll get word to Sheriff Riley. He'll know what to do. They can't just put a man in jail like this. In a day, this will all be over and Carter will be back."

Ray, Wheeler's overweight assistant, helped Carter onto a horse, then drew his own gun. He mimicked Ludlow's stance as best he could.

Bailee clung to Carter's leg, wishing he would tell her

what to do. *Stay here* and *stay safe* didn't seem like enough.

She looked up at him, but the sun robbed her of a clear view of his eyes. She shifted until she could see his face. "Did you do what they say you did?" The words were out before she could stop them. The moment they were said, she would have pulled them back if she could. But it was too late.

Carter's blue eyes turned to steel. She felt the coldness between them as quickly as if they'd both fallen into icy water. He was so still, she thought . . . she prayed . . . he hadn't heard her ask the question.

"I never asked you!" His words were no more than a whisper of wind between them, but they slapped across her face just the same.

August jerked the reins of Carter's horse, and the men rode toward the gate as though bullets were flying around them.

Carter's words echoed in Bailee's mind as tears ran down her face. "I never asked you," she repeated, trying to make sense of the words.

Then she knew. When he met her, he never once asked if she was guilty of the crime she not only was charged with, but confessed to. Yet, even so, he never questioned her. No wonder he wasn't surprised Zeb Whitaker was alive. He never believed she killed the man. Or if he did, it hadn't mattered.

"What are we going to do?" Lacy asked.

Bailee looked around. Samuel and the others were waiting for the answer.

Bailee straightened her shoulders. "We're going to make a plan," she said, knowing she had to do this right, "and then I'm going after my husband."

Everyone offered to help at once, even Samuel.

Papa Farrow stepped in front of her and bowed. "My people will help. We are not good in a showdown or gunfight, but we have skills in moving unnoticed and retrieving things. We will go retrieve your husband for you."

Lacy laughed. "I'm not much good at anything that I know of, but you're not going without me. If I'm mad enough, I can fight. I'd like nothing better than knocking that Ludlow more senseless than he already is."

TWENTY-THREE

By NIGHTFALL ALL THE CHILDREN WERE TUCKED away safely in the orchard with their fathers on guard. Carter had been right when he'd told Bailee to hide in the trees if trouble came. They'd been planted, not in rows, but in circles, making it almost impossible to find someone who didn't want to be seen.

Papa Farrow objected when Rom wanted to go into town with Lacy and Bailee. But if they planned to see Carter, they needed to enter town as quietly as possible, and Rom was a master at playing a shadow.

They waited until dark to start out so the night would act as cover. Samuel hitched his own wagon because, with the cover, someone passing might think he was traveling alone.

Bailee left lanterns burning bright in case Zeb was watching the house, he would assume she was still there. She even took the time to build a small fire in the stove so smoke would circle into the night.

As soon as they reached town, Lacy planned to go straight to her father-in-law and ask for help. With any luck, he could get a telegram sent to Sheriff Riley.

Bailee needed to see Carter. Once she knew he was all right, they'd think of some way to get him out. So her only mission in town would be to break into the jail.

Samuel's job was to drive the wagon. Once they got to town, he'd hide it behind the newspaper office. From Lacy's apartment window he could see the jail and be ready for whatever happened.

Rom, on the other hand, would scout around, listening for anything that might prove helpful. Wheeler was a talker and a drinker. Bailee bet Rom could find him bragging over whiskey in one of the saloons.

The plan was simple. Everyone would scatter and meet back at the apartment at midnight. It would probably be tomorrow before they could get things accomplished, but by dawn they'd know where they stood.

Bailee watched the night sky as they rode toward town. Only a sliver of a moon lit the way, and no one talked as they huddled in the back of Samuel's wagon. Like Bailee, they were lost in their own thoughts.

It was no plan at all, she decided. Even if Lacy got a telegram off to Riley, he was probably too weak to travel. If he came back, he'd only be one against three, maybe four if Zeb showed his face. Lacy's father-in-law might be a nice man, but he was old and crippled. He'd be of little help. Wheeler and his partners probably wouldn't let Bailee see Carter, and if they did, Carter probably wouldn't talk to her after she'd hurt him so with her question. Even if Rom did hear something, he most likely wouldn't remember enough English to repeat it exactly.

Bailee fought back tears. "No plan at all," she whispered.

Lacy seemed to believe they'd think of something when

the time came, but experience had taught Bailee she wasn't good at saying or doing the right thing without thinking it through. Her life was a string of calamities due to no regard for caution, and tonight promised to be no exception.

They pulled into a sleeping town, Bailee's hopes low. Part of her wished she'd stayed in the orchard with the children, but she knew she couldn't sleep without at least trying to apologize to Carter. She needed to explain about her past even if it meant telling him everything. Once she knew he wasn't angry with her, they'd think of something.

Lacy, Bailee, and Rom climbed silently from the wagon and melted into the night. Lacy to the boardinghouse where her father-in-law lived, Rom to the shadows near the saloon, Bailee to the jail.

"Midnight," Samuel whispered, as if anyone needed reminding.

Bailee pulled her shawl around her head. It wasn't cold, but she felt somehow protected from the night with it covering her. The hour was far too late for respectable women to walk the streets alone. She kept her head low and her steps quick.

A light shown from the jail window. She had the odd sense of coming home as she entered the office/jail where she'd spent a week. Sheriff Riley never bothered to lock the door to the cell when Bailee and the others stayed there, so no bad memories hung over the place.

Smell was another matter. From the moment she opened the door, Sheriff Riley's pipe tobacco greeted her, along with the odor of years of boiled coffee. Tonight, other smells blended with the familiar. Unwashed bodies. Whiskey. A lingering hint of violence.

Bailee stepped inside the office and pushed the door

closed. She noticed the large cell was locked tonight. The bars dividing the office reflected the light of a single lantern atop the sheriff's desk.

Ludlow sat with his feet propped beside the light. Empty coffee cups cluttered the usually neat counter, and a stack of unread mail weighed down one corner of the desk. Ludlow didn't look up at her as he lazily cleaned his huge Colt.

" 'Bout time you got here," he mumbled as he swung his chair around and let his feet hit the floor with a thud. "I'm mighty thirsty—"

He didn't finish the sentence when he spotted her. First surprise, then irritation registered in his scarred face. "What do you want?"

Bailee searched beyond the bars for Carter. "I came to see my husband." She saw a dark form on the cot against the far wall, but it didn't move.

"Have to come back when it's daylight." Ludlow stumbled over his words as he stood and blocked her view of the cell as if she didn't have the right even to look. "It's too late for a visit tonight."

Bailee took a step, trying to see around the man to Carter. Was her husband asleep? Or unconscious? Surely if he were able, he'd at least move.

"I insist!" Bailee straightened her shoulders. "I have a right to visit."

Ludlow widened his stance. "You can insist all you like, but you're not seeing him till morning. Wheeler didn't leave no orders that there could be visitors tonight. If he didn't tell me, I ain't doing it."

"But I have to know if my husband is all right."

"He's fine." Ludlow looked like he couldn't care less if she believed him. He touched his badge as though trying to think of the right words a deputy should say. "Now, get out of here before I lock you up for bothering the law."

Bailee stood her ground. "I'm not leaving until I've seen my husband, so don't try to threaten me." She pointed her finger at him.

Ludlow frowned. "I said leave or I'll arrest you. I got the right, you know. This badge says I do."

"No, it doesn't!"

"Yes, it does!"

Bailee moved a foot closer, still just out of his reach. "You wouldn't dare arrest me, you no-good drifter. That piece of tin doesn't mean anything. You're no more the law than Wheeler is."

"Yes, I am."

"Then prove it."

Ludlow took the bait. He grabbed her arm with one hand and the keys to the cell with the other. "I'll show you what I can and can't do."

He pulled her to the cell and opened the lock, then shoved her inside with enough force to send her halfway across the floor.

"Now you can just stay there till you rot, for all I care." He tossed the keys on the desk and stormed to a box nailed high that served as a shelf near the stove. A whiskey bottle replaced the coffee tin that usually rested there. Ludlow helped himself to a long swig. "This job ain't as easy as Wheeler said it'd be," he mumbled, then raised his voice to add, "and you don't give me no more trouble or there'll be hell to pay, lady. Hell to pay."

Bailee forgot about the idiot she'd been talking to and moved into the back of the cell. Her hand brushed along Carter's shoulder as he lay facing the wall. He was warm and she could tell he was breathing, but he didn't roll toward her. Something was wrong.

She knelt. "Carter?" Her fingers brushed the familiar line of his arm. The muscles were tight, unyielding.

"Carter?"

"Go away," he answered without moving. He didn't sound as if he'd been asleep.

"I'm here to help," she whispered back as her fingers brushed his hair. She could feel dried blood mingled in the strands.

"How? By getting locked in here with me?"

Bailee frowned. Maybe it wasn't the best of plans, but at least she got to see him. "Are you hurt?"

"I'm fine."

He said the words so flatly she knew he lied. She wanted him to roll over and open his arms to her, but she understood why he didn't.

"I'm sorry," she whispered, brushing his shoulder with her fingers once more as though she could brush away the pain the question had caused him.

"Why? Because I'm not hurt or because you aren't sure I'm not a criminal?"

"I'm sorry for ever asking the question."

"You've only known me days. Maybe I asked too much thinking you could believe in me. After all, I'm only the husband you chose from a hat, one choice better than staying in jail." His words were hesitant, rehearsed, meant to hurt.

Bailee fought back tears. She deserved his anger, but that didn't make the pain any less. Could it have been only hours ago that he'd spoken to her with passion and told her he wanted her? Now, not the world, but her words had made him pull back from everyone, including her.

"Carter, I—"

"Hush up in there!" Ludlow yelled. "Or I'll gag you both. Ray's forgot about relieving me tonight, so I plan to sleep here, and I don't want any noise bothering me." The sound of whiskey being gulped followed.

Bailee leaned her forehead against Carter's shoulder, but he didn't move. He'd pulled away from her, locking himself in a cell she could never enter.

She stood and moved to the other cot. There was no use trying to talk to him.

An hour passed, then another. By now Lacy, Samuel, and Rom must be wondering where she was. She stood and looked toward the lantern. Ludlow was sound asleep at the desk, his Colt resting across his legs.

Silently she crept to the window and waited. If they were looking for her, one of them would check the jail eventually, and the only window safe to peep into was the barred one.

She didn't have long to wait. Rom's dirty fingers wrapped around the bars, and he pulled himself up the outside wall.

When she touched his fingers, he stiffened. Slowly he pulled high enough to meet her gaze. He didn't bother with unnecessary words.

"Tell Lacy and Samuel I'm fine," Bailee whispered. "Tell them to get some sleep. There's nothing more we can do tonight. Carter is all right for now."

Rom nodded and slowly disappeared from view. His fingers slipped from the bars.

Bailee pressed her back against the cool adobe wall and relaxed. There was nothing to do until morning. She knew Carter was all right, and she was probably safer than anywhere else she could be. Zeb Whitaker wouldn't think to look here. She closed her eyes and tried to remember to breathe.

The warmth of Carter's nearness pressed against her a moment before his body leaned into her.

Bailee stiffened, startled that he'd moved so close without making a sound, then relaxed as his fingers slipped into her hair, destroying the bun she'd tied at the base of her neck.

She opened her mouth to speak, but his lips covered hers before she could get a word out. His kiss was hard and demanding without the tenderness she'd grown to expect.

His fingers twisted into fists, tangling her hair inside them as his body pressed her against the wall, boldly telling her of his need for her.

Shock and passion pumped through her veins. She could almost taste his anger at her as his kiss bruised her lips, but there was something more, far more.

He needed her. Far down in the very core of his being, he needed her . . . and her world crumbled about her when she realized he hated himself for it.

TWENTY-FOUR

From his cell window Carter watched the moon disappear behind shadowy buildings. The night had grown cold as it always did on the plains. Another few hours and it would be daylight. Another few hours and he'd have to say something to Bailee.

Rubbing the wrinkles from his forehead, he tried for the hundredth time to remove the smells and noises of the town long enough to sleep. But it was hopeless. The only relief from the horrible odor of too many people living too close together had been when Bailee came near. Then his senses filled only with her.

The ugly town, the stench, even the constant rumbling of sounds vanished when he pulled her close. The memory of her was stronger than all the reality he'd known before she tumbled into his world.

He glanced over at her sitting on the cot, her eyes still wide open. She needed sleep, he reminded himself, and he had to think, but at this rate neither would reach any goal tonight.

When she glanced in his direction, their eyes met and

held as if they no longer had the strength to look away. The longing for each other was so great, it hung in the air like hundred-year-old spiderwebs, distorting all else around them.

She stood, a dream walking toward him. He waited until she was only inches away, before he pulled her to him as he had earlier.

She responded like clay in his arms as he touched, letting him mold her, handle her. And he touched her boldly, almost angrily at first, then with more passion than he'd ever known. The memory of every embrace they'd ever shared washed against his body in a tangible wave of pleasure as he stood before her collecting the nearness of her with every sense.

She made no protest when he moved his hands over her clothes, cupping her breast tightly in his fingers as he kissed her, daring her to object. His last words had been spoken in anger, yet she accepted his silent hunger with a longing that matched his own.

They stood beside the barred window, oblivious to all but each other. His hands claimed her as his with the daring of a man betting all he had on one roll of the dice.

He broke the kiss suddenly, bracing himself for her reproach.

She'd whispered his name, driving him more insane than he thought it possible to be and still breathe. He heard no objection to his actions, only a need for him to continue.

There would be no casual embrace, no friendly kiss. Their longing for each other had gone far beyond such. She'd become a basic need to him, and her responses told him she felt the same.

He'd pulled her deeply into the blackness of the cell and kissed her more gently.

Vaguely Ludlow's snoring registered, and he knew they were alone, blanketed by night. Long, lazy kisses followed as she relaxed against his body. Their movements became a slow dance that flamed a fire building inside each.

Giving her time to breathe, he buried his face against her neck and tasted her throat, unbuttoning her collar until he could feel the swell of her breasts. Then he returned, hungry for her mouth, not giving her time to speak as he took her breath away once more.

When he moved to her throat, he felt the pounding of her heart against his lips as he unbuttoned another button of her blouse. The knuckle of his first finger slipped between her breasts and he pushed the material low, longing for the feel of her flesh in his hand.

She made a slight sound, and he wasn't sure if it was pleasure or fear.

He broke the kiss abruptly with only an ounce of reason remaining and waited for her to tell him to stop. When he saw her smile, his hand slipped beneath her blouse and claimed her breast, covered in thin cotton. As with the kisses, his action was bold, almost a challenge.

She leaned her head back against the cool wall and sighed, allowing him to explore. Her arms rested limply on his shoulders as she opened her mouth slightly in invitation. There was no challenge in her soft sigh, only pleasure.

He bent in to kiss her, trying not to think of how deeply he wanted her. Since she opened her blouse to him in the orchard, his hand ached for the feel of her flesh. All the anger he felt for her couldn't compare with the longing to touch her.

And he did without hesitation. The buttons of her garment gave easily as he took his time, letting her know how dearly he wanted to caress what she'd offered for his view.

Slowly breaking the kiss, he let her breathe deeply, while he moved his hand down her skirt, pulling the material up until he reached the flesh of her leg.

She didn't say a word, but jerked slightly as his hand moved over the soft skin of her thigh. He pushed her stocking below her knee then let his fingers glide up her warm skin.

He told himself she was his wife for this lifetime. And there would be nothing between them but her own doubts. He couldn't make her believe in him, but he could let her know that very soon she'd be completely his.

His fingers tugged to open her legs. The softness of her skin made him waver, as pure pleasure washed over his senses. Her rapid intake of air brushed his cheek as she trembled against him, then shifted and parted her legs.

Her hand shook as it crossed shyly over the torn material of his shirt. They were beyond words now, and somehow the knowledge made him more comfortable. They crossed together into a place neither had ever ventured, but both knew it was time to go.

All the anger he'd held toward her vanished as he hesitantly brushed his fingers across the thin undergarment she wore.

She trembled once more as his hand covered the warmth of her. No one had ever told him about the intimacy between a man and a woman, but suddenly he knew. He'd been a fool when he'd married her, thinking he'd sleep with her only to have children. There would be far more between them than an occasional sharing of beds.

"You'll sleep beside me," he whispered against her ear as he pressed his hand gently over her, "every night of our lives."

She raised her fingers to his hair and pulled his mouth against her lips, kissing him in answer.

His hand, resting over her most private part, left no doubt that there would never be any rooms between them. When his fingers moved to explore, she jerked in surprise, but he held her tightly, pressing her back against the wall and continuing his discovery until she jerked once more with pleasure.

He'd meant to give her time to answer, but the warmth of her drove him mad. He kissed her wildly, starved for the taste of her. When he finally pulled away, they gasped for breath.

For a while, they both stood in the darkness, an inch away, not touching. He could still feel her warmth, smell all the smells that made her, taste her on his lips, but he didn't touch her again.

When she could breathe normally, she slowly straightened her clothes. Smoothing her skirts as if he hadn't bunched it to her waist, redoing the buttons of her blouse where he'd twisted them free.

He glanced toward the lamplight and saw that Ludlow was still fast asleep, an empty whiskey bottle beside his chair.

Carter guessed he should probably stand back, give her room, but he didn't want to put any more space between them than he must.

"Did you . . . like what we just did?" He had to know,

before she had time to convince herself of a lie.

"Yes," she answered softly without looking up at him.

He wanted to ask her if he did it right, if he pleased her a fraction as much as the feel of her pleased him. But he didn't dare. He was afraid to let her know how much she meant to him. She wasn't a part of his life; somehow in a day she'd *become* his life.

"There is more." He said an inch away from her ear as he fought the urge to close the distance.

"I know." She rubbed her cheek against his jaw.

"But not here. Not in a jail cell."

She brushed her slightly swollen lips feather-light across his, touching the words as he spoke.

"At home," he mumbled, praying he had the will to wait. Loving Bailee would never be something he'd hurry through.

Her lips grew confident.

"In my bed," he said against her mouth.

She kissed him gently. He wanted to reach for her, lean into her, flatten her against him, but he stood perfectly still, waiting for her to advance this time.

Her mouth tortured him, lightly brushing his lips with a promise. When her tongue tenderly trailed over him, he fought for control.

It crossed his mind, what little he had left, that he'd held her boldly, aggressively taking what he wanted, almost demanding that she accept his passion. Now she was getting her revenge by enjoying his agony.

Her hand rested over his heart as she leaned closer and pressed her lips against his in a chaste kiss.

Carter had gone too far beyond such a kiss to allow it to continue; he opened his mouth and deepened her offering.

They kissed like that for a long while, then he held her until she fell asleep. Twice, she'd tried to talk. Both times he silenced her with his touch. There would be time to talk in the morning.

When he was sure she was asleep, he wrapped her in the blanket and stood, his mind too full of thoughts even to close his eyes.

He wasn't angry at Wheeler and his two helpers. They were just trying to get what they thought he had . . . Zeb's gold. If Zeb ever had any. But surprisingly, he was still angry at Bailee. She should know him well enough to believe in him.

Life made no sense to Carter. How could he want her so dearly when she didn't trust him? How could his body ache even now to hold her? He'd never done anything to cause her not to believe in him. He'd never lied. He'd never tried to deceive her. Yet the first time she was tested, she doubted him.

Part of him wanted to grab her by the shoulders and demand an answer. Part of him wanted to hold her forever, never allowing her to talk to him. That way he'd never hear the betrayal he'd heard this afternoon in her voice.

He lifted her hand that rested outside the blanket and cupped her fingers over his. Without thinking, he began to sign, slowly moving his hand.

The words he couldn't say, might never say to her, whispered in movement. Words of love. Words of promise. Words of forever.

TWENTY-FIVE

Dawn crept into the cell, a thief intent on stealing dreams born in the night. Bailee slowly opened her eyes to the sight of dust dancing in a beam of light. For a long while she watched the tiny particles drift in the still air as if trapped in winds that left them without control.

That's how she'd felt since the night months ago when she'd thought to frighten a thief and murdered a man instead. Though all the world looked calm around her, she was caught in whirlwinds beyond her strength, drifting, tumbling. Now, with the dawn, another storm would hit and she wasn't sure where she might end up, or even where she belonged.

When she finally glanced beyond the light, Carter slowly came into focus. He was sitting on the bunk opposite her, leaning his back against the bars, one leg drawn up to act as an elbow rest. His face was more bruised than it had been when he'd left the ranch, but he'd cleaned the blood away. Sun-browned skin showed through the rips in his shirt. As always, his blue eyes anchored her to his world.

Bailee sat up, tried to straighten her hair, and mumbled, "Morning."

He didn't say a word as he studied her every move. She couldn't help but wonder if he watched her all night.

She wasn't quite ready to face him. The memory of what they'd done in the darkness of the cell drifted across her mind. She wondered how people could do such things at night and still face each other in the morning. A shadowy touch that was so much more than a touch. Passion cloaked in darkness that warmed her still. A need that bloomed only in the stillness of midnight lingered now in her thoughts.

Bailee crossed to the water bucket by the cell opening and drank a full dipper of water with her back turned to Carter. She noticed Ludlow beyond the bars. Sometime during the night he'd slid off the chair and now lay spread-eagle on the floor, snoring softly while he drooled.

Judging from the light, Bailee knew she didn't have much time. Wheeler, or the fat one called Ray, would be here any minute, and her time with Carter would be over. She turned and faced him, having no idea what she'd say.

He straightened as she walked toward him and moved over a few inches so she could sit beside him.

"I'm sorry—"

He stopped her with the touch of his fingers on her lips. "We've no time now," he whispered.

Bailee nodded. They had far more to worry about than something she'd said yesterday.

He brushed her cheek with a stroke so light it made her feel beautiful and cherished for the first time in her life.

He looked at her as if she were the only woman he'd ever seen, or wanted to see.

"As soon as Deputy Wheeler returns, I want you to talk your way out of here just like you talked your way in last night."

His words sounded practiced, and she wondered if he'd ever speak to her without thinking about exactly what he would say. It was almost as though he had to translate his thoughts from another language.

Bailee opened her mouth to object, but his fingers stopped her once more.

"It won't take Wheeler long to figure out that I don't have any gold beyond the few coins I collect when Samuel sells the chairs I make. Once he believes the truth, he'll let me go."

Bailee wasn't sure it would be that simple.

"That leaves Piper, Lacy, and you to worry about. Piper's family may already be in Childress waiting for her, not knowing where else to go. If Zeb is looking for you and Lacy, he'll head toward my ranch . . . or here. I've tried to deny it, but both of you would be better off somewhere else."

Bailee shook her head, refusing to think about leaving him. She almost felt the winds coming again, sending her tumbling into the unknown.

"If you can make it to Fat Alice, you'd have both sheriffs to protect you, assuming they're recovered. Alice said she runs a boardinghouse, so she'd likely take in two more ladies."

"But, Carter, you don't know . . ." How could she explain about Fat Alice?

"I know she helped me once, and I think she'll do so again. If anyone knew where your friend Sarah went, I'd worry about her, but if the sheriff didn't know, the odds are good Zeb won't. She should be safe enough for the time being. Fat Alice's is a place Zeb will never think to look for you."

Bailee didn't want to leave. She had friends to look after and Carter to take care of. He wasn't a fighter, he was a farmer. He had long days of work ahead of him in the orchard. He needed her at home to help.

"The train leaves at noon. I talked with the boy called Rom just before dawn. He and Samuel will get Piper and meet you at the station. Try to get on the southbound unnoticed."

Bailee leaned against his shoulder. "I don't want to leave you." She also didn't see how she and Lacy could board the train in broad daylight without half the town knowing.

He put his arm around her and held her so tightly she could hardly breathe. There was something he wasn't telling her, she knew it, but wasn't sure she wanted to ask.

"I'll come get you, or send word. If the plan fails there's another place you'll be safe. It took me three winters to build. Not even Samuel knows about the passage."

Before he could say more, Mrs. Abernathy clamored through the office door, waking Ludlow. He stumbled to his feet, waving his arms as though he could fight off the devils in his dreams.

When Ludlow saw it was only the old woman who brought food to prisoners, he tried to act sober. He went about straightening his vest as if it were all that was amiss in the rubble of his grooming.

She looked at him with disgust. "Get out of my way, you saloon waste. There's a prisoner here and I aim to collect my twenty-five cents for feeding him."

Ludlow stepped aside. He frowned at the old woman. Everyone in town knew the sheriff pistol-whipped him once for being disrespectful to Widow Abernathy. Ludlow held his words, though it constipated him greatly.

"Well!" she shouted. "Get the keys and let me in. This tray ain't getting any lighter."

"What about my breakfast?" Ludlow whined as he followed her orders.

"You ain't locked up. Go get your own breakfast." She passed into the cell, then added, "And wipe that drool off your face or they'll think you're the world's tallest spittoon."

Mrs. Abernathy nodded at Bailee without seeming the least bit surprised to see her. "In again are you, honey?"

Carter pulled a stool up so the old woman could set her tray down.

"I'm here to get my husband out," Bailee answered, remembering how the old woman complained every time she had to bring food to Lacy, Sarah, and her while they were in jail.

"Doin' a great job." Mrs. Abernathy chuckled as she sat on the empty cot and waited for her tray. She'd learned years ago that it was easier to wait than to have to return for the dirty dishes.

She pulled out a small tin of snuff and a thin branch the length of a pencil. After chewing on the end of the twig for several minutes, her few remaining teeth shredded it. She circled the newly made brush in the snuff and stuck in her mouth.

They heard Ludlow splashing like a catfish in an inch of water at an old washstand the sheriff kept in one corner of his office.

"I brought extra victuals, thinking you might be hungry,

boy. If there ain't enough, I'll bring for two come lunch-
time."

Bailee was shocked. In the week they'd been in jail,
Mrs. Abernathy had never brought anything extra. Once
Lacy had asked for more salt, and the old woman reminded her jail wasn't a restaurant. Her usual breakfast
of biscuits and watered-down gravy had changed to a
plate of sausage and eggs large enough to feed a family.

Carter leaned forward. "Thank you," he said simply,
"but my wife won't be here at lunch." He met the old
woman's stare. "Can you help get her out of here?" he
whispered so low Ludlow couldn't have heard.

To Bailee's surprise, the old woman nodded once, then
returned to chewing on her twig and blotting any brown
liquid that darkened the corner of her mouth with a ragged
handkerchief. Bailee had heard that snuff deadened the
pain from rotting teeth, but no woman she'd known back
home used it.

Carter ate as if he were truly starved. Bailee guessed
he hadn't had anything to eat since breakfast the day before. She felt a moment of jealousy that he enjoyed another's cooking so much, then called herself foolish.

Bailee ate one of the biscuits. They were fresh from
the oven, not day old as Mrs. Abernathy always brought
before. She thought about how she could explain to Carter
that she wasn't going to leave him no matter who he en-
listed to help her escape.

Ludlow moved too close to the bars for them to talk.
The scarred man looked miserable. He was hung over and
hungry and forgotten by his friends. After he glanced at
the door several times, Bailee read his mind easily. He
wanted to leave, but was afraid to abandon his post.

When Carter finished eating, Mrs. Abernathy gathered

up the tray and nodded at Bailee. "Come along, honey. We'll see if we can't find that husband of yours a shirt to wear that isn't ripped. A gentleman like him shouldn't have to wear a shirt that's falling off his shoulders."

Bailee frowned in confusion, but stood while Ludlow unlocked the door. "I don't—"

Carter pressed his hand against the small of her back. "You're going," he whispered in more the tone of an order than a request.

She glanced over her shoulder at him. His hand almost pushed her forward, but in his eyes she saw a plea.

"She ain't going nowhere." Ludlow let Mrs. Abernathy pass, then blocked Bailee's way.

"Yes, she is," the old woman corrected. "We can't have a man in jail half undressed. Look at that shirt."

Ludlow stared at Carter's shirt as if he'd missed something. "It's not so bad. I've worn worse."

"Well, Sheriff Riley won't tolerate a prisoner being all bloodstained and battered. I aim to tell him just how men are treated when he's away."

The mention of Riley made Ludlow scratch his head. Fear flickered across the layer of dumbness that usually clouded his features.

The old woman didn't give him time to think. "Get out of our way, you gully rubbish. The lady is going with me, and I'll not hear another word. Everyone knows it's not proper to have a man and a woman in the same cell, even if they are married."

Ludlow wanted to argue, but he wasn't sure what to say. He had no charge to hold Bailee on other than bothering him, so he moved out of the way.

"I'll send someone over with a clean shirt, and I don't want you touching it. After all, you're just a deputy's deputy, nothing more." Mrs. Abernathy stormed across the office with Bailee only a step behind. "And before I leave, I'm obliged to say that I'd cut my fingers off if I couldn't get my nails any cleaner than yours, Mr. Ludlow."

He was looking at his hands when Bailee stepped through the door and into the morning sunshine.

"Thank you," she whispered when she caught up with Mrs. Abernathy.

"Didn't do it for you, honey." The old woman kept up a fast pace. "Did it for the dummy's boy. Though I never like folks calling him that. His mother weren't no dummy. You could see it in her eyes. She was one of those rare folks who sees and tastes and feels everything in this life."

"You know Carter?" Bailee was surprised. She guessed everyone in town knew of him, but she really never dreamed he'd talked to this woman.

"Don't know him, just seen him all his life. He used to come into town with his ma and pa. I had eleven kids then, none old enough to earn a full day's wage, and my man had up and left me figuring California was safer then getting caught in a war."

She didn't look at Bailee as she continued. "Living got mighty hard that first winter he was gone. Three of my babies died that year. Carter's ma would always drop off food at my back door when she came to town. Sometimes fruit and nuts, sometimes potatoes, carrots, and eggs. She weren't like some folks in town wanting to be thanked every time I passed them. She'd slip up to the door and hurry away like silence was a part of her. I'd see her husband grin at her as he pulled her quickly into the wagon and drove off."

"When Carter's folks died, I figured I'd seen the last

of the food. But a few years later the fruit started appearing again on my back porch. Peaches mostly and nuts in the fall."

She stopped suddenly and looked up at Bailee. "There ain't much I wouldn't do for your man, and all he ever asked me was to get you out of jail. Ludlow's lucky he didn't argue or I'd have taken him to the ground in a fight, if it had come to that." She raised an eyebrow. "You know what your man wants you to do, honey?"

"Yes," Bailee answered. "But I don't know if I can leave him."

"He's thinking of what's best for you."

Bailee nodded. Of course he was thinking of what was best for her, but was it best for him?

"Do what he asks. I'll be near if you need my help. My house is right there." She pointed to a shack that looked like it might fall down if the wind got up.

"I'll be fine." Bailee knew whatever she asked, if it were within the old woman's power, she would do.

"Then get to it, honey. I've got a shirt that belonged to one of my sons. Best one he had next to the one he was buried in. I'll take it over to Carter along with a little Navy Colt my oldest boy brought back from the war."

On impulse, Bailee leaned down and gave Mrs. Abernathy a kiss on her wrinkled cheek, then rushed off in the direction of Lacy's apartment. The old woman was right, she had to follow Carter's request. Maybe if he knew she was safe, he'd be able to think about keeping himself out of harm's way.

Lacy was near panic when Bailee arrived at the print shop.

"I was so worried you wouldn't get out, or you wouldn't stop in here, or you wouldn't be alone." Lacy wound her way through the cluttered shop as she talked.

Bailee thought of catching her and begging her to settle down, for Bailee could barely keep up with her.

Lacy told about Samuel sleeping outside of her apartment all night. He'd seen a huge shadow of a man moving in the alley, but no one came close enough for Samuel to get a look at him.

Rom had hidden in the corners of the saloon until the town grew quiet, then he'd climbed halfway up the stairs to a place where he could see the front of the jail and waited like a guard.

When they reached the little upstairs apartment, Lacy added, "Samuel and Rom left at dawn to fetch Piper. I'm packed and ready to go along with you. Between the two of us, we should be able to take care of Piper until her father shows up in Childress."

She stopped with her hand on the knob. "I almost forgot to tell you, Sheriff Riley sent something to you." Lacy fought down a giggle. "I'm not sure what it is, but it arrived a few hours ago by stage."

Bailee entered the apartment, trying to guess what the sheriff would find so important that he would have it shipped to her.

Sitting at Lacy's table was a ragamuffin of a girl in her early teens. She had long chocolate-colored hair that flew in all directions and huge brown eyes ringed in the black remains of makeup.

Bailee threw a questioning look at Lacy, then moved closer as the ragged girl stood.

"I ain't afraid, if that's what you're thinking." The child stammered as Bailee advanced. "I c-come a-toting lead."

Lack of sleep and the fear of the past few days fogged

Bailee's brain. She could think of nothing to say to the strange creature.

"Sheriff Riley didn't send me, like I told this lady." She pointed to Lacy. "I come of my own free will. I was worried about my friend Carter McKoy."

She watched Bailee closely, as if expecting her to start yelling at any moment. "I know how some wives feel about women like me, but you don't need to worry. I ain't here to take him away from you. Once I know he's all right, I got money for the train back home."

"Who are you?" Bailee knew she was being impolite, but one sentence was all she managed to get out.

"Nellie Jean," the child said. "Nellie Jean Desire, but folks mostly call me Two Bits. I'm a good friend of your handsome husband. In fact, last time I talked to him, he invited me to Sunday dinner."

"She's lying," Lacy whispered in Bailee's ear.

"Am not!" Two Bits snapped. "I was the one who helped him saddle Smith's horse and pointed him toward home. If it hadn't been for me, he wouldn't have known which way to go." She winked at Bailee. "He's one fine slice of man, but he don't know nothing about the world. You'd think he was born in a bucket and ain't found his way out yet."

"She knows Carter," Bailee whispered with a smile.

"Maybe, maybe not," Lacy answered. "Most of the men I've met in this part of the country are short on brains. No offense to your man, Bailee."

Bailee stepped closer to the girl. "Did you notice what he does when he's nervous and can't think of what to say?"

"Sure," Two Bits answered. "He moves his hands in

some kind of little patterns. I seen him doing it when the girls were operating on Riley."

Bailee jumped forward and hugged the girl wildly. She had to be the one who'd helped Carter.

"Hey!" Two Bits squealed. "Don't go drippy-eyed on me. I just come to check things out."

Lacy wasn't convinced. "How'd you find me? How'd you know Bailee would come here?"

"Riley told me to look over the print shop first." Two Bits frowned at Lacy. "I ain't traveling alone. I got the biggest Texas Ranger with me you ever seen. He come along looking for some little girl named Piper Halloway, but he told Riley he'd keep an eye on me. I'm suppose to meet up with him at the station ever time a train leaves today. He says if I have my business done, I can ride back with him."

"We're going along with Piper." Lacy finally accepted the girl. "I've grown attached to her, and I'd like to see her back in the arms of her family." Lacy left out that she and Bailee were also running from a killer.

Bailee glanced at Lacy's bags scattered around the room, and realized she had nothing but the wrinkled clothes on her back. The girl in front of her looked to be in the same predicament. Unless she'd stuffed clothes into the small knit bag by her chair, she was wearing her wardrobe.

Lacy read Bailee's mind. "We've time to stop at the mercantile before Samuel returns with Piper. You can get a few things against Carter's account. I'll send a message by one of the men downstairs to tell the ranger we have Piper and we'll meet him. If he's as huge as this one claims, he shouldn't be hard to find in a town this size."

Bailee agreed. She had no idea how long she'd be in

Childress. Surely Carter couldn't mind her buying just a few things more.

She turned to Two Bits. "Carter would like to see that you get a new dress, also. Would you consider going shopping with me?"

"I can pay for my own, if I needed one." Two Bits looked down at her dress. "Course, Fat Alice says never turn down a gift from a man, so I guess I could let him buy me one, long as it wouldn't make you too jealous."

Bailee smiled. "I'll try to hide my feelings."

An hour later she stood at the corner of the train platform with Lacy by her side. Two Bits was walking the platform showing off her new outfit to the morning like there was a crowd watching.

Bailee heard the tingle of spurs and turned as a tall man jumped on the platform and moved toward them. There was power in his movements even though he couldn't have been out of his mid-twenties. He had blond hair and intelligent brown eyes. He wore no badge, but Bailee guessed who he was.

"Ladies." He removed his hat. "Is one of you Mrs. McKoy?"

"I am," Bailee answered, liking the way the man showed her such respect.

"I'm Jacob Dalton. I understand you have a little girl traveling with you by the name of Piper."

"We might have."

"I'm here to see she gets home safely." He glanced at Two Bits. "As well as all in her party."

Two Bits winked at him. "You married, cowboy?"

"No." He smiled. "I was kind of waiting for you to grow up. You look mighty fine, Miss Nellie Jean."

"Thank you, Jacob." She straightened her new dress.

"I'm growing as fast as I can, now that I know you're waiting on me. I'll be there before you know it, so don't go getting killed."

He laughed. "I promise."

As the train pulled to a stop, they saw Samuel walking across the tracks with Piper in his arms. He'd hitched his wagon behind the mercantile. The bed was loaded down with another shipment of peaches.

The child looked frightened; Samuel looked worried.

They bought tickets and boarded as the whistle blew for "All aboard."

Bailee hung back from the others, hating the thought of leaving, but knowing Carter would want her safe with the sheriffs in Childress until Zeb Whitaker was rounded up.

She patted Samuel's hand as she stood on the platform. "Everything is going to be all right," she reassured him, wishing she could believe her own words.

Samuel didn't look at her. "I got peaches to unload, then I'm heading back to the ranch. Carter wouldn't want the place left."

"Thanks," Bailee stepped on the first step leading to the passenger car. "Take care."

The train jerked, preparing to start, as gunfire thundered from the direction of the jail.

Bailee glanced at Samuel. The old man with his poor hearing hadn't noticed the sound. He turned and headed back toward the mercantile.

TWENTY-SIX

"WAS THAT A SHOT?" LACY WHISPERED FROM JUST behind Bailee. "Thank the Lord we made it on the train." She looked inside at the almost empty car, expecting trouble to come charging down on them at any time.

Piper and the Texas Ranger were picking out seats, a few older women had already settled in to talk, and a gambler slept on the last bench.

The train shifted beneath them. There was no time to hesitate. "Lacy?" Bailee leaned close to her friend. "I have to go back to Carter."

Bailee moved past Lacy and ran to Piper. Kneeling beside the little girl, Bailee waited until Piper looked at her before speaking. "I have to stay with Carter." Bailee said the words slowly. "You'll be all right with the ranger and Lacy."

Tears welled in the child's eyes.

"You'll be safe soon." Bailee fought back her own tears. "But I have to make sure Carter is safe now."

Piper nodded.

"Want me to stay in town and help?" Two Bits leaned around the ranger. "I can shoot."

Bailee smiled at Two Bits. "I need you to see after Lacy and Piper now, but when this is all over, you will come back to dinner."

Suddenly Two Bits caught the teary-eye disease that seemed to be spreading. "I'll think about it. You'd better hurry if you're leaving."

Bailee kissed Piper's cheek, then ran back to the platform where Lacy still waited.

"You can't go!" Lacy grabbed Bailee's arm trying to hold Bailee on the train. "You have to stay with us. You have to be safe. Carter said so."

"I can't," Bailee whispered, moving away. "I know you and the ranger will take care of Piper. Get her to her father, then wait until I send word. You'll be safe from Zeb. I have to find Carter. He may need me."

Lacy understood. She forced her fingers to let go of Bailee's arm.

Bailee jumped off the step just as the train rolled.

She lifted her skirt and ran toward the jail. Several other people were ahead of her. When she reached the entrance of Riley's office, the first thing she saw, over the heads of several people, was the jail cell door standing wide open.

Pushing her way past the onlookers, she rushed inside the office. Ludlow lay facedown in a puddle of his own blood, one hand gripping his gun, still in its holster. The only sign of Carter was his torn shirt tossed in a corner of the cell.

"What happened!" Deputy Wheeler yelled as he bombarded his way into the office. He rushed too fast and stepped into the blood before he looked down. Swearing, he wiped his boot on a crumpled newspaper.

No one answered Wheeler's question. A man in a barber's coat knelt beside Ludlow and poked at him with one finger.

"Someone get help!" Wheeler shouted at no one in particular. "We got a man bleeding." He seemed more concerned with getting bloody newspaper off his boot than with his friend.

"I'm the nearest this town's got to a doc," the barber answered. "And I say someone get the undertaker."

Wheeler turned on the man. "You ain't no good at anything but pulling teeth and shaving. What makes you think you're suddenly a doc?"

"It don't take schooling to know a man's got a bullet plumb through the center of his chest." The barber rolled Ludlow's body over.

Bailee stepped back, not wanting to see the wound.

Wheeler looked as if he might explode with anger. He searched the crowd until he found a wide target. "Ray! I thought you were supposed to be here at dawn. What's going on? Why was Ludlow still at the office?"

Ray had the good sense to look terrified. "I must have overslept."

Bailee slipped behind two men as Wheeler stormed around the room. "Did anyone see anything?"

Everyone in the room shook their head. This was a town steeped in a tradition of nobody ever seeing anything as far as gunplay was concerned.

She moved closer to the door behind the crowd. She held her breath, hoping to become invisible.

Ray must have figured he was already fired, because he

spoke. "Carter McKoy was in the cell. He must've escaped and kilt Ludlow."

Wheeler looked as if he might slap Ray. "How does a man with no weapon, who's locked in a cell, escape?"

"Maybe he had help?" Ray spoke up, proud of his reasoning powers.

Bailee was out the door before anyone noticed her. She'd heard enough. If she stayed a moment longer, she'd be the one Wheeler questioned next. She ran down the alley and glanced across the road to where Mrs. Abernathy's shack stood.

After pounding on the door several times, she realized the woman either wasn't home or was refusing to help. Bailee wouldn't blame her for not helping. She didn't owe Bailee anything. But if Carter ran this way, she would have helped him, and, if he were inside, he'd let Bailee in.

Bailee tried one more time. Hoping.

Panic threatened to overtake her. Shouts echoed from the direction of the jail. She darted behind the old woman's house and headed through first one alley, then another to the mercantile. She didn't allow herself even to breathe until she saw Carter's work wagon parked behind the store. The boxes of peaches had already been unloaded and the tarp thrown in the back behind the bench seat.

Bailee scrambled beneath the tarp a moment before Samuel stepped from the back of the store with a load of supplies. She slowly scooted to the far side beneath the wagon's seat and peaked through the cracks in the side boards.

"I don't know about you picking up Carter's supplies!"

Mr. Willard shouted at Samuel. "I ain't never let no one sign for him before, except his wife."

Samuel offered the box back.

Willard quickly stepped away, afraid he might miss a sale. "No. No. I'm sure it's fine. I was just talking. After all, you did bring in his load of peaches, so it must be all right. You been doing work for Carter McKoy for years."

Samuel nodded and shoved the crate in the back of the wagon. As he pushed it to the front, Bailee's hand slipped from beneath the covering.

She froze, knowing he had to have seen it.

To her surprise, Samuel pulled the tarp over her fingers and tied the box down as though having a body in his wagon was nothing new.

"I'll be back with more peaches in a few days," Samuel said calmly. "You can settle up with Carter when he gets out of jail, but I'm keeping a count of the number of crates."

Willard agreed, but he wasn't really listening. He was staring down the street at what appeared to be a mob flooding toward them. "Wonder what's going on?" he said to himself. "Thought I heard a shot a while back. You reckon there's trouble?"

Samuel didn't bother to look. "I've no interest in what folks do in this town or any other. I got work to finish back at Carter's place."

Willard waved him off without even looking in his direction.

Bailee heard the crowd moving closer, but from her hiding place she couldn't see them. She guessed Wheeler was leading them.

Slapping the horses into motion, Samuel maneuvered

the wagon down the street toward home. Bailee heard the shouts of men fading behind her.

They traveled for half an hour at a slow steady pace before Samuel said, "You can come out now. Ain't no one around."

She crawled from beneath the sweaty tarp and climbed over the bench. "Are you sure I'm safe?"

The old carpenter nodded. "Where's Carter? I half expected him to be under there with you."

"I don't know. He was in the jail, but now he's gone and Ludlow has been shot. The town is all looking for him. They think he killed Ludlow."

Samuel only seemed mildly interested in her ranting. "What do you think?"

Bailee froze. She wouldn't doubt Carter again. She wouldn't! "I don't think he did. But if he shot Ludlow, he had good reason."

Samuel nodded. "I think the same."

They didn't say another word until they reached the ranch. For several minutes all was quiet, then the Gypsies came from every direction to greet her.

Old Papa Farrow took both her hands and welcomed her back. They all wanted to know if Piper got on the train safely and if the deputy had decided to let Carter come back home.

Bailee told them all about Piper and the ranger, but collapsed in tears when she tried to talk of Carter. She had no idea where he was; he might even be lost. All she knew for sure was that the entire town seemed to be gunning for him. She stayed behind to help him, and she'd run before she found him.

"You're safe here," Samuel said. "None of us will tell a soul you're on the place. I'll even tell Old Man Willard at the store that I'm worried about you disappearing. If I know him, he'll tell the rest of the town."

Everyone agreed. Bailee's safety depended on it.

She wasn't sure how she got to bed, but Bailee curled beneath the covers and cried herself to sleep thinking that somehow she'd let Carter down again. Wherever he was, she should be with him.

That thought hadn't crossed Carter's mind as he stood in Mrs. Abernathy's tiny kitchen and strapped on a holster with double Colts.

"Do you even know how to use handguns?" Mrs. Abernathy asked as she poured him a cup of hot coffee.

Carter grinned. "I've been learning a lot of new things lately." He lifted the coffee cup. "I'm a fair shot, but don't know about drawing a weapon. Most of the time, when a gun was necessary, a rifle would do the job around the place. I don't know if I can hit anything with these."

"Then go in shooting." Mrs. Abernathy laughed. "That'll confuse 'em."

"Are you sure you saw my wife get on the train?"

The old woman raised her hand, palm up. "I was heading home from delivering your shirt. So I was pretty far away, but I swear I saw her step on the train with that girl Lacy. Then I heard that gunshot and started running toward the jail. When I looked back, the train was gone."

Carter closed his eyes, remembering how he'd run from the jail when Ludlow and Zeb started fighting. He'd almost turned back when he heard the shot, but suddenly the old woman ran toward him like a guardian angel. She'd pulled him out of sight and down into a gully, then sneaked him back to her house after the mob passed.

"You saved my life today," he said, not knowing how he could ever thank her.

"Course I did, but don't you worry about it. That's what friends do for each other." She shoved back a tear. "But I didn't do it so you could go off getting yourself shot running after Zeb Whitaker."

"I have to settle it once and for all," Carter answered. "I can't have Bailee living in fear that he'll come get her any day. And since I'm the only one who knows he was in the jail with Ludlow this morning, he has to come after me as well."

The widow shook her head. "He ain't no easy man to kill."

"Neither am I," Carter answered, remembering how Zeb stormed in the sheriff's office and demanded to know if Carter stole his money. He ordered Ludlow to open the cell so he could have a talk with Carter.

Ludlow tried to tell his friend that they were already handling the problem of Carter and only expected a small share for their trouble. Maybe half.

All at once Zeb and Ludlow were arguing.

Ludlow opened the door to the cell just as Zeb pulled his gun. It happened so fast. Ludlow demanded his share. Carter darted out the door. Zeb must have fired. Carter heard the man swearing he'd get Carter before the sun set.

"Well, if you're going," the widow interrupted Carter's thoughts, "I'll pack your supplies. You'll need food and warm clothes."

"No peaches," Carter said as he finished his coffee.

"No peaches." Mrs. Abernathy laughed. "I can find you a horse over at the stable. Mosely bought a bunch from the army the other day, but he's been too drunk to count them."

TWENTY-SEVEN

October air arrived packed in a chilly dampness, but Carter paid no mind as he listened just beyond the light shining from Fat Alice's window.

"You want to go upstairs, Ranger Jacob? It might feel real good to get out of this cold. There ain't no outlaw going to come crashing into this place this late. Winter's coming on, and a bed's a warm place to be on a night like this."

Carter heard Nellie Jean from where he stood in the shadows of the porch.

"No, thanks," a low voice answered. "I'm waiting to marry you, remember. I don't want you going upstairs with no one including me before then, you hear."

Nellie Jean sighed. "Oh, all right. I was just a-hoping you were ready. Fat Alice says I won't be grown for at least another two years. That's a long time to wait downstairs."

Carter heard Nellie Jean go inside, slamming the door behind her.

Jacob laughed, then lit a cigar and said in a low, calm voice. "You still there, Stranger?"

Carter didn't answer. How could the ranger know he was standing at the corner of the porch? It was a moonless night. He'd been standing in the same spot for an hour waiting for the young ranger to came outside.

"I figure you're not out to do me harm, or you would have already been shooting." The ranger turned toward Carter. "So you might as well show yourself and say what you come to say."

Carter took a step forward. He didn't waste time with introductions. "I'm going into Hell's Lookout after Zeb Whitaker tomorrow. I talked to Riley last night, and he thought you might want to come along."

The ranger relaxed against the post on Fat Alice's boardinghouse porch. "I might. Now that Piper is safe back with her father, there's a strong chance I'll find my train robbers the same place you'll find Zeb Whitaker. A federal marshal wired me that they want to question Whitaker for a robbery and murder of a rancher near Santa Fe. He'd be mighty obliged if I showed up with the man."

Carter moved into the pale light filtering from the window. He heard a piano playing and smelled dinner cooking. Just the slight aroma of homemade bread made him miss Bailee so bad his gut twisted. He'd looked for Zeb for two weeks and all he'd done was go in circles. The old buffalo hunter seemed to have fallen off the earth. Hell's Lookout, wherever it was, would be his last hope.

The ranger pointed toward the window. "Real quiet at Fat Alice's tonight. Every night, I guess, since two sheriffs decided to homestead in her parlor. She may have to go respectable if they don't get well soon."

He tossed his cigar in the dirt past the porch. "You hunting to kill Zeb Whitaker, or help me bring him in?"

"Seeing him behind bars is good enough. I just can't let him frighten my wife any longer."

The ranger nodded. "Fair enough. We leave at dawn, Carter McKoy."

"How . . ."

Jacob grinned. "I haven't stayed alive three years as a ranger without knowing who the good guys are."

Carter moved back into the shadows. He walked silently across the tracks to where he'd made camp. Though he knew he'd be welcomed at Fat Alice's place, he couldn't bear to go inside. He needed the comfort of being alone with his thoughts of Bailee.

Tonight it had been one month since he'd married her. One month, Carter thought, the night they'd agreed that their marriage would truly start. He never would have believed one woman could come to mean so much to him in such a short time.

He should be home holding her in his arms, not dirty and cold and miles away. But he couldn't go back, couldn't rest until he knew that she was safe.

He'd seen Lacy the last few mornings. She was taking care of both sheriffs and happy to stay right where she was until Zeb was behind bars or dead. When Carter checked on her, she had a hundred questions about Bailee and he'd had to stand there and say he didn't know any of the answers. Lacy's father-in-law had wired her that even Samuel was asking about Bailee's whereabouts. Lacy told him how Bailee stepped off the train that day, going back to help him, then vanished.

Carter decided he must have missed Bailee by moments. He'd crossed the alley to Mrs. Abernathy's with the gunshot still ringing in his ears. According to Lacy, Bailee had jumped from the train and ran toward the jail at the same time.

Not bothering to build a fire, Carter rolled up in his blanket and tried to sleep. He didn't notice the cold or the hardness of the ground. The only ache that registered in his tired mind was in his heart. He needed his wife by his side.

A little after dawn Jacob Dalton stepped from Fat Alice's with two cups of coffee. He handed Carter one. "You have any idea where we're headed?"

Carter liked the ranger's honest stare and economy of words. "No," Carter answered.

"Riley swears there's a hideout about fifty miles from here, just below the caprock. Those that have seen it call it Hell's Lookout. Years ago it was little more than a line shack for sheep farmers. Now there's nothing but snakes nesting in the place. If Zeb Whitaker is still in Texas, he's probably hiding there. It would take an army to go in and dig him out from the front, but two men might be able to cross behind and drop in off the caprock."

Carter finished his coffee. He didn't want to go, but he'd seen the way Zeb looked at him. The old buffalo hunter wanted the gold he thought was his, but there was more in his stare. Zeb Whitaker wanted Carter dead. Carter blocked his path to another he wanted to kill: Bailee.

Carter wished for the thousandth time that he knew she was safe. Maybe she knew someone he didn't. Some place she could hide where Zeb would never think to look. But how could *he* ever find her?

Jacob set his coffee cup on the porch swing. "You ready to ride, farmer?"

"It's Carter," Carter corrected. He'd lived enough of his life being called names.

"Carter it is." The ranger smiled and nodded once.

They were almost the same size and age, but until this moment Carter knew the ranger hadn't considered him as an equal.

They rode west, kicking up dust in the frosty air. In the past two weeks Carter's body had grown leaner, and his skills on horseback had sharpened. He was equal to Jacob's pace.

Sheriff Riley stood at the window with Nellie Jean and watched them go. "I wouldn't want to be Zeb Whitaker."

Nellie Jean lifted her chin. "He's a dead man for sure. He don't have a chance up against my future husband and my good friend."

Riley laughed. "You giving up the nightlife, Two Bits, and settling down?"

"I ain't decided for sure. Time my chest comes in, Jacob may be a little long in the tooth. Men are like lace, I figure. Some last and others fray after a few washings. I'll have to wait and see how he does."

From almost out of sight, Carter swung the horse he'd named Traveler around and waved once to Riley.

"Take care of Bailee, if I don't . . ." he whispered, unable to finish. All his life he'd survived for no reason but to keep living. Now he had something to live for. Now was not the time to think of dying.

"Come on, Traveler," he whispered as he guided the horse with his knees. Somehow, naming the animal that Mrs. Abernathy stole for him made Carter feel closer to Bailee. She'd managed to name everything on the place but the chickens. "When we get back home, I'll buy you from Mosely." He patted the animal's neck. "Provided we get home."

Traveler rattled his reins as if he understood the promise.

TWENTY-EIGHT

THE WIND TURNED COLD ON THE PLAINS AND howled with the coyotes long into the night. Bailee tried to act as if it didn't bother her, but each day the sound wore at her nerves more and more.

Papa Farrow and his family finished the harvest. Samuel took most of the fruit to town, while Bailee spent days canning. The little storage cellar overflowed with food for the winter.

When the wind turned and blew from the north, the Gypsies became restless. It was time for them to move on. Though they wouldn't allow Bailee to pay them, they did accept her oxen and wagon laden with food as a gift. On the third day of October they left, promising to come back and visit. But their promises were hollow, carried on winter's breath.

Suddenly days that had been busy and full of conversation were silent. Except for the wind. Always the wind. Bailee told herself she was used to spending her days alone, but worry over Carter flowed through every thought.

Samuel refused to step foot inside Carter's home for more than one meal a day. He spent the rest of his time in the bunkhouse making the chairs he'd later sell in Fort Worth. Even when he joined her, Bailee soon grew tired of trying to engage him in conversation. He was a man who wore his solitude proudly.

When she first returned to the ranch, Bailee made Samuel tell her all the ways Carter protected the land. A windmill that turned only when the back gate was opened. An apple that fell off a shelf in both the barn and by the cabin door when someone crossed the front road. Dirt plowed regularly to mark any footprints near the house. The way the trees circled, confusing anyone who tried to enter from the creek side of Carter's land.

There were others, Samuel admitted, but he'd never asked about them.

Words that Carter whispered to her kept haunting Bailee's sleep. *There's a safe place at the ranch. It took me three winters to build. Even Samuel doesn't know of the passage.*

On the sixth of October Bailee locked the door against the night air and returned to sit by the fire. She'd had Samuel latch the vent space Carter crawled through before. She didn't want to mistake him for an intruder again.

She'd been married a month, but there was no Carter to share her bed. He'd vanished, and with each day that passed she realized he might never come back. Maybe he killed Ludlow and figured he'd hang for the crime, so he lit out for California. Maybe he witnessed the murder, and knew if he came forward, he'd suffer the same fate.

Carter wasn't a coward, Bailee reminded herself. And he wasn't a fool. If he said there was somewhere on the ranch where she'd be safe, then she'd find it. And there she'd wait. She'd wait forever, if need be.

At first she had roamed around as if on an egg hunt looking for the prize. That didn't work. Then she divided up the ranch and searched a different location each day. If Samuel thought her mad, he didn't comment.

Finally she'd tried logic. Carter had called it a passage. He said he built it in winter, so that eliminated all areas outside. He also told her he did it without Samuel knowing. That crossed off the barn and bunkhouse.

Bailee rested her head against the back of her chair and studied the fire as she thought. The passage had to be big enough for him to pass through, and it had to start from somewhere in the house.

She'd scrubbed every inch of the floors and walls except in the cellar. Calmly she stood and walked to the cellar, lifting the lamp from the kitchen table as she passed.

When she reached the cellar, she sat the lamp down and carefully moved her hands along the walls. No shelf moved. Nothing was out of place.

She'd almost given up when she rested her hand on the wall and looked around for an idea.

The wall shifted slightly. A movement she might not have noticed if she hadn't been searching. Her heart pounded in her throat as she tried again.

It didn't give when she pushed, but slid easily sideways. Suddenly Bailee saw a shadowy passage tall enough for Carter to walk through without having to bend.

She'd found his private home. On this night she'd keep her promise to sleep in his bed, even if he wasn't there with her.

• • •

Carter closed his eyes almost a hundred miles away and thought of himself walking the very passage that eluded Bailee. He could feel the wood against his fingertips as he tapped his way through his secret rooms. The cool, earthy smell filled his nostrils, telling him he was home. The feel of his books. The silence within his rooms.

But when he opened his eyes, he wasn't home at all. He was lying in the mud a quarter of a mile from a group of shacks known as Hell's Lookout. The buildings were so run-down and smelly it was impossible to tell which one was the outhouse. He and Jacob Dalton watched all day and counted twelve men coming and going from the place.

Dalton seemed to think those were good odds, twelve to two, which had Carter questioning the man's reason.

They moved closer about sundown. The men inside the little settlement started drinking soon after noon when a woman pulling two mules arrived with supplies. She must have stayed willingly, for every now and then Carter heard her laughter clank through the night air.

"We give them time to get drunk," Jacob whispered, "and then I go in from the back and have a look around. If these are the bank robbers, they won't have bothered to clean up. I'll probably find the baggage car's safe right where they cracked it open."

Carter wanted to say all he was looking for was Zeb Whitaker. Maybe they should go after help before advancing on all twelve men. But the ranger didn't seem to think he needed any further assistance. Jacob had opened the corral gate when they'd moved closer at sundown, and most of the horses were probably halfway back to Childress by now.

"If there's trouble or you hear gunfire, ride in shooting.

That will distract them enough for me to get away."

"You say you've lived three years as a ranger?" Carter had to ask. With this plan Jacob would be lucky to live the night.

When the ranger had suggested riding their horses down a cliff just before dawn, Carter thought he was kidding, until Jacob kicked his mount and began the slide. Carter followed and now figured if he lived through the bone-jarring descent, he could make it through the night.

"Trust me. We've got surprise on our side." Jacob fought to keep his laugh low.

Since surprise didn't carry a canon, Carter wasn't overjoyed to have it on his side. But the ranger was set on his plan, what little there was of it. So they waited as the men inside drank and the rest of the horses in the corral wandered off.

About midnight Ranger Jacob Dalton slipped into the camp, with Carter waiting fifty feet away in the last cluster of trees near the buildings. For a while Carter listened for the slightest sound that Jacob had given himself away. But all he heard were shouts from the men and the woman's laughter.

At one point Carter decided if he had to start firing, he'd shoot the woman first, for her laughter grated like sand in his veins. After living off the land for days, he was in no mood to be kind.

Carter thought he saw Zeb Whitaker step out on the porch of one of the shacks, but hair and hides seemed to be the dress in this place.

The man on the porch lit a cigar. The light only flickered across his features for a moment, but Carter knew he'd found his man.

All at once gunfire rattled from the back of one of the

buildings. Shouts followed. Anger! Surprise! Pain!

Carter swung up on his horse and grabbed the reins of Jacob's mount. "Into battle!" he shouted at Traveler. With a loud yell he hoped would echo, Carter charged into the cluster of buildings at full gallop, not realizing he hadn't pulled his weapon until he was ten feet from the shacks.

The man on the porch stormed forward, prepared to face Carter head on. But the ground was muddy. The huge man twisted, almost falling, just as he fired, sending lead blazing into the air.

Carter reached him in a heartbeat. He jumped off his horse, frightening Traveler even more than the gunshot had. The horse reared. Carter hit the mud, flat on his back, clawing to free his Colt from the holster.

As if in slow motion he watched Traveler's hoof swing into Zeb Whitaker's head. The big man jerked backward, his weapon raised to fire at Carter.

Carter scrambled to his feet. In three steps he was standing over Zeb. He grabbed a handful of Zeb's matted hair and raised the scoundrel's head from the mud to the light spilling from the house. Zeb Whitaker gave no response. The horse had knocked him out cold.

"You got him!" Jacob shouted as he fought his way out the door. "I came up clean looking for the train's vault. Load Whitaker up and lets get out of here." Jacob was easily winning a fight with two drunks as he moved toward Carter. The drunks seemed to think running at the ranger until he slugged them was a grand way to fight.

Carter lugged Zeb's body over the woman's horse, left tied to a dilapidated hitching post. He bound the buffalo hunter's legs and hands beneath the animal. In pulling the reins free, he demolished the post and set the two mules loose. They kicked and ran, disappearing into the night with the supplies the woman hadn't unloaded.

"Let's ride!" Jacob shouted as he raised his gun in the air and fired, sending any remaining horses scattering and any outlaw left alive rushing for cover. "Since there's no evidence of the train robbery, we must be in the wrong rats' nest."

Suddenly a woman's scream outsounded even the gunfire. When she paused, she swore that she'd kill everyone.

"Hurry." Jacob looked worried for the first time. "She'll be out any minute."

Carter had to dance with his mount to catch the stirrups. He had no doubt this was also Traveler's first battle.

Carter finally swung up and grabbed the reins of Zeb's horse. They galloped away into the cool night.

They thundered across the open country as if the devil chased them. Carter struggled with the reins of Zeb's horse. The animal was half wild and didn't take to a lead well. Carter hadn't had time to put on his gloves, so the leather strips cut into his hands.

With the first light of dawn, the ranger slowed, searching the horizon to see if they'd been followed. Zeb's low moans and swearing had polluted the silence for a few hours, but both Carter and Jacob acted as if they weren't hearing a thing.

Jacob suddenly laughed. "That was great fun! Let's go back and do it again tonight. Those small-time cattle rustlers never knew what hit them. It'll take days for them to round up their horses and sober up enough to try and figure out what happened."

Carter didn't comment then, or later when Jacob tried to make him a hero, claiming he had Zeb already beaten on the ground by the time the ranger could get outside to help.

Carter tried to deny it, but Jacob continued telling the story for his own amusement, adding to it each time. Carter McKoy would be legend in another few tellings.

When they reached the outskirts of Childress, Carter said his good-byes. He knew the ranger and Riley would take care of Zeb Whitaker from this point. All he had on his mind was turning toward home.

He knew the way. He'd made it a few weeks before in the rain. Only this time Carter didn't push himself or his horse. There was no hurry. Lacy had checked almost daily with her father-in-law; no one had seen Bailee. If she wasn't there waiting for him, his home was just somewhere to rest. It was no longer where his heart dwelled.

When he rode onto his land, he took a long breath, welcoming the smells. As before, he crossed the creek and came up by the orchard. The harvest had been completed and the trunks of the trees banked with straw against the cold. In the short time he'd been gone, the trees had turned color, dying off to winter.

He saw no light from the house and only a small one from the bunkhouse. Samuel was still here. He'd be gone before the last leaves fell.

Carter led his horse across the yard, knowing he wouldn't wake the old man. The barn was empty. Papa Farrow and his people had moved on.

Rubbing Traveler down, Carter caught himself talking to the animal, thanking him. "You're fit to be named after a general's horse," Carter said as he gave the horse an extra scoop of oats.

All seemed in order. All except for Bailee not being here. At the washstand by the well, he stripped and washed. He couldn't stand the thought of putting back on any of his filthy clothes, so he wrapped a towel around himself. If Samuel should wake, he'd think Carter had reverted back to the days when he used to do the wash naked.

Carter knew the house would be locked. He hadn't had time to take a key those weeks ago when Wheeler pulled him to the barn. Now, he felt along the porch railing for the extra one. Henry the Eighth sauntered over to him in welcome and waited, expecting Carter to rub his ears. Carter frowned, then obliged.

When the door swung open, the warmth of the house surprised him. Someone had been there recently. For a moment he thought it might be Bailee. But she would have heard him. She would have run to greet him.

He glanced back to the bunkhouse, wondering if Samuel might have been inside. But if he had, why wouldn't he have stayed there, and not also had to heat the bunkhouse?

Carter checked the door to the bedroom. Maybe Lacy was here? She'd had time to travel back here since he'd seen her.

But the door was open, and he saw the outline of an empty bed. No one was there.

Everything looked to be in place. His stack of clothes were missing from the corner of the pie safe where Bailee put them when she finished washing them. Maybe Samuel had given them to the Gypsies.

Maybe he'd given them Bailee's wagon, Carter thought, remembering it was missing from the barn. Or maybe she'd gone.

He glanced at her china, her tablecloth, her candlesticks. She hadn't left him. At least not willingly. She wouldn't have forgotten her things. He allowed himself to breathe, and the weeks of tiredness flowed into his bones.

He crossed and lifted the cellar door, thinking tonight he would finally be able to sleep in his silent rooms. And, as every night, Bailee would be there beside him, if only in his mind.

TWENTY-NINE

Bailee heard a slight tap, first near the opening of the passage, then at the entrance to Carter's bedroom. The trifling noise would never have awakened her if she hadn't slept in total silence every night since she found Carter's underground rooms.

Snuggling deeper beneath the covers, she listened. Her eyes were wide open, but she couldn't even make out a shadow in the blackness.

From the moment she found his private rooms, she'd felt Carter near. She understood him so much clearer. And she missed him far greater.

It occurred to her that maybe she should wait until Carter brought her into his underground world, but when she found the passage, she could wait no longer. She needed to feel him with her. Though he might never say the words, she knew he loved her, and somehow in the darkness she believed it was true.

So she'd moved her things down beside his, rearranging his world to include her. She'd thumbed through his books and spent hours looking at a signing book his mother must have drawn that rested beside his bed. With simple strokes Carter's mother had shown the hand movements for hundreds of words.

The rooms were safe and welcoming, until now.

Something moved near the bookshelves, as though tripping over the carpetbag Bailee hadn't found a place for yet. Something fell to the floor with a wet plop. Something breathed.

Bailee froze. She was not alone.

Frantically she retraced her steps. She'd locked the door, hadn't she? She'd closed the trapdoor when she'd walked down the steps to the cellar. At least she thought she had. She'd closed the passageway. Of course she had.

Or had she?

Could the intruder be an animal that had somehow burrowed into the walls? Or a mouse? Mice found their way everywhere.

She was almost sick with fear when the side of the bed gave to a sudden weight. If it were an animal, it was huge. And it was between her and the lamp.

Carter stretched his arm out and relaxed into the softness of his own bed a moment before a scream three inches from his ear frightened him out of a few years of his life.

He was up, fumbling for matches as the scream came again, echoing off the walls. It didn't occur to him that he was totally nude until after the match flickered to light.

Bailee stared at him with huge frightened eyes, and he stared back until the match burned his finger.

They were in blackness once more. Silence. He listened. She didn't even breathe.

"I'm sorry," he finally managed to stammer as he

reached for his clothes only to find them gone from the peg where they were kept.

He stumbled over what might be a rug where no rug had ever been before and opened the top draw of his dresser. Lace and silk greeted his touch, not cotton as he'd expected.

He pulled open the second drawer. The same.

At the third drawer he decided he must have somehow crossed through the wrong passage. This wasn't his home. Nothing was in the right place.

Trousers flew from nowhere and slapped him across the face. "Thank you," he mumbled as he untangled them from around his neck.

"You're welcome," came a whisper from the blackness.

He pulled on his trousers before she found the matches and lit the lamp.

He wanted to pull her to him and hold her so tight she'd know that he'd never let her go. But he didn't. He couldn't. She was mixed in with every thought he had, every breath he took, yet he couldn't cross the three feet that now stood between them. He'd seen the fear in her eyes.

"You're safe." Bailee pulled the covers close around her. "I was worried." She didn't look up at him.

"Zeb's behind bars," Carter said, thinking he should tell her that first. The beauty of her made his mind foggy. She was even more beautiful than the picture he held in his memory. How could he have ever thought her plain?

"I missed you so," she whispered. "But I felt near you once I found your passage."

"I didn't kill Ludlow." He didn't want her still worrying about that. Maybe she thought he was a killer? Maybe that's why he saw such fear when she first looked at him.

"It took me some getting used to, the darkness and all."

"The ranger helped me find Whitaker, and they're going to charge Zeb with Ludlow's murder." Maybe she hadn't noticed he'd been naked. He figured his odds were about a million to one, but maybe if they just talked, everything would be fine.

"Lacy's still in Childress as far as I know," he said. Bailee didn't seem to be listening.

"Since this is where you sleep, this is where I'll sleep." She played with a thread on the quilt.

Her hair shielded part of her face from him, and he could almost feel the softness in his hand. But he couldn't touch her. Not until he knew she wasn't afraid of him.

"I'm the only witness. So I'll have to testify." Maybe she thought he was still nude. Maybe that was why she hadn't looked at him.

"Our month is up," she said, not paying any attention to what he was talking about. "It has been for several nights."

He watched her, suddenly aware of what she'd said. "Bailee?" he whispered. "Look at me."

Bailee smiled, glad he'd finally started to hear. She stretched her hand toward his as he sat on the bed. The sight of him was enough to stop her heart. His beard had grown an inch since she'd seen him. He looked leaner, more tanned even in the flicker of the lamp. But his eyes were still the same wonderful shade of blue and they still made her feel as if they could see all the way to her soul.

He was the one man who made her feel, who made her alive. She wouldn't stay with him because she had to marry him to be out of jail, or for any other reason. She would stay with him because without him there was no life inside her heart.

"Our month is up," she whispered once more.

Carter placed her fingers over his hand and signed a single sign.

"I love you too," she answered.

"How did you know what I said?" He moved his fingers along her arm trying to convince himself she was truly with him.

"I listened with my heart." Her gaze locked with his.

All at once any space between them was too much. He pulled her close, kissing her with a touch so light, so cherishing.

She curled into his embrace, seeking his warmth as he surrounded her with his arms. For a while he cradled her gently, touching her hair, tasting her lips, caressing as though each touch was newfound and a first.

Her hands moved over him hungry for the feel of him. They'd both made love too many times in their minds. They needed more, far more, tonight. She couldn't find the words to tell him how much he meant to her, but slowly she began to show him.

When he straightened to pull off his trousers and blow out the lamp, he heard her giggle softly and knew no matter what mistakes he made in making love to her tonight, it would still be perfect.

"I want to love you by touch," he whispered against her ear. "My mind would be overloaded with senses if I could also see you."

She laughed against his cheek. "I've already seen quite a lot of you already." She'd never be able to tell him how shocking—and beautiful—the sight of him had been.

He silenced her with a deep kiss that left him starved for more. Awkwardly he pulled off her gown and lowered his body against hers. The silk of her skin against his made his heart pound so hard he was sure he bruised his ribs from the inside.

Slowly, as he'd longed to do, he moved down her body, kissing, touching, tasting. She was shy at first, pulling the covers, trying to move away. When she hesitated, he returned to her lips and kissed her until her body grew warm and needy for his caress. Then he continued his journey of discovery. He listened to her every sigh, noticed her every move as he learned to please her.

When there was no more resistance, no more hesitation, no more shyness, he parted her legs and came home to his wife.

She arched her back and cried out, then wrapped her arms tightly around his neck and held on as they rode passion's journey together.

When he collapsed on top of her, neither had enough energy to speak. Carter lay drowning in the wonderful way her nearness surrounded him so completely. He didn't know or care where he was. He raised slightly and pushed her damp hair from her face, wishing that he'd left the light on so he could see her now.

"Carter?" She stretched beneath him. "Do you think we did it right?"

He smiled. "I'm not sure. We may have to try again." He rolled from her and pulled the covers over them both, then slid his hand beneath the quilts and spread his fingers wide over her abdomen.

For a while she lay perfectly still, absorbing the feel of his hand moving in slow motion over her. Sometimes he just felt her, sometimes his fingers moved in sign.

"Talk to me, Carter," she finally whispered.

He trailed his fingers between her breasts. "I like the way you feel."

"Good," she answered, running her hand along his rib cage. "I like the way you feel, also."

"I've missed you by my side." He kissed her gently, knowing she was waiting for him to tell her more. "I want you next to me."

"For all my life," she answered, knowing it may have taken her a month, but with her words she'd just sealed her wedding vows. "I'll be your wife."

They made love again, slower this time, joining both bodies and hearts. When they collapsed in each other's arms, Bailee was too exhausted to move. She drifted into a perfect sleep. Safe and warm and home.

Carter moved his hand against hers.

"I love you, too," she whispered.

And felt him answer, "Forever."

EPILOGUE

February, 1884

DEAR FATHER. BAILEE STARTED THE LETTER FOR THE fifth time. "I can't write him again. I just can't," she mumbled. She had little hope her father would reply to this letter when he hadn't answered the other two she'd sent.

Carter looked up from the wooden chest he'd been building and tried to decide if she was talking to him or herself again. With a winter storm threatening, he chose to move his latest project into the living area so that he didn't have to keep fighting the icy wind crossing to the bunkhouse.

The thought of getting snowed in made him smile. He had plenty of firewood, food, and Bailee.

She stared at him and wrinkled her brow.

Before he could think of an answer to her comment, the apple tumbled off the shelf by the door. Bailee no longer panicked at the signal. In the months since Zeb Whitaker went to prison, folks had started stopping by. The sheriff, Lacy, when the roads were clear, the neighbors. At first Carter had stood on the porch as if on guard, but finally he'd welcomed them in for short visits. Come in for coffee, he'd say, always making her smile.

Now, out of habit, Carter reached for his rifle and walked to the door.

Bailee picked up the apple and began cleaning up the writing supplies. She knew the letter would wait another day, another week. Even when mailed, it would probably be like the others, never read or answered. With each day her father was proving he'd meant what he had said when he told her she was dead to him. She could almost picture him tossing the unopened letter in the wastebasket as he entered his house.

"Carter!" came a shout over the wind. "Put down that rifle you got pointed at my heart and unlock the door."

"Sheriff Riley," Bailee said unnecessarily as Carter unbolted the door.

She grabbed her shawl and followed him to the porch.

"Welcome," Carter managed to say as he held the sheriff's mount.

"Come in, Sheriff," Bailee added. "We've hot coffee."

"I've no time, thank you." Riley was bundled up in a mixture of wool and hides. "I'm just passing by on my way home. Lacy asked me to drop off your mail if I made it out this way." He handed Carter a packet. "I'll stop in come spring and visit. Right now I just want to make it back to town before the snow hits."

He stared at Bailee for one last second. "Still want to be married to this man? I haven't had time to mail the license to Austin, but I will soon as I get back."

Bailee grinned. "I'm his wife for life, Riley. You can stop asking."

The sheriff nodded. "Take care of her, Carter."

Carter moved close to Bailee and waved the old man on his way. She may have taught him to tolerate company, but his favorite time was always when they left.

While she hung up her shawl, Carter slit the twine on the bundle of letters. It had been almost a month since he'd traveled to town to pick up the mail. Flyers, a note from a bookstore, a letter from Piper's father, and one letter addressed to Bailee Grace Moore McCoy.

Carter handed it to her without a word. For a while he didn't think she planned to open it. She just stared at the bold handwriting.

"It's from my father," Bailee finally whispered. Slowly she opened the envelope as if unwrapping a package and read the single sheet of paper.

Carter watched her out of the corner of his eye as he went back to his work.

She must have read the note ten times before she finally crossed the room and knelt in front of him. "My father wants me to come home."

He fought for control. He wasn't sure his heart would beat if she left, but he didn't know how to tell her how much he loved her. "Will you go?" he asked without meeting her eyes.

Bailee laughed as if he'd said something funny. "No, dear. I am home."

Turn the page for a preview
of Jodi Thomas's romance telling Sarah's story

Coming soon from Jove Books

ONE

Texas 1883

SAM GATLIN REMOVED HIS RAIN-SOAKED SHIRT THEN folded his trousers neatly over the chair before he turned and noticed his new wife had slipped from the bed. She'd disappeared, along with one of the Colts from the holster he'd hung on the rusty bedpost moments before.

The pale lightning of a dying storm blinked in the small room offering him enough light to see. Far away thunder only echoed, barely a rumble through the night as it blended with the tinny piano music of the bar across the street.

He was bone tired, so cold he would never get warm and now, he had lost the woman he just married. She couldn't have gone far, not in these cramped quarters. He stood between where he had set her atop the covers and the door leading into the hotel's hallway.

She was either under the bed, or folded into one of the dresser drawers.

It was little comfort to discover his new bride might be

insane as well as armed. But bad luck had been running a blue streak through his life lately, so he did not bother to be surprised by the possibility.

He knelt on one knee and stared into the shadows beneath the iron railing of the bed frame.

"Now look, miss . . ." he began, knowing she was no longer a *miss* but forgetting the name the sheriff used several hours ago when Sam paid her fine, got her out of jail, and married her. "There's no need for you to hide."

You would think she'd have the good sense to be grateful that he coughed up the money to save her from a life behind bars. But she hadn't said a word since they left Cedar Point. He might as well have bought a china doll for all the company she had been on the trip.

The barrel of his Colt poked out from under the bed.

"It's been a long night," he mumbled without moving. They'd driven through the worst storm he had seen in years in a flimsy rented buggy. "I'd like to get some sleep in the few hours we have left before dawn."

No answer.

"Lady." *Lady* didn't sound right. A man can't go around calling his bride *lady*. Sam straightened his large frame hating the way his body always ached when he had to jam himself into a buggy. Man was meant to ride on a horse, not behind one. If he had been alone today, he would have braved the weather on horseback. But his new bride looked so weak a dozen raindrops would have probably drowned her.

Sam decided to take the direct approach. "Get out from under that bed, lady. The sheriff said you've been married before. You should know by now what's expected on a wedding night. Stop this foolishness and climb under those covers."

The barrel pointed at his heart. It occurred to Sam how her first husband might have met his end.

She had looked like an angel when she'd stepped up and pulled his name from a hat back in Cedar Point. He'd won. A bride for the price of her fine. He thought it fair when he read about the wife lottery. Three young women had confessed to a murder, but the sheriff hadn't found the body they'd admitted to killing. So, in the name of justice and because the county couldn't afford to hold them indefinitely, Sheriff Riley held a lottery.

"I'm not goin' to hurt you." Sam tried to sound kind, but kindness was not something he wore easily. "I've never hurt a woman in my life," he added, then decided that didn't make him sound much better.

He thought he heard her sniffle. If she didn't show some sense they would both catch pneumonia. The room offered little warmth, only a block from the icy wind. The owner downstairs laughed when Sam asked if the room had a fireplace or a tub.

"Come out and tell me what's the matter," Sam said like he wasn't too tired to care. He already knew the problem. The lady figured out she truly married him and would have to look at him every day for the rest of her life. All six-feet-three, two hundred pounds of him. And if his size didn't frighten her, wait until she found out what he did for a living.

He pulled his wet shirt back on hoping to cover a few of the scars across his chest before she noticed them.

"You are not going to touch me," came a whisper from beneath the bed.

"Well, of course I'm going to touch you. That's what husbands and wives do. They touch each other. Everyone knows that, lady." Maybe she was simple-minded. Sam remembered old man Harris's daughters who'd grown up down the road from him. They were all fine looking girls, who developed early and fully, but there wasn't a complete brain among them. Their pa's only hope of getting them married off was to encourage it while the girls were too young and shy to say more than a few words.

Sam hadn't thought about his bride being turned that way when he decided to marry. He just thought about how much she looked like an angel with her pale blond hair and light-blue eyes, and how loneliness trailed behind him like a heavy shadow. It had been so long since he'd said more than a few words to anyone, or ate a meal across from another person. He wasn't sure he knew how to act. Half the people in Texas thought him the devil, so why not marry an angel?

He tried again. "Look, miss, if you don't want me to touch you, I won't for tonight. I give you my word. Come on out from under the bed." He thought of adding that he wasn't all that interested in anything but sleep, but he didn't want to hurt her feelings.

She didn't move.

"You could keep the Colt if you like. Just for tonight, of course."

The shadow shifted. "What's my name?"

He'd been afraid she might ask that question at some point. "Mrs. Sam Gatlin." He smiled, proud of himself.

"My first name?"

He didn't answer. There was nothing he could say that would hide the fact he'd been only half-listening to the sheriff who married them. That he had been staring at her and that had taken most of his attention.

Sam walked over to the chair and started putting on his

trousers since it didn't look like they would be crawling beneath the covers anytime soon.

The wet wool had grown cold and stiff. He tossed his trousers back over the chair and grabbed one of the blankets from the bed.

Sam wrapped it around his waist. The barrel of the Colt shook. He guessed she was as cold as he. "Come on out, Mrs. Gatlin, and get under the covers. I won't come near you if that's what you want." His new bride made no sense. Why would she marry him and leave town with him if she didn't plan to be his wife? She acted like he had abducted her and forced her here.

As he pulled the blanket up over his shoulders, she slipped out from beneath the far side of the bed.

"Sarah," she said. "My name's Sarah and I won't hesitate to kill you if you come closer, Mr. Gatlin."

Sam sat down on the chair and folded his arms, locking the ends of the blanket around him. "You've killed before, have you?"

"That's right." She lifted her chin. "A man we met on the way to Cedar Point." She took a deep breath as though she'd said what she was about to say one too many times in this lifetime. "Because we were three women, Zeb Whitaker tried to steal our wagon and take my friend Lacy away with him. We all three clubbed him with a board Bailee brought to Texas for protection. So, we all killed him."

The angel lady fascinated Sam with her sunshine hair and her soft southern voice. She was so beautiful, even now, damp and tired and barely able to stand while she confessed. He found it hard to believe such a creature could swing a board hard enough to hurt anyone.

"Why didn't you shoot him?" he said more to keep her talking than out of interest.

She slipped into the bed, covered herself, then wiggled out of her wet dress. "I would have if I'd had a gun, but the wagon master took all our weapons when he threw us off the wagon train. I guess he figured we'd be dead soon and didn't want to waste a rifle."

Her dress hit the floor with a wet plop.

She was good, he thought. Her story became more unbelievable by the second, but she wasn't backing down. He'd hunted outlaws who were like that, so good at telling lies they made people want to believe them even when proven false.

"What wagon train?" It wouldn't take him long to trip her up and find the truth.

"The last one to leave Independence for California last summer. They called it the Roland Train with a wagon master by the name of Broken-Hand Harrison. I don't remember much more. First my husband got the fever a few weeks out, then my baby. They both died while we were moving across Kansas." A tear rolled down her pale china face. "If Bailee and Lacy hadn't saved me, I would have died too. I had a fever so bad I didn't care one way or the other if I woke up every morning."

"Bailee and Lacy?"

"The two women kicked off the wagon train with me. Broken-Hand thought I had a fever that would spread, so he didn't want anyone around me, but Bailee let me ride in her wagon." Her words slowed as she warmed beneath the blankets. "Everyone figured Lacy for a witch just because all the folks she nursed had died, except me. Some said she danced with the moon, but I never saw her do that."

Sam watched his wife lean her head against the pillow and close her eyes. The sheriff mentioned something about her feeling better since she'd had regular meals, but she looked as fragile as cottonwood seed blowing in the wind.

"What about the one named Bailee?" he said louder than he'd intended.

She jerked as if in the moment while she had paused, she'd fallen asleep. "The wagon master thought Bailee killed someone back east, but she's a real nice person, even if she does have this habit of clubbing men when she's angry. Maybe whoever she killed needed killing as bad as Zeb Whitaker did."

The angel closed her eyes again. Sam watched her grip on the gun relax. He waited a few minutes, then stood and carefully lifted the weapon from her hand and pulled the covers over her shoulder.

For a moment, he thought of returning to the chair. But the empty space beside her invited him.

He spread his blanket atop her and moved to the other side of the bed. When he slipped beneath the covers, he smiled for the first time in a long while.

Come morning, he would probably face the wrath of Sarah for taking up half of her bed. He almost looked forward to the clash. But right now, in the cold dampness of the tiny room with music filtering in from the saloon across the street, he felt almost at peace lying by her side.

Sam turned his head and studied her in the shadows. She was too beautiful to be real. The lady had no idea yet, that she didn't have a chance of bending him around her finger. No woman ever had, no woman ever would. Within a few days he would let her know how their marriage was going to be. He would set the rules and she'd follow. She'd give him a home to come to, a place to rest between battles, and he'd keep her safe. She'd do his cooking and cleaning, and he'd see that she had enough to eat. What more could either of them want from the other?

Sarah shifted, moving toward his warmth. In sleep she lay her hand atop his heart.

All thought drained from his mind as frail, slender fingers slid through the hair on his chest and then relaxed as though her touch had found a home.

Breathe, he reminded himself. Breathe.

TWO

Sarah Andrews stretched beneath the layers of blankets and opened her eyes to sunshine filtered through ragged curtains. For a moment, she had no idea where she was. Shadows dominated the room, except for where one intruding beam of light sliced across the dusty floor to her bed. The air smelled musty and damp, as though the place had been shut away for a time.

She listened as she had all her life. Listened for the day's approach. "Be still," she told herself. "Don't move. Don't make a sound and you might hear dawn tiptoe in."

Granny Veasey, a neighbor near where Sarah grew up, whispered once that if Sarah sat still long enough, she could hear the changes in the world, the changes in her life. And Sarah tried. She always tried, yet she could never hear them. She sensed change coming, sometimes she swore she almost tasted it, but she never heard anything. Not dawn tiptoeing, or spring yawning, or age lurking.

Granny Veasey was a crazy old fool for believing such

things. But, listening became a habit with Sarah, just the same.

She stretched, enjoying the silence. Yesterday had been endless. First, she endured being raffled-off in the sheriff's lottery. Then a strange man with dark hair and black eyes swept her away, and the sheriff, her friends, even the town melted in the rain.

Sarah glanced around the room, just in case the dark-haired man hid somewhere in the shadowy corners. "No," she said to herself. "I'm alone. Probably abandoned again."

It had become a way of life for her. When she had been only a few days old, someone left her on Harriet Rainy's steps. Sarah imagined her mother had been the one and how she must have held her close one last time before she disappeared. Her mother might have prayed that whoever lived inside the farmhouse would open their hearts to a child, not knowing that Harriet Rainy didn't have a heart.

Years later, Sarah thought she finally found a place to belong when she married Frank Andrews. A family. The dream of a home of her own. But within a year he succumbed to a fever. Even the baby she delivered shortly before Frank's death hadn't stayed with her on this earth. Her tiny daughter left before Sarah had the strength to give her child a name.

A few weeks later, Broken-Hand Harrison deposited her, and two other women, in the middle of the wagon trail to find their way back to civilization. However, after being in Texas for days, Sarah felt sure she was nowhere near finding a civilized world.

Now her new husband, a man named Sam Gatlin, had abandoned her in a shabby hotel room.

It had been raining when they stopped last night, but she'd seen what little there was to see of the town. A few stores, a two-story hotel, a saloon and a livery. When she asked the clerk the name of the place, he'd said no one had bothered with a name. The local resident added that the mercantile had once been a trading post for the first cattle drivers and buffalo hunters. Back then everyone called it the Scott's Stash, but no one thought that was a proper name.

Slipping from the bed, Sarah searched the room. Her husband had taken everything, even the wet dress she'd dropped on the floor beside the bed. Only her tattered, muddy shoes remained.

She didn't have to be still and listen to life's changes. They shouted at her this morning. Her situation would have to get better before she could die. She wasn't about to be buried in her worn petticoat with so many patched holes the hem looked like cheap lace.

"I should just kill myself," she mumbled old Harriet Rainy's favorite refrain. But without a gun or knife, Sarah would have to jump out the second floor window and drag herself back upstairs, over and over, before the ten foot fall finally broke her neck.

Last night she should have shot the cowboy who married her while she held his Colt in her hand. What kind of man chooses a wife from a jail cell? He either had something seriously wrong with him, or he was as dumb as kindling. If she had shot him during the storm, folks might have thought it thunder. Maybe she could have escaped with his guns and sold them. Or robbed a bank, assuming she could find one in this town called Used-to-be-called-the-Scott's-Stash. Now that she found herself on the path to a life of crime, Sarah saw no need to stop.

She tried to remember what Sam Gatlin looked like. Tall, very tall. And strong. He'd carried her as though she were made of straw. And mean, she decided. He definitely had a mean look about him. And eyes so dark they looked black when he watched her. His jaw was square and set. She'd bet a smile never crawled across his face.

Sarah fell back on the bed. She'd married the devil. It was her punishment for tricking Frank Andrews into marrying her when she knew she didn't love him. He'd been a good man, he deserved more than a wife who cringed every time he touched her. She hadn't even cried when he died. What kind of heartless woman doesn't cry when her husband dies?

Sarah shook her head. "Me." She answered her own question as she continued analyzing her crimes.

"Then I clubbed Zeb Whitaker," she mumbled. Killing a man, even a worthless one like Whitaker, couldn't be a good thing to do. Now, her sentence would be spending the rest of her life married to a cold, heartless man who stole her one dress. With her luck, she'd live a long life.

There was no choice for Sarah other than to believe that Harriet Rainy had been right. Maybe she was a worthless nothing who washed up on the porch one night during a storm.

Someone shouted from down the hall.

Sarah listened. A woman swore and ordered a man out of her room. Footsteps suddenly thundered toward Sarah's door.

She panicked and pulled the covers over her head. Maybe he wouldn't get into her room. Maybe, if he did, he wouldn't notice her beneath the covers.

The door creaked open. Someone stomped in.

Sarah tried to be perfectly still. Maybe if she didn't

breathe the intruder would simply go away.

"Mrs. Gatlin?" came a man's voice that sounded vaguely familiar. "I hope this is the right place and that lump in the bed is my wife. I forgot to look at the room number when I left and guessing which room is not the healthiest game to play around this place."

Sarah peeked out from under the covers. Sure enough, there he was, the demon she'd married. He didn't look any less frightening in daylight than he had last night. So big, she could cut him in half and still have two fair-sized husbands.

When she didn't say a word, he tossed her the bundle he carried.

"Your dress was ruined, so I got you another one." He watched her closely with his black eyes.

"Thank you," she whispered as she glared down at the plain brown dress with not even a touch of lace at the collar. It reminded her of old Harriet Rainy's clothes, simply cut, made of coarse linsey-woolsey. Harriet always combined cotton for the warp yarns in the loom and wool for the weft. Serviceable fabric. Warm. Scratchy. Ugly.

Sarah didn't want to put it on. Afraid that if she did, she might somehow come an inch closer to sharing old Harriet's hatred for life.

"They didn't have much of a selection." Her new husband waited for her to respond. "It'll be warm. We need to get going."

She couldn't bring herself to touch the material. Somehow, an inch at a time, she'd finally sunk to the bottom. She had nothing, not even her own clothes to wear.

A tear slid down her cheek. She still had her pride. What little belongings she'd gathered from her first marriage had been burned when the people on the wagon train thought Frank was sick with the fever. The dress she'd worn last night was all she owned and it was little more than a rag. But it was better than this.

"Thank you for the offer, but please bring me back my dress. I'll wash it. My dress will do fine."

Sam Gatlin raised an eyebrow and looked like he might argue. "I can afford to buy my wife a new dress."

"Not this one," Sarah whispered. "I won't wear this one." How could she ever tell him about the old woman who raised her? She barely knew his name. She'd never be able to describe memories of running to Harriet Rainy and folding into the skirt of her scratchy dress, only to have the old woman jerk her up by the arm and slap her. "I'll give you something to cry about," Harriet would shout. "I'll show you fear."

Sarah steadied herself, bracing for a blow. He looked like the kind of man who would beat his wife. If so, she might as well find out right now.

To her surprise, he turned and walked out of the room without another word. Sarah pulled a blanket over her shoulders and ran to the window in time to watch him go into the saloon across the street.

He's a drunk, my devil husband, she thought. That was plain. What kind of man goes into a place like that when the sun isn't even high in the sky? Frank Andrews might have bored her to death some days with his talk of farming, but he never drank.

She looked at the dress still spread across the bed. If she put it on now, she could run. Who knew how many miles she could be away before he sobered up enough to notice?

Moving closer to the bed, she stared at the dress. It had been handmade by someone without skill. She was foolish not to put the garment on with the room freezing. But she couldn't. If she did, she'd disappear.

Curling into a blanket, Sarah sat on the uneven window ledge watching clouds crowd out the sun. Noises from the other rooms drifted around her, but she paid them no mind. She didn't care what happened in this no-name town.

Sarah drifted to sleep, leaning her head against the rain-cooled windowpane.

She longed for the dreams that took her away as they always had. Dreams of color and light.

A tap sounded on the door, startling her. When she jerked, she almost toppled off the window ledge.

Stumbling, Sarah hurried to the door. "Who is it?" She knew it wasn't her husband, he would have just turned the knob and entered. That is, if he remembered the room number.

"Let me in, hon," a female voice whispered from the other side of the door. "It's Denver Jones. I'm the owner of the saloon across the street."

Sarah knew no Denver Jones, but she opened the door a few inches. "Yes . . ." Sarah managed to say before a huge woman shoved the door wide and hurried in.

"There ain't no time for introductions." Denver was large enough to be named after several cities, with hair the color of a harvest moon and eyes rimmed in black paint. "You'll just have to trust that I'm a friend of your husband's and you got to get him out of town fast."

Sarah could only stare as Denver grabbed the ugly brown dress and headed toward her. "Your man's been stabbed in the back by a no-good, low-life, cattle-stealing, worthless . . ."

The dress went over Sarah's head, blocking out the rest of Denver's description.

When Sarah finally fought her way through to the neck opening, she asked, "Is he dead?"

Denver snorted a laugh. "If he were dead, hon, we wouldn't need to be getting him out of town, now would we?"

Sarah nodded as if seeing the logic. "Shouldn't we be taking him to a doctor?"

"Ain't no doctor for fifty miles. You'll have to take care of him. Charlie, the bartender, is loading a wagon for you now." The huge woman stared directly into Sarah's eyes. "You can drive a wagon, child? You don't look strong enough to carry a half-full bucket."

"I can manage."

Denver pulled her along as Sarah frantically tried to slip into her shoes. "Good. Don't worry about the doctoring. Just plug up the hole as best you can and give him whiskey until he stops complaining. That's always been my method of treating gunshots or stabbings. It seems to work about half the time."

"But shouldn't we doctor him before we try to move him?"

"Hon, if he's not out of town fast, he'll be dead for sure in an hour. There's probably men strapping on their six-shooters right now itching for a chance to gun down Sam Gatlin, and they don't give a twit that he's been stabbed in the back and already bled a river." Denver paused at the bottom of the stairs and patted her ample bosom in an effort to breathe easier. "Don't you know? Your man is a legend in these parts."

Sarah wasn't sure she wanted to know what kind of

legend. Her gut feeling told her whatever his claim to fame, it wasn't good.

Denver towed Sarah out the hotel door as panic flooded Sarah's brain. "But where will I take him?" She didn't even know the man, or like him for that matter. How could his life suddenly rest on her shoulders? She wasn't even sure which way was north from here much less how to take him to safety.

Denver stopped so quickly Sarah bumped into her back. The strange woman turned around and whispered, "You'll take him to Satan's Canyon. No one will find you there." Denver stared at Sarah as though gauging her bravery. "If you can't get him there, we might as well bury him now, for he's a dead man."